The first book we write we dedicate to our nearest and dearest, then we go on to dedicate different works to those who inspired the stories. But it always comes back to the same people we started with: those who love us even when we're up all night writing because the spirit moves us and then put up with us when we're crabby the next day because the spirit has left us.

I love you, my dear, and thank you for not insisting I keep a normal person's hours or even my loose hold on sanity all of the time. I wouldn't be me if not for you.

Into the Light

Book 2, The Admiral's Elite
by HK Savage

Chapter 1

"Tell me, Captain, did you get what you needed?"

"I thought we were past that whole 'Captain' thing." He captured a drop of sweat on the back of her shoulder and brought it to his mouth. A slow lick and it was gone.

"Fine then, *Michael.*" She shivered, feeling a stir in her stomach and lower despite her exhaustion from the last hour's activities. Her voice was lower, husky. "Answer my question. Did you get what you came for?"

He chuckled. The vibration where their bodies touched sent another shiver down her spine. "I wouldn't say I didn't *enjoy* all that." His hand, back to tracing her curves, glided over the tiny silver scars that crisscrossed her body. Most humans would never see them they were so light. Michael's wandering hand dipped below the sheet he'd pulled over her cooling body. "But that's not actually why I came to see you."

Becca craned her neck and leaned back, sliding off of Michael's chest so she could see his pale face. Blue eyes met her hazel gaze and darkened as his hand reached the small of her back and her breath caught involuntarily. "You mean you were gone for three days and *that* wasn't why you came to see me?" Her lover's appetites were comparable to her own and Becca knew having him back in her bed was the first thing *she'd* wanted upon his return.

Michael's other arm curved around her back and tightened to drag her, painfully slow, up his chest until her hair fell down onto his face. The hint of black stubble permanently frozen just under the surface of his cool skin failed to catch her sandy brown strands and, barely long enough, they slid down onto either side of his cheeks. "Well, I did want that and I'm not quite done yet." That stray hand started to drift.

Becca sucked her lower lip in between her teeth. "I'm hearing a 'but' coming." Not to be outdone, she sneaked a hand between them and grinned when he forgot to breath.

Michael took a breath to speak, even if he didn't need it for any other physiological reasons, nor had he since 1944. "I was supposed to tell you that Admiral Black wanted to speak to you about something."

The mention of their scary as hell leader was as effective as a cold shower. Becca brought both hands back up and propped herself up on Michael's chest. "Do you have any idea what it's about?"

His lips tightened and there was a quick flash of

something on his face before he hid it. "No, he's asked me not to say anything. He wants to fill you in himself."

Becca knew from being inside of his head that, through some sort of metaphysical mystery, Captain Michael Rossi was connected to Admiral Black and unable to disobey him. Not like many people risked disobeying the admiral. Aside from being the most terrifying single being she'd ever met, Becca heard rumors from the others about some Homeland Security officer who'd started digging into Black's history and turned up in a psych ward shortly afterward. Two months ago she'd found she was able to "jump" into other people's heads and see what they saw, hear what they heard. Thus far she'd only been able to jump into Michael and their fellow unit member, Captain Ryan Hallbeck. Several secret experiments she'd conducted revealed that those were the only two she could manage jumps into for some unknown reason. She had no idea the hows or whys it worked or why it was only them. Michael had shared blood with her to save her life twice and they were having sex. Lots of it. But Ryan was a fellow member of their unit, nothing more than a friend. How she had managed a jump into him and not their other unit member, Gabrielle, or some random person on the street was still unknown.

She knew Michael wondered what she'd been privy

to while in his head. Thus far they'd avoided talking about it other than her initial assurances that she'd only been able to use his senses. That was true, only she'd been able to pick up some other things too. Like the sensation that his head was in a vice when he'd tried to disobey Black's orders to sacrifice Becca for the greater good. A sound tactical decision, it just wasn't one to Michael's liking. And Black had punished him. Somehow.

Dragging her thoughts back to present, she blinked and tried to look like she was thinking about her upcoming meeting with Black. "Huh, well, I guess I'm supposed to go downstairs, then?"

Blank and silent, Michael nodded slowly.

"When?"

"Sixteen hundred."

Her eyes lifted to the red numbers beside them and she sat up in a rush, the sheet pulling away to leave her exposed. Becca hardly noticed. "When were you going to tell me that? It's almost three."

"That's over an hour. Are you worried about what you're going to wear? Maybe the commute?" He folded his long fingers over his flat stomach, covering the top of the trail of dark hair leading down below the dark sheet. "There's a lot we could do in an hour and still have you ready in time." His voice sounded sleepy, impossible for the undead but incredibly sexy sounding regardless.

Becca had to drag her eyes and mind back north of the cotton divide. "Well, no, I just don't want to go showing up in front of Black looking like I've just been rolling around with a co-worker." She still wasn't convinced Black was a hundred percent okay with "inter office" relationships, even though everyone *was* sleeping with someone. Fellow unit members Ryan and Gabrielle had been doing it too, but they certainly didn't flaunt it. The only times Becca saw them touching openly was when they were on a mission and out of the admiral's sight.

A pale shoulder rose and fell. "Honestly, it isn't like he doesn't eventually find out everything anyway."

The defeated undertone caught Becca's attention and she frowned. "Did something happen while you were gone?"

There was only a second's hesitation. "No, nothing you need to worry about."

Her eyes dipped again to a freshly healed scar along Michael's ribcage. With his supernatural healing ability that could have easily been yesterday instead of the month it would take a human to heal to that point. One thing was certain, it wasn't there when he left. His arm shifted and it was hidden. "If you say so."

Gone was the easy familiarity that had grown between them in the last few weeks of their budding relationship, replaced, once again, by the giant pink elephant that had just walked into the room: Michael's mysterious tie to Black and whatever it was he'd been hiding from her since that last big mission when she'd almost died. Michael didn't like talking about it and no one else knew what all he'd done other than give her an unusual amount of his blood to heal her from what should have been fatal burns encompassing most of her body. Getting the little information she had only left more questions, as did her inheritance of more than a small amount of his hypersensitive senses and inhuman strength.

That had been two months ago and she hadn't seen any signs of those side effects fading. According to everything she'd been learning about the supernatural world in the two months since, she should have been back to normal. Or at least as normal as she ever got; second sight, prescient visions, danger warnings, whatever you wanted to call what she had and why Black found her a useful addition to his special unit of monster fighters. It had occurred to her that Black might have some answers for her, but she figured if Michael was trying to keep her away from the admiral then she would respect that and refrain from asking. For now. Eventually, she had to get some answers or forever wonder how close she was to being what he was. Half of her expected to wake up one morning with fangs and blood lust.

She shivered but didn't make a move to get up. "I should start getting ready." Questions or no, it felt good to be lying in bed with him.

"Yeah, me too. He's asked me to be there." He tapped a finger on his stomach.

Another look at the digital display and five minutes passed. Finally, when it was clear neither would be adding anything new to the conversation, Michael slid out of the bed and grabbed his black boxer briefs off the floor. Zipping up his pair of the black cargo pants they all wore, he walked toward the door, slowing and grabbing his black t-shirt off the end of the bed on his way. "I'll see you down there."

Becca offered him a tight smile, which he returned before slipping out the door and shutting it quietly behind himself.

"K," she said softly after he'd gone, wondering if he heard her through the ancient wooden door. Kind of hoping he would.

Chapter 2

With ten minutes to spare, Becca hit the bottom of the twisting stone steps that led from the cold, formal estate above to the state-of-the-art command center in the basement. The lack of lighting in the open space didn't obstruct Becca's vision anymore. With a self-conscious blush, she thought of the duration of their session upstairs and realized that in addition to her senses, her endurance had been enhanced by Michael's blood donation. If no one else had figured out the unusual extent of her enhancements, they would soon. Would they worry about her ability to handle it? She didn't need them to question her ability to do her job and handle the stress; being human already handicapped her somewhat. Maybe they would think it was a good thing, her being more like them, she considered with an unusual surge of optimism. Or not, reality followed on the heels of the cold slap of air as she passed into the room where they awaited her.

Her hands smoothed any possible stray hairs back into her ponytail then down the front of the black jacket she wore over her black fatigues. The others were all either too hot blooded or beyond the point of caring about the cold temperatures in the house to bother with the added layer, but not Becca. She still thought it was too cold in here to believe that outside the front doors lay the baking California desert, only a short drive from San Diego.

"Rebecca." Admiral Black's cold voice ended her mental wandering with the subtlety of a straitjacket. Quiet and drawn out, his summoning left her with all the revulsion of a slimy swim through the sewer system.

Becca's eyes searched the dimly lit space to find Black easing out of his office, a nearly invisible opening in the wall on the far side of the room, and gliding forward to stand at the head of the long rectangular black table in the center of the room. An overhead set of lights washed his alabaster skin clean of details until she got close. A thick bunch of tan folders were set neatly on top of the black surface.

"Admiral Black, Sir." Becca refrained from saluting when she reached the far end of the table; she learned in the beginning they didn't do that here.

Obsidian eyes showing no whites, only an expanse of flat black set into white skin and topped with equally under-pigmented short hair, regarded her without expression. By some trick of the light, the immortal, soulless creature appeared strained. Could it be? She shook off the thought as impossible.

"Please, take your seat, Rebecca."

His towering six-foot-four frame stationed at the

head of the table was even more daunting when she sidled up the table to take her usual seat on his right. She tried not to be obvious as she scanned the room for Michael.

"I have asked Michael to give us a few minutes alone, if you don't mind. We have not had the opportunity to speak without his company for some time." Tapping a long white finger on his pointed chin, he appeared to think for a minute. "Not since you returned from the hospital, I believe." Those flat black eyes turned toward her and his thin lips tightened into what might have been a smile. On him it was more of a grimace. Then, gracefully, he folded and took his seat.

That simple act had her heart racing. Becca had never seen the man sit before, much less smile. It freaked her out even more than his hovering aloofness. Keeping herself from making direct eye contact for long enough for him to manipulate her mind, she glanced to his nose and back every few seconds.

"Calm yourself, Rebecca. I assure you, you have nothing to fear from me." The corner of his mouth twitched again. Another smile. "We have not had an opportunity to discuss how you are finding things here with us. You have had ample time to settle in and see how things are done here, I trust."

If the admiral wasn't the admiral, Becca might have been tempted to laugh. It wasn't like she'd had a choice in her place here. Once Black decided he wanted someone that was it. It didn't matter whether she liked it there or not. One thing was for sure, if she had to be around the chilling admiral as often as she had her previous commanding officers, she would have had a breakdown or at least developed a nervous tic or ten by now. Fortunately, she had Michael acting as a buffer between them. While that would have bothered her in her old unit in the Navy, it didn't so much now. The less time she spent with Black the better, and Michael was her immediate supervisor. That was another can of worms entirely and not one she could open while she was with Black. One stress case was enough, thank you.

"Things are fine, Sir. Everyone is teaching me about the sorts of creatures I'm encountering and we train every day we aren't on a mission."

Black blinked. With his coloring and lack of visible corneas it lent him an uncanny resemblance to a snake. "Yes, Michael has kept me apprised of your progress. He reports that you are a quick learner. What has it been, five missions in two months? All presenting different obstacles, none quite so challenging as the one that nearly cost us your gift." His white fuzz covered head wagged, more disturbed by his unit's possible loss than the pain of the human who wielded said gift. Trust Black to leech any hint of sentimentality out of something. "However, I did not ask *what* you were doing. I asked *how* you are doing."

"Uh…" Becca's heart and mind went into overdrive. Immediately, she tried to calm herself. The fact that her eyesight wasn't dancing lent her a tiny modicum of solace. If she were in danger from the admiral, her preternatural sight would have let her know. Only recently she'd discovered she could somewhat control how debilitating the effects were and since mastering that control, she hadn't lost her vision for more than a few seconds at a time. That didn't stop her stomach from clenching nervously now. She feared she knew where this was leading. They hadn't spoken about the new twist on her ability since she'd jumped into Michael right in front of the their scary boss. If her damned vision hadn't been so blurred at the time with her lover and old partner about ready to face off, she would never have done it. Now she realized what a mistake it had been. "It's good, Sir. Everyone is very helpful and I find the work challenging as well as rewarding."

The black eyes narrowed slightly. "Thank you for the sanitized version, Rebecca. However, I know that you are an intelligent woman. You know very well what I am asking you. Have you learned more about this jumping ability of yours?"

Chapter 3

His voice never rose. It didn't have to. Becca caught the uptick in intensity. That Black knew she called it jumping meant he'd gotten it from Michael. She couldn't be angry he'd told. He had to. And that was exactly why Michael asked her to tell no one, including him, about how it all worked. That she was unable to tell him she understood why, that she knew Black could pry anything out of him and he would be powerless to resist, troubled her. Her thoughts turned to the new scar he carried and inwardly she winced. He was her ally here. He had been from day one, even if there were a few hiccups. Out of a need to keep him from the further punishment sure to be doled out if he continued to defy Black's information requests, she complied.

"I haven't jumped since the fire demon, Sir." That much was true. Sure she'd tried on a number of unwitting participants. Random people on the street, in a restaurant, even Gabrielle, all to no avail. Thus far only Ryan and Michael were open to her, and with no one to ask about how it all worked, she had no clue how to proceed.

No sound came from the admiral's seat and Becca let her eyes rove nearly all the way up to the soulless eyes, catching herself when they hit the top of his cheek. From her indirect scrutiny she could see that he had gone "dead" in that that creepy vampire way of his. A little voice inside her head reminded her Michael could do it too and she shook it off. Michael was a different kind of vampire. He was caring. He had a soul. Other than Black's unexplained desire to help keep the monsters from outright attacking humans, he'd shown no signs of any sort of compassion at all.

Miracles happen. A shoe scuffed on the stone at the base of the steps and Becca could breathe again.

Black didn't move. "Michael, well timed."

***

As he approached, Michael's expression remained blank, giving away nothing of the carefully controlled feelings he wrestled. His nature threatened to flare, had been doing so since Black altered his request that he leave them alone for fifteen minutes before he join them. A quick flick of the eyes and he saw that, although clearly stressed, Becca was unharmed. She moved and he caught a flash of faint silver lines spiderwebbed over her cheek from the mission that nearly took her from him. Gritting his teeth, he held back his vampire need to take his woman far from where Black or anyone could touch her. It was impossible. Black could find her anywhere and Michael couldn't take one step if Black ordered him to stay. His rage threatened to compromise him and, falling back on

21

skills developed over many years, he quieted his body and mind. "I've come as you requested, Sir," he said, benignly. "The others are on their way."

Black waited several heartbeats before switching the subject. "I wonder, Rebecca, if Michael has informed you as to the nature of our business in Washington?" A faint glimmer of amusement twisted his lips and Becca caught sight of his fangs. Unlike Michael's, Black's never fully retracted. It was an age thing, Michael had told her. "I'm confident his first stop after returning was your quarters?"

Blood rushed to her cheeks and Becca ducked her chin. With her hair up, Michael could watch the red wash over her face. "We didn't discuss the details of the trip, Sir."

A deep rumble from Black's chest sounded vaguely like laughter, maybe the closest the sick bastard got. "Then tell me, my dear, what did you do?"

For some reason Black was endlessly amused with the fact that they were sleeping together. He was actually pleased; he'd even told Michael to bed her to secure her loyalties. After some initial adjustment issues, she believed him when Michael reassured her that his desires were entirely his own.

"All due respect, Sir," Michael spoke up from the

other end of the table where he stood by his chair.
"Our visit was personal and your affairs were not
the subject of our private discussions."

The admiral averted his gaze from where Becca
squirmed and stared at his second in command.
"Then I will leave the subject matter of your visit to
my imagination."

Michael was grateful the admiral had yet to show a
sexual inclination toward anything. If he wanted to
take her, Michael would surely die trying in vain to
protect her. The rapid heart rate of the sole human
in the room was the only response to the admiral's
crude insinuation. Both of them waited for the
admiral to move on.

"Rebecca, you are new to us and might not
comprehend our unique relationship with the rest of
the United States government." Black resumed his
standard upright position and pushed his chair aside
with a foot.

Becca's eyes followed the admiral, careful not to
touch his eyes for more than a second at a time. She
remembered what Michael had told her about his
ability to get into her head with anything more than
that. Thus far she hadn't asked if he had the same
capabilities and he hoped she wouldn't. It would
pain him to have her compare him to the vampire
that ruled them all.

"You have seen firsthand that we serve the needs of our soldiers, protecting both human and otherwise among our ranks as well as civilians around the world."

She nodded. That was true. Confounding as he may be, Black had proven he would go to any lengths to protect those serving. Especially the supernatural beings who found places within their ranks. With their strength and intelligence, the military had shown itself to be a perfect match for many non-humans; Special Forces and wet work being a particularly well-suited destination for those with certain thirsts.

"We recently learned there are those in Washington who question the relevance of our work." He let that hang.

Her uncertainty at where this was going was visible in her pinched brow. The freckles he could see in the bright light and the puzzled expression made her look young and Michael felt that same protective instinct he'd gotten the first time he met her, helpless in a hospital bed.

"Your recent discovery of this new ability of yours affords us a rare chance. It would be helpful to be 'inside,' so to speak, to determine the source of this sudden dissension."

Predictably, her frame tightened and the glance she aimed his way was glazing already. Her sight was warning her the danger of Black's proposal, or maybe it had more to do with what might happen if she couldn't perform. His own insides twisted at the thought of the admiral bringing harm to her.

Becca took a deep breath through her nose and lifted her chin. "I'm not certain how it works, Sir. It's possible I wouldn't be able to jump into a stranger, on command."

Leveling a heavy gaze upon her, Black gave her objection no regard. "Your goal over the next two weeks is to figure out how it works, master it, and be ready to use it at *my* command."

"Hey Mike, when did you get back?" Ryan called, moving to take his seat across from Becca. Gabrielle sashayed a few steps behind and took her seat beside the big Marine.

Ryan's casual air was clearly meant to distract and diffuse. He was the only one who got away with that sort of thing, though typically he was more subdued in front of Black. It must have been pretty obvious the tone their little "catch up" session was taking.

Black tracked the newcomers with a pointed stare. Michael cast another appraising glance her way and she caught it. Becca lifted an eyebrow and widened her eyes in question. He raised a shoulder, subtly trying to let her know he hadn't known this was coming. It was unknowable if she believed him or not. He wished it could be otherwise and hid his disappointment in himself that he wasn't the man she deserved.

Their exchange ended when the admiral opened his mouth. "Now that we are all together, I would like you to familiarize yourselves with our next mission." Gliding in his creepy way around the table he passed out the files, pausing a moment longer behind Becca. She sensed without knowing what he'd done exactly, that something had transpired between Michael and himself. It had only taken a second but the mood of everyone at the table changed. Frowning, Ryan gave Becca a curious look confirming her suspicions it involved her. Gabrielle feigned boredom. And the heat rolling off of Michael was palpable. Becca shot him several nervous sideways glances.

"Is there something you would like to say Michael?" Black had resumed his position at the head of the table and leaned forward, putting his features directly under the overhead light. He glowed, eerily wraithlike.

The vampire climbing its way out of Michael gnashed its teeth, demanding blood. Black openly challenged him on the flight back from D.C. He was going to use Becca for something. Did Michael have an issue with that? The knife Black put between his ribs hadn't been what stopped him from objecting more than he had. It was the damned bond Black controlled him through. There was no stopping the admiral from using Becca, she was one of his soldiers now like the rest of them. But Michael already struggled to make absolutely sure he was able to offer protection against those he could defeat, while letting her believe he was treating her the same as the others in the unit. She was intelligent. Eventually she would figure out something changed while the admiral and he were in D.C. And as much as a part of him wished he could tell her, Black had forbidden his mentioning his new plans for Becca, he also dreaded it. There was no chance she would believe him to be anything other than a weak coward for doing nothing to defend her from Black. As her commanding officer and lover it was his duty. Too soon, his only happiness in over half a century was going to come crashing down and he was powerless to stop it.

"No Sir. I believe I've expressed my opinion already." From his periphery he caught Becca's sharp intake of breath and the direction of her eyes. He could almost see her picturing the fading scar that would be gone entirely the next time he fed.

Thankfully, Black let it go. He was confident he'd made his point and everyone at the table knew Michael was allowed a certain amount of leniency given his elevated position in the unit. They couldn't know why Black chose him as their leader though they were more than willing to keep him as the go between. No one wanted to spend any extra time with the admiral if they could avoid it. That was the only reason no one had discovered his ties to Black thus far. Only Becca had gotten close enough to him to be in a position to be suspicious. And this jumping ability had him shaken. If she guessed at the depth of his supplication she would withdraw for self-protection, if not for disgust. How could she not? He was half a man, or monster; unable to exercise his own will. And if she didn't guess the cause of his compromised strength, she could only believe him a coward. It was only a matter of time before she left him. A strong woman could only want an equally strong man, and he was not that. He wished he could tear his dead soul from his chest and break the bond he would obey until his end.

Leaning back, Black removed himself from the light and let his hands drop by his sides. "If you will turn your attentions to the case files..." He went on to briefly outline the details of the crime scenes, what little information they gave about the potential creature they were facing, and when they would be leaving. The crime scenes were standard issue psychopath complete with disemboweled bodies and removed hearts. Of course there were pictures. Because the hearts hadn't been found, the police assumed the killer was keeping them as souvenirs. Black believed they were being eaten which indicated an animal, maybe a were. Or a demon.

All eyes turned to Becca at mention of the last. Staring at her file, she avoided looking at any of them and kept her shaking hands beneath the table. They all sensed her systemic panic, her faint scars were still easily visible to all non-humans present. He vowed to keep her safe from this one.

"Wheels up at zero-seven hundred."

Chapter 4

Their briefing complete, all were excused. Becca pushed her chair back and gathered her file under her arm. She made her way as quickly as she could without running to the stairs, half expecting to be called back for more one on one time with the admiral. The spot between her shoulder blades itched from all the eyes surely fixed there. A quick stop in her room to toss the file she should be reading on her bed, and Becca did a quick change into running clothes. She left her iPod on her dresser. She wanted to clear her mind and a quiet run in the desert was more likely to do the trick than a head full of driving bass.

Minutes after she'd stepped out the front door, Becca felt peace returning to her frayed psyche. The sun was on its way down, tinting the few wispy clouds brave enough to be near it to glowing pinks and oranges; a tiny line of silver luminescence on the undersides. Early spring brought with it the first signs of life. Browns, grays, and pale woody greens were brightening to vibrant peeks of yellow, lavender, and even the lightest hints of pale blue through the bland landscape. The cacti were budding. Everything was readying for a brief yet vivid display that would be peaking within the next few weeks. Even the scent of dust and dry earth was starting to give way to the occasional sniff of something living. Not sufficient to identify yet, but enough to whisper that it was on its way.

By the time Becca returned the sky was deep blue and already dotted with a handful of stars. The now visible half moon had risen and was casting its white glow on her shoulders as she mounted the cold gray steps to the estate. Its grand outline stood dark and jarring against the starlight. Whoever had decided an English estate belonged here in the desert where Spanish styling and earth homes were prevalent was beyond her. Probably the admiral, Becca thought with a roll of her eyes. It most likely never occurred to him that he might want to fly under the radar, being what he was. After who knew how long as a giant pasty monster, he'd probably forgotten it was even possible to do such a thing. She shivered as the evening cool mixed with sweat and her date with a hot shower became primary in her thoughts.

Becca was wrapped in a towel and combing her hair when there was a knock at her door. Assuming it was Michael, she bit her lip to hide her smile and felt her body stir. It wasn't just his stronger senses she'd borrowed for the time being. Becca put her comb on the dresser, one hand on the doorknob, the other readying to drop her towel, when she opened it and gasped.

Amber eyes, carefully deadened to feign her standard general disinterest rolled. "Jesus Becca, put some pants on."

Backing up, Becca did nothing to stop the female werewolf's forward momentum into her room and sat hard on her bed while Gabrielle leaned against the door she closed behind her. "And to what do I owe the pleasure, Gabrielle?" Becca didn't call the woman by her nickname, Gab, like the others did. It didn't seem right, nor had the familiarity been offered.

Always the suspicious one, Gabrielle went straight on the offensive. "What the hell was that downstairs this afternoon?"

Her hands clutched the towel, top and bottom. It was the only armor she had shielding her from Gabrielle's onslaught. It felt woefully inadequate under the circumstances. The spots beginning to cloud her vision agreed. "What are you talking about?" Becca wrangled her emotions to get them under control before her warning system got the better of her.

Body rippling forward with the grace of a predator, Gabrielle moved off the door and approached the bed. Becca forced herself not to scoot away. The last thing Gabrielle needed was more evidence that she was weak, and human. "Michael's thing with

Black. What's he getting all caveman about? And why was Black taunting him?"

"Taunting him?" Becca was clueless.

Again the eye roll. "Oh come on." Tanned hands rested on perfectly curved hips clad in black fatigues that looked so much better on her Becca wondered if she had hers tailored. "He waited until he had Michael's undivided attention and got down, close enough to your neck to be sure Michael got the picture. You're his." Leaning back, Gabrielle crossed her arms over her enviable chest. "Any particular reason those two are having a pissing contest over you?" The way she said the last made it abundantly clear Gabrielle's previous friendly overtures toward Becca were going to be her last.

Shaken to think the admiral had gotten close enough to bite her, making a point of showing her vulnerability to her only protector, Becca was nearly blinded with the overwhelming warning of impending danger. Breathing became difficult and she clutched at her stomach. As panic overtook her, Becca's defenses shattered and cold fear flooded her.

There was nothing from Gabrielle for a long moment while Becca struggled to regain some functional bit of her senses. The combination of fear and Black's earlier assignment came back to her and she had an idea. Using the visual of Gabrielle's honey blonde hair visible outside the blinding bright light washing out her face, Becca focused on her and jumped.

Or she tried. Nothing happened. Fearful she wouldn't be able to complete the admiral's assignment within his deadline, terrified that meant he would make good the implied threat everyone but she had seen at the briefing, Becca's heart went into overdrive. The sides of her ribs ached as her heart thudded hard within its bony cage, threatening to tear her asunder and leave her body broken like the victims in the case file. Surely that was what the admiral had planned if she proved less than useful. He never kept anyone around he didn't need and he had no patience for failures. Shadows joined the bright spots in a laser show of yin and yang just for her. Where her hands had been white knuckled clutching at her towel, they came away to break her fall as Becca fell backward.

"Shit. Becca? Are you all right?" Anger gave way to concern and Gabrielle reached out to shake the girl by the shoulders. "Don't have a heart attack on me." Was she old enough to have a heart attack? Her supernatural hearing told her the organ was going far too fast to be good for her. Maybe if she passed out she'd calm down. Unsure what else to do, Gabrielle sat down next to her and patted her shoulder awkwardly.

It didn't take long for her relief to come. The wooden door flew open to reveal a very pissed off vampire glowering at her. Normally he didn't scare her and Gabrielle typically made sure to show Michael he couldn't intimidate her. But years of seeing what fangs like those could do and not being a masochist, Gabrielle hopped to her feet and held her hands out in front of her. "Michael, I swear I didn't do anything." Both of them glanced over at the human struggling to breath. She was making weird groaning noises and her towel had fallen open. Nudity was normal in the world of a werewolf, that wasn't what caught her eye. Gabrielle stared at the flesh that had been burned to a crisp only two months before. Michael had really done it. He had brought her all the way back with scarring barely visible even to a creature with enhanced vision like theirs. And even those were fading. Eventually she would be flawless, she was sure. He was stronger than she thought. That had to have left its mark on the girl. She couldn't be completely human anymore. Gabrielle determined to keep an eye on her, watching for signs of transformation or servitude. Would Black allow Michael a human servant? And was he really willing to turn his lover into a servant to save her? There were ramifications for these sorts of drastic overtures.

"What did you do to her?" Michael appeared next to Becca. His hands reached out to take his woman and in a blink, very gently, cradled her nude body to his chest. "Becca, can you hear me? You have to calm down."

Amazed at this side of her formerly emotionally closed leader, Gabrielle watched as he cooed to her, hands stroking her hair. The gentle side of the admiral's whipping boy brought Gabrielle's suspicions to heel. The admiral was a typical crazy-ass vampire in that he coveted things. It was possible he didn't like the fact that his underling had found something that divided his attention and was asserting his control. Unlike Gabrielle and Ryan who were smart enough to keep their sex lives private, these two were stupidly obvious about the fact that they were together. And seeing the fear in the captain's eyes, both at the admiral's threat and now that his human was in trouble, she realized that the admiral most likely didn't care for the distraction Becca caused Michael. He must really value that whole "prescient sight and future visions of danger" thing she had. Or was it this new "jumping" thing she could do? Honestly it freaked the crap out of Gabrielle. She didn't want the woman in *her* head. What if she could poke around while she was in there? She was getting twitchy watching for some weird tickling or foreign jabbing feeling in her head when she was around the human. Nobody got in and poked around in there.

"Get out," Michael growled low and dangerous, yanking Gabrielle back from her thoughts.

Blinking at the naked human lying prone, she could hear the heart calming under Michael's ministrations. Not yet ready to go and wanting to see more of this curious relationship, she took a half step toward him. "I'd like to help."

He was having none of it; typical vampire. Selfish creatures that smelled like dirt and ash, her lip curled in distaste. Narrowed eyes burned almost black as he hissed at her. "You've done enough."

Then Becca made a funny choking sound and Gabrielle was forgotten. "I'm here. You need to calm down. Breathe for me. Can you do that?" His hand touched her forehead and again the heart slowed.

Curiously, his touching her seemed to have a profound effect and Gabrielle had the feeling she was seeing something she wasn't meant to.

Reinforcing that vibe, Michael glanced up at her. "I told you to get out." This time, his human was out of danger and he was not going to be distracted from ejecting her.

Gabrielle saw that it was time and she carefully backed out, shutting the door on them. Standing outside her room, she ticked her fingernail against her teeth, thinking. "Hmm."

Just then, Ryan happened to come up the stairs. He smelled of apples and peanut butter. The display of power, loyalty, and the girl's surprisingly attractive form had Gabrielle in a mood. Stepping forward to put herself in his path, she put a hand in the middle of his amply muscled chest and purred. "What are you doing right now?"

A broad grin cracked Ryan's strong features and he reached out behind her to playfully grab at her ass. His physique was enviable. He'd been a Marine, and a good one, before he'd been infected. The years of shifting back and forth between human and wolf had left him even broader and firmer than in his purely human life. "I have an idea."

Gabrielle slid her hand down his t-shirt and scratched lightly over the front of his pants. "Me too." Securing her fingers in his waistband, she turned and led him down the hall to his room on the other side of Becca's. If she were more self-conscious she would have been grateful for the thick walls of stone that deadened almost all sounds. But, as Michael had just made evident, not all was silenced from supernatural ears.

Back in his room, Ryan let Gabrielle take control, as
she was wont to do. Shutting the door, she pushed
on his chest and he let his body follow her direction
toward the bed until the mattress hit the backs of his
knees and he plopped down. She was on him in
seconds, all teeth and nails.

Ryan thought about making a joke about how
revved up she was until she caught his throat in her
teeth, a gesture more wolf than human and he
sniffed. She was close to changing; her control was
thin. They weren't supposed to change in the house.
It wasn't close to the full moon, but still. It wasn't
safe, this close to a human, when she was this
jacked. Sexual desire could easily shift to the desire
for the kill when they were in their animal form.
Ryan knew he would have to let her burn off a little
juice with him to avoid trouble. He would have to
change and go for a run after this so he could heal.
She was going to leave marks.

He wasn't wrong. Fingers tipped with claws tore his
shirt from his suntanned shoulders, leaving thin
trails of blood in their wake. Instead of her violence
cowing him, Ryan felt his body waking, responding
in kind. His teeth grew while he willed his snout to
stay back. He wanted to stay human with her; it was
more personal. Taking her shirt in both hands, he
ripped it open and grabbed her lean arm, pulling her

toward him until she sat astride his hips. Elongated canines scraped her throat, asking her permission.

Arching her back, Gabrielle gave in but not without a price. Her claws tore his back in long raking trails. Groaning, needing more control, Ryan pushed off the bed, taking her with him and backed her up against the wall. Roughly, he tore at her pants while she ripped his zipper in two. Not taking the time to unlace their boots, he turned her around and pushed himself into her, feeling her readiness as he slid inside.

Growling, she reached around to grab onto his backside and help him drive into her. He knew she would want it rough in a mood like this and the scent of blood in the air had him needing to bite something. He snuffled at her collarbone and she tossed her long honey blonde hair off her shoulder and tipped her head, allowing him access. Getting close, Ryan reached around her front. One hand tweaked her nipple, twisting it painfully to make her clamp down harder on him and the other found its way between her legs to bring her to the edge he was already riding.

Claws dug into his ass and she clamped her core down on him hard. Pulling back his lips, Ryan lunged forward and drove his canines into her shoulder to hold her while he pounded into her at a punishing speed. Gabrielle ducked her head and took it, panting and flying over the edge seconds after she felt his release pumping inside her.

The explosion faded and she came back to herself, feeling Ryan's tongue cleaning her shoulder where he'd drawn blood. With a satisfied moan, she pushed back and hinted that she wanted up. He eased back to allow her a little breathing room. His hands were slower to let go and they, as well as his tongue, continued to work languidly on her hypersensitive skin.

"Was that what you were thinking?" He teased her with his tongue, bringing his hips forward; making hints that he was willing to help her if she wanted to work at it some more.

Twitching at the sensations he was causing, Gabrielle pulled away and faced him with heavy lidded eyes. "Couldn't you tell?" She checked the flesh under her nails and winked. "I think we could both use a run. Are you too tired?"

Ryan knew they weren't done yet. She was going to be looking for more as soon as they were out the door. Impersonal sex was what she could handle and he was okay with it. He tortured himself wondering if she was like this with the other guy. The one she called out for in her sleep sometimes. Luc. He hid his displeasure by ducking his head and shaking out his shaggy auburn hair, peering up at her through it. This was the woman he'd chosen, baggage and all. With a smirk and a wink he leaned down to unlace his boots. They were his only pair and he didn't want to lose them somewhere in the desert.

Chapter 5

"How long was I out?" Becca blinked back into the world, horribly embarrassed but no worse for wear. "Tell me Gabrielle didn't see me faint?" She put her hands over her face and groaned.

All signs of tension he'd been showing in the meeting were gone from Michael's face as, chuckling, he pulled her hands away and held them. "If it helps, she felt guilty when she thought she killed you."

"No, that doesn't help." Becca breathed deeply into her sore lungs. She felt like she'd swallowed half a swimming pool and then coughed it back out, leaving her chest stretched and sore. Pushing herself up to a sitting position and leaning back against the short, squared-off wooden headboard, Becca let her shoulders slump. "I thought we were getting somewhere, Gabrielle and me. Now she thinks there's some sort of thing going on between you and the admiral and I'm in the middle." Her eyes searched his face, not missing the shadow that crossed it at mention of the admiral. Gabrielle was right, there *was* something going on there. "Michael," she stopped him before he could argue, "she told me what he did during the meeting." Hazel eyes held his darkening blues. "What's going on?"

"It's a power play, nothing more." He leaned in and kissed the corner of her mouth, lingering.

Becca studied his features, carefully controlled and giving no sign that he was telling nothing but the truth. She felt her insides burn in warning. "Okay, if you say so."

Reclining beside her, Michael pulled her onto his chest. Becca nestled her head under his chin and sighed. After their false start, when she'd believed Black to be behind Michael's romantic interest in her, he promised no secrets. As far as she knew, he'd honored that oath these past couple of months. It seemed they'd come to the end of their run; Michael had just lied to her. Of that she was certain.

***

Studying their files gave everybody who needed one an excuse to keep quiet on the plane ride to their next mission in River Falls, Wisconsin.

"Pack warm," Ryan cautioned them, confessing he'd been a Midwesterner before joining the service before the war. Although which war or which state he wouldn't say. "It's spring in Cali but it'll be a few more months before the ice is off out there."

Becca had gone through her pack that morning at five, waking early and creeping down to the command center to have some alone time. Michael had gone back to his room some time in the night after she'd fallen asleep and she wanted a few more hours before they ran into each other again.

The night had offered perspective; that any lies Michael told were the result of whatever gag order the admiral had given. And that was exactly where she kept getting stuck. Could anyone have a relationship where the admiral was involved? He had his hooks in all of them in different ways; he could manipulate each one.

Somewhere over Colorado Becca nodded off, not to wake until rubber hit tarmac in River Falls. Staring out the porthole-sized window of their private jet, Becca frowned. Snow, and lots of it, lay in piles all around them with endless stripes of white and black along the runways from planes melting their way through the ice that had covered the ground since November. Arching her back and reaching over her head, she stretched and settled back until they reached the hangar.

"Alright folks, we're here." Gabrielle's voice crackled over the PA system. "Grab your shit." She had a different sort of pilot's speech for her departing passengers than your typical pilot.

Becca wondered if she'd been in the Air Force or maybe a Navy pilot before meeting the admiral.

They were all from different branches of the service. Admiral Black seemed to pick the attributes and it didn't matter from where he gathered. Michael and Ryan had been Marines, Becca Navy. One could guess Black was Navy as well because of his title, only no one knew for sure. Maybe he just liked the sound of it.

The seat across from her shifted and Michael stood, blocking the light. The next few minutes were filled with the sounds and easy conversation of old acquaintances deplaning.

"Hey Mike, maybe while we're here we can make snow angels," Ryan teased.

Michael shot back something about Ryan being too warm; he'd have an unfair advantage for clean outlines. Ryan, not one to give up the last word, said something back about it not being his fault he was so hot.

As usual, a car was waiting for them. This time they had a dark blue SUV with tinted windows. Unlike the myths, Michael could walk in the daylight but that didn't mean it didn't hurt. Packs in the back, all four loaded up with the men in front and women in back; they were on their way.

Once the flat expanse of the airport was behind them and they were out on the main highway, Becca was struck with the beauty of the landscape. Rolling hills rose on either side of the road. In some parts, elevated bridges carried them over narrow rivers littered with ice, cutting through the farm fields below. The skeletons of trees, shrunk by distance and accentuated by the evening's shadows, offered negligible cover for the black and white cows patiently waiting for food or some sort of distraction from the desolate white surrounding them. It was her first trip to the middle of the country and Becca ached to see it in bloom. The green would be breathtaking. There was so much countryside, so much distance between houses. Even the towns were a fraction of the size of those she was used to on the West Coast. Up ahead a white cliff face overlooked a bend in the road. A lone tree stood sentinel from the top, watching the traffic below.

Just after the bend the land below changed, opening to a wide valley hemmed in by pale, jagged-faced limestone cliffs on either side. Michael navigated the vehicle around the cloverleaf exit and after a few more twists and turns, brought them to a long, two level building with a black and white sign designating the location simply as "Motel."

The lot was open. They parked in the center giving them some amount of privacy, though in a small town such as this they were guaranteed to get some extra attention. Ryan went in alone to check them in. With a black knit hat and blue parka over his jeans and boots, he could almost pass for a big-shouldered local country boy. Maybe he was before the Marines got a hold of him, he sure never was small.

Fifteen minutes later they had split into couples, their usual when on the road, and were settling into their rooms. Absently Becca wondered if Black didn't mind them pairing off because it was more cost effective that way and snorted at the thought of the admiral caring about cost.

Michael looked up from where he was laying a cooler with his "on the road" supply next to his pants in a drawer. Not wanting to talk yet, she smiled and turned her attention back to her own unpacking and effectively closed the door on any conversation.

When everyone was unpacked they all met in Michael and Becca's room. Not a fancy motel, their room had two queen beds and slightly more floor space than Ryan and Gabrielle's king suite. Suite was the motel's term, not theirs. Becca curled her legs underneath herself and scooted her pillows over to lean back on the headboard. Michael stood at the foot of the bed, arms crossed. Ryan and Gabrielle lounged casually on the farther bed. Becca couldn't help but wonder if they'd already had a quickie, if that was why they were so relaxed. Or maybe she and Michael were just that tense by comparison.

All having had sufficient time to study the files, they brainstormed. The attacks were random by all counts. The places varied from outside a bar to the middle of a farm field. The choosing of its victims also had no apparent rhyme or reason. The youngest was a recent high school graduate while the oldest had been a semi-retired farmer coming in from checking on his livestock. A variable the admiral's people considered that the regular police didn't, lunar cycle, also offered no insight. The only real pattern was the time of attack. Full night, and the victims were always alone. All of them had occurred after the Winter Solstice as well. Five kills in just under three months.

"Okay, so what do we know about our potential demon?" Michael caught his eyes from wandering to Becca at mention of the same type of creature that had nearly killed her, though not before she caught his slip.

The way they held their breath when someone said demon had Becca's teeth on edge. "How do we know it's a demon? What if it's some other sort of thing that likes to," she fought the lump in her throat while she shut down her mental pictures of the last demon she met, "eat people parts?" She'd read about human serial killers who did horrible things like that. Dahmer was a known cannibal and Gein used skin to make lampshades. She mentioned as much.

"Because of the screams," Gabrielle answered first. Seeing Becca's confusion, she went on. "Locals reported hearing a woman shrieking on the nights those people were killed, but not all the victims are female. Ryan called the DNR and there aren't any mountain lions around here. I doubt it's a shifter, they aren't known for going after humans. It could be a werecat of some sort although with the kind of frenzy we're seeing with the victims the moon would be a more consistent factor. " She shrugged. "Nothing else sounds like a woman screaming, so it's got to be demonic. There are a couple of them that use shrieks to freak out their victims. Part of the game for them."

A game. No matter how many creatures they'd gone after, nor how many humans she'd apprehended as an MP, Becca couldn't get past the sick way some hunters toyed with their prey. Her stomach clenched and a few spots appeared in her vision before she shut them down.

"Ryan, Gab, you can keep tabs on outside tonight. Becca, you and I are going to do some bar hopping and see what we can find out from the locals," Michael said, assuming his role as their leader.

Hearing her name brought her focus back to him and Becca couldn't help her irritation at his pointed efforts to avoid eye contact. It wasn't until the other two left and they were alone that she felt free to speak. Very quietly, keeping her blood pressure as well as her voice down, Becca addressed him. "When am I going to be able to put it behind me?"

Michael stopped flipping through his file, tossing it down at the foot of the bed before he stuck his hands in his pockets and looked at her. The denim shirt and tan trousers looked good on him. Strong forearms showed where the sleeves were rolled up partway and his hair hung down on his forehead in thick black waves. "It hasn't been that long, Becca. These things take time."

"I haven't had a nightmare in weeks." She felt her lip sticking out in a pout and sucked it back in.

Shaking his head, Michael didn't let his gaze break from hers. "I'm not just talking about the fire demon. It's everything. Two months ago you didn't know about any of this. Now you're a fully functioning member of the unit. We've been on what, six cases counting this one and you've seen things that shouldn't be possible. You lost Danny." He watched her closely, knowing his words hit home.

Michael was right. As much as she wanted to pretend this was all routine and it was no different than her previous post investigating cases on base, it *was* different. She'd seen vampires, shape shifters, werewolves, even a sea nymph. That wasn't counting the fire demon who had melted the human shell he'd possessed right before her eyes. She barely got the others out before he burned the house down around them. It wasn't her intention to get caught in the house with it. The pain had been horrible. She would never forget the smell of her hair and flesh being charred before she passed out from the smoke. Tears pricked at the backs of her eyes and Becca rolled them up, willing them to stop. "I've always pulled my weight, haven't I?" She hated to think they were back to considering her as less than an equal or believed her to be incompetent like they had in the beginning.

"Each one of us has been new. You're no different."

"Yes, I am," Becca maintained stubbornly.

Head tipping, Michael came close to rolling his eyes. Not something he typically did. "You know what I mean. Coming in here, doing this, hunting things like ourselves, that's hard in a different way than what you've done before."

Feet going numb from lack of blood flow, Becca slid over to stretch her legs out in front of her on the bed. Her eyes stayed on her wiggling feet. "How so?" The discussion of how they'd come to their roles in Admiral Black's elite force was one she'd been hoping to broach for some time. She'd come in as the newbie serving with three veterans. "How is it hard for you?"

She heard him inhale deeply as he lowered himself to sit on the corner of the mattress, body turned to face her. "Some people choose to become like this." He rubbed at a finger, studying his palms with singular focus. "None of *us* did." A chunk of hair fell and blocked her side view of his eyes, keeping Becca from seeing if emotion colored his irises. "All of us served before we were changed and that calling did not end with our humanity. Serving with Black affords us the opportunity to continue to do some good, to use our altered selves to help instead of hiding or losing ourselves in our monsters. The ones we hunt, they aren't that different from any of us. The only thing that separates us is who chooses our targets." He didn't address the fact that Black also had found some way to keep all of them; that none could leave the unit.

Feeling Michael's words resonate, Becca was silent. Before she could try to come up with some sort of intelligent remark, Michael put his hands on his thighs and pressed himself up. "We should get going. There are a lot of bars for a small town."

Chapter 6

Their third stop, *Sneaky Pete's* was much the same
as the previous two. The twenty-something kid
working the front desk at the motel had
recommended it for some local color. They hoped it
would be *and* be a bit more used to outside traffic
than the others if the motel was recommending it.
Barely longer than the six stool bar along the back
wall or wide enough to accommodate the row of
three narrow tables on the other side of the aisle, it
was easy to scan the place for anything out of the
ordinary. A few seconds in and they realized the
only thing out of the ordinary in there was them.

No dancing spots or sick stomach, Becca trusted
they wouldn't come to any harm and gave Michael
an encouraging grin. Her early warning system was,
after all, why the admiral brought her on. It had
saved all their skins several times and the unit
looked to her for guidance often before entering a
potentially dangerous situation.

Michael led the way to the second to last stool
giving her the option to sit on either side. She knew
he would prefer to keep himself between her and
the bar and didn't want to needle him. Taking her
seat at the end, she set her purse down on the bar
and turned to keep an eye on the lone occupied
table. Only one other patron sat at the bar two chairs
down to bring the building occupancy to a grand

total of five, including the bartender. A wall mounted jukebox was playing CCR, loud in the empty space.

Their elbow room disappeared quickly, the music picked up in speed and volume, and it got crazy noisy. Within half an hour, right about the time they were considering leaving, a steady stream of people began trickling in and didn't stop for the next two hours. Becca was grateful for the man beside her and bar behind providing a small buffer from the press of people all around. How so many could fit inside was a mystery. There had to be thirty people. There was no way they were in compliance with fire code. Fire. An involuntary shudder sent ice racing down her spine.

Michael ran a hand up her arm and leaned over to whisper in her ear. "Remind me when we get back, I still want to take you dancing."

"You do?" She tipped her face up to see if he was serious or if he was merely trying to distract her after sensing her discomfort.

The corner of his mouth twisted. "I made a promise, Becca. I always keep my promises."

Becca felt the tension leak from between her shoulders as she allowed herself a brief daydream. What would it be like to dance with Michael? If he

was half as good at dancing as he was at some of
the other things he could do with his body… she felt
herself flush.

He chuckled beside her.

"You did that on purpose." She felt her own mouth
twitch.

Michael's soft laughter moved her hair. Then their
moment was gone as the front door opened and a
gust a cold air blew against their feet.

"Hey Josh," the bartender called over the crowd to a
round-shouldered kid who looked barely old enough
to be there, even if he was large enough to pull a car
with his teeth.

The towheaded kid raised his chin to the rail thin
bartender. "I'm thirsty, Pete."

Grinning, Pete wiped his fingertips on the white rag
hanging over his shoulder and disappeared into the
little room beside the bar. When he came out, brown
beer bottles hung from his fingers like ornaments.

Josh and two of his equally large friends made their
way through the throng, reaching above the heads
of two young girls giggling over light green
martinis. One doe-eyed giggler ogled him hungrily.
Taking the beers and handing them back to his

friends, Josh smiled at the girls before giving Pete his money.

"Figured you might be in again. Still not safe out there."

Michael and Becca both heard the bartender's cryptic comment even with the noisy chattering all around. Hiding their interest behind bored expressions, they listened in.

The big blonde head shook and frowned. "No, we'd rather be drinking around the bonfire and taking the girls for four wheeler rides but a little groping's not worth dying for."

The bartender looked grim. Even the giggling twins sobered at the mention of the creature haunting their town. "I heard the last guy they found was all cut up." The doe-eyed girl joined in. Her friend took a hurried gulp of her green concoction.

"I got a friend with the sheriff's." Josh's expression darkened. "He said they're *all* that way. Each one they find has stuff missing too. It's pretty sick."

"And gross." The quieter of the girls chimed in over the rim of her glass.

Leaning in Pete let his eyes fall on each one and, instinctively, they brought their faces closer.

"There's an Indian fella that comes in here sometimes." He pointed a thumb over his shoulder. "Lives on the reservation. He called it some sorta spirit. Said in his grandpa's time they had one feeding on their tribe. He said they sent a warrior out into the woods to wait for it and when it came he chopped its head off with an axe and burned the body."

Doe Eyes gasped and covered her mouth. "Oh my God."

The men ignored her. Their eyes were locked; sharing in some unspoken manly hunter exchange about what needed doing.

Michael's cool hand on hers below the bar startled Becca back to her body. His face came close to hers and he started nuzzling her neck. "I know what we're looking for."

An involuntary rush of goose bumps tightened her skin. Whether it was his words or merely his breath on her flesh, Becca couldn't tell. The woman in her wanted to go back to their room, even the car, while the soldier in her knew they had work to do. "Should we go?" She hoped he didn't notice the hoarse catch in her throat or the way her heart had picked up.

In answer, he slipped a twenty onto the bar's pocked wooden surface. Pete noticed immediately and gave him a nod. Standing up, Michael shrugged into the coat he'd rested on his chair before helping Becca into hers. His hands didn't linger; his touch was perfunctory. Feeling ashamed for considering putting her wants before the welfare of the town, Becca ducked her head and tucked a hair behind her ear, giving herself time to breathe. For the first time, she hoped the effects of her heavy blood ingestion would wear off soon. She couldn't handle the raw nerves and constant state of arousal much longer. She worried she'd make a mistake that would end up getting someone hurt because she was thinking about what was in Michael's pants and miss something that could get them killed.

Outside, the breeze had picked up. The crisp chill helped to return her reason. She pulled it deep into her lungs, grateful for the mild burn the sudden cold brought to her nostrils and brain. Michael waited patiently by the truck, his hand on her door. Tossing him a tight twitch of the lips that hardly passed for a smile, she bobbed her head and he opened it for her. Stepping inside with a sigh, Becca sank into her seat and let her heavy shoulders fall into the cool leather.

Michael was silent until they were back in their room and he was removing his coat. It wasn't for comfort, his body temperature couldn't be altered by any amount of clothing. The only way for him to change it was to ingest warm blood. Becca ignored the twinge she felt at recalling how much she herself had consumed. It might have saved her life, but still, it was disturbing to think she'd sucked stomachfuls directly from the source. On the few occasions she'd gotten up the nerve and asked how much it had actually been, he'd only shrugged and told her he'd given her "as much as it took." Ryan had been the one to hint that it had been "a shitload." However much that meant.

****

He watched her features, not missing the exhaustion in her bearing. There were the beginnings of dark purple bags under her eyes even though she'd slept on the plane. Yet he'd sensed her reaction when he'd touched her in the bar. And just the night before she'd been insatiable. He didn't know any other humans who had consumed enough blood to feed three starving vampires as she had. But from what he knew of the transference of power through blood, she should be virtually inexhaustible. Still, all signs pointed to a body in decline. Michael frowned.

"So, what is this thing?" Becca sat down on the edge of the bed, not bothering to take off her coat. "Are we going out to hunt for it?"

Michael did some fast figuring. The wolves were already searching the area. Becca wasn't up for an all nighter. "No, I think we should leave Ryan and Gab to track it. If we go running around out there we might confuse the trail."

"How could they confuse *us* with whatever *this* thing is?" Becca squinted up at him.

"Because it's a vampire." He leaned against the wall and regarded her steadily, hands securely jammed in his pockets. "Like me, and you smell like me right now."

Becca grimaced, not commenting on the fact that she smelled like a vampire because the blood of one was a part of her. "Who eats hearts and doesn't drink blood?" She grunted. "I read the reports. None of the police reports say anything about puncture wounds *or* blood loss." She tipped her head to the side. "Well, other than what they lost when their chest cavities were ripped open." Her lip curled.

He bobbed his head slowly. "This is a different sort of vampire. It's an ancient subspecies."

"There are different kinds of vampires?" Becca's eyes fixed on him. "Did you evolve or something?"

"More like *de*volve in this case." Michael bounced himself off of the wall using only his shoulder blades. "If I'm right, this is a windigo. It bears almost no resemblance to what you think of as vampire." He watched the wheels in her head working on this new information.

"I guess that depends." She met his gaze evenly. "I've met a few of you now and already I can see differences."

His brows rose and she went on.

"Look at the admiral. He's crazy tall and I've never seen his skin color change like yours does when you feed." She shrugged. "Maybe he doesn't have to eat as much as you because of how old he is." Her observations received a minor chin dip of approval from him. "And he's got those eyes."

Michael could see the discomfort she tried to hide and gave her a half smile. He understood. Black's most frightening feature was his flat, expressionless gaze. They bored into one's soul, while at the same time making one wonder if he was paying attention at all. That and the fact that he never blinked were unnerving to say the least.

"And then Vanessa, she was more like you but," she paused, considering, "but a little like the admiral too."

Once again, Becca's ability to wrap her head around the nuances of this world's bizarreness without judgment fascinated him. Her place in his heart was cemented. It would hurt him deeply to lose her. "You're right, she was much older than me. Not as old as Black."

"So this thing is different than that? It's not an age thing?"

He ran a knuckles across his jaw, a habit he'd never lost from when he was human even if his stubble was frozen under his skin. "A windigo is barely classified as a vampire. I've heard others call them zombies, sometimes demons. The body is skeletal, the fangs longer and the thirst for blood has been twisted." In his mind's eye he pictured the one such creature he'd faced decades before in Germany's Black Forest. Describing only a few details, he left out the most disturbing. "It doesn't go for blood in the conventional sense, it gravitates to the organs. This one seems to have zeroed in on the heart."

"So how do we kill it? Does it have the same weaknesses?"

"Yes, it's more sensitive to light though. Like a freshly turned vampire." His mind was working through the possibilities as he filled her in. "We might be able to find it during the daylight hours if we can find its den."

"Okay. Then when Ryan and Gabrielle get back, we'll all sit down and figure out how to find it and then we'll kill it."

Chapter 7

The wolves hadn't had any luck finding the windigo. Gabrielle, according to a reliable source, was in a foul mood and had gone directly to bed leaving Ryan alone to knock on their door at sunrise the next morning. The slamming door woke Becca just before Ryan's knock. The exhausted Ryan took Michael's revelation in stride.

"That explains the smell. It was worse than a vamp." He wasn't too tired to take a cheap shot. "Like you, except all decayed and unwashed."

"You found it?" Becca was getting a drink of water from the bathroom sink and popped her head out around the door.

He was shaking his shaggy auburn hair. The werewolves' hair continued to grow. Their bodies were alive versus their undead counterparts. "No, but I think it just wanders aimlessly all night. The stink was everywhere; we couldn't follow it. We went in circles all night."

Becca felt her heart stutter. "Could there be more than one?"

"No," Michael sounded certain.

"Just 'no'?" Becca asked, curious. "How can you be so sure?"

"Because there would have been more bodies," he answered without wavering.

Becca wasn't put off by his direct response. She'd grown up with direct. A therapist would have something brilliant to say about Michael's similarities to her father. To which she had a smart comeback, her father didn't drink blood. "So where did it come from? Why is it striking *now*?"

"They are a winter borne creature, migrating at the end of the season and going into torpor during the warm months."

"So we have to catch it before spring or it's gone until next year?"

"I've never run across one of these things." Ryan yawned, removing himself from the conversation. "This is Mike's forte."

"We have to check in with the local police. See if there's something in the files that might give us some history." Michael's hand dropped to his pocket. "There's something not quite right here. The attacks aren't sloppy like they should be. They're too random and far apart to be just one acting alone."

The water got stuck in her throat and Becca temporarily lost the ability to swallow. "I thought these things were like zombies."

"You said there was only one." Ryan ran a hand through his hair, leaving it gripping the back of his head. One hand remained propped on his hip, pushing his back forward, and he stopped stretching.

Becca put down her glass and pressed her point. "You know, brain dead versions of vampires wandering through the woods taking the occasional victim. You mean someone can *use* these things? Like some sort of attack dog?"

"*Anything* can be conditioned to follow simple commands." Michael was already dialing his phone. "Even a brain dead zombie vampire," he told her without the slightest hint of levity.

Ryan, on the other hand, guffawed loudly, offering no apology when Michael cut him an impatient scowl. "I'm sorry Mike, that just sounded too funny. Thanks, I needed that after a whole night of pissed off Gabs."

Becca caught the strain in his voice and got annoyed for the millionth time with Gabrielle. The woman was an absolute bitch, how Ryan managed to like her even some of the time astounded her.

Thinking the double meaning of the term brought a titter bubbling up. Immediately she bit her lip to kill the grin that went with it and Michael withheld the glare she imagined was coming.

Holding his phone up as an explanation, he made his way past where Ryan leaned by the door, and closed it behind him.

Instead of returning to his room for the sleep his body was screaming for as evidenced by his unusual flat affect, Ryan crossed the room and fell on his face on the nearest bed.

Becca gave him a few seconds to finish groaning. "Do I need to ask how last night went?"

The baby blue floral coverlet muffled his encore groan, but he held both hands up over his head in an "oh my God" gesture.

"I'm sorry you ran all over the place following that thing. Michael thought if we went out there he'd confuse the scents."

The shaggy head rolled so that he was facing Becca with his eyes closed. "I would have chased that damn dead thing all night. It's Gabs. She's making me crazy."

The subject of Gabrielle's attitude wasn't a new one for Becca to ponder, but it *was* a new conversation for her to have with Gabrielle's boyfriend. She was careful with her answer. "I'm sure she was just tired. I mean we got in and you guys went right out and were running all night," she justified.

Ryan made a sound. "That explains *one* night, not *all* of them."

Becca knew better than to take the opening. Even if Ryan was mad today, he might not be tomorrow and he would remember whatever she said. "Well, everybody deals with things differently. Maybe Gabrielle has some worries about the two of you. Have you tried talking to her?"

Big green eyes opened slowly and Ryan lifted his head. "Can you see Gabrielle seriously *talking* about her problems?"

Thankfully he didn't expect an answer. Becca kept her lips pressed tightly together.

"Besides," he went on, fully in therapy mode, "we don't really talk about stuff. We pretty much work together and screw. It's all she'll give me."

"That's not true," Becca was really uncomfortable with the turn their discussion had taken and was hoping her phone would ring or Michael would come back. Maybe a meteor would come crashing through the roof. "I've seen you two talking when we're not working."

Rolling over onto his side, Ryan propped his head on his hand. "We talk about work or what a bastard Black is when we're out of earshot. It's never anything personal." He focused on his hand, splaying it out to cover two giant white polyester flowers. "I've tried to talk to her, to get her to talk about stuff I hear her say in her sleep." He clenched the flowers in one fist. "She mentions people."

Becca's thoughts turned to her own situation. Before Michael she'd never spent the night with a man, fearing what she'd say in her sleep. Worried her sight would rear its intrusive head, suck her into a vision, and freak out the poor guy next to her. Not Michael, he knew what she was from the start and accepted it. A part of her felt violated on Gabrielle's behalf. "She was probably just dreaming. You can't hold that sort of thing against her."

He continued, softly, to himself. "How can I be jealous of someone she dreams about? Some guy that's probably dead by the way she calls out for him."

Finally, the doorknob turned and Michael walked in. He took in Ryan's position before questioning

Becca with his eyes. Feigning ignorance, she raised her shoulders and dropped them.

"Ryan, why don't you get some rest in *your* room."

A grunt and the big Marine was on his feet, roughing up his hair. "I'll go sleep, but I don't know how restful it'll be." He shuffled to the door, pausing before he opened it. "What'd Black say? What's our next move?"

"He's making a call to local PD letting them know we're working the case. Becca and I will go to the station and see if there's something else in their records that didn't make the files."

He was giving Becca a queer look. What had Black said that he couldn't tell her? She was sure that was it. He always got that sort of sick look when Black swore him to secrecy. She'd learned to recognize it. He had it a lot lately and, maybe it was paranoia, but she feared it was about her.

After Ryan left she watched Michael pace the room. Up and back three, four, five times before she had enough. She got up and stopped him with a hand on his chest. "Michael, what is it?" Becca smiled gently when he evened out his face. "Don't hide from me. I know Black told you something."

The lack of a reaction was confirmation enough.

"And I know he told you that you can't tell me."

He blanched. Another confirmation.

"I grew up with secrets." She pointed a hand at her chest and smiled again, "Marine dad, remember? I know there are things you can't tell me." He didn't need to know how she knew. She was fairly certain he hadn't told her about Black's grip on him for the simple fact that he didn't tell *anyone* about it. "Black trusts you with a lot of secrets about how all this works and I get that. I'm not going to ask you to betray that trust just because we're involved. I only bring it up because I can tell it bothers you." The other hand joined the first. Her fingers spread out to cover his taut chest, rock hard with tension. "And I want to tell you that I trust you too." Taking a deep breath, she looked him directly in the eye and willed her next words to be true. "I know you won't do anything that will get me hurt no matter what Black says. Any of us." The appearance of several dancing spots in her vision brought tears to her eyes. Quickly she blinked them back.

Surprisingly restrained, Michael frowned at her and then smiled tightly. "Thank you. I appreciate that."

Before she could say more, he took control. "I would assume you packed something appropriate for bluffing our way into a police station?"

"Of course," she answered lightly.

The River Falls Police Station was an attractive modern building with lots of glass, stone, and brick. The front wall facing the street curved outward, an architect's attempt at making the building seem innocuous. Oddly, despite a commonly held misconception that a police station was a loathsome place, most weren't. Especially those built after the 1990's when Public Affairs decided to make the push that police are our friends, not the enemy. River Falls had obviously bought in. Their headquarters looked more like a library than police station.

Getting out of the truck first, Michael gave the place a long look while Becca came around the back to join him. Both of them had packed non-combat attire and, when they entered, Becca could read on their lips and minds, "Feds are here." She kept her expression light but blank, allowing one hand to sweep over her suit coat even though she knew there were no wrinkles. She'd left her black wool overcoat in the truck. Thank goodness for modern materials. A little spandex in a pantsuit did more than just allow for a shoulder holster it kept the rumples of travel at bay as well.

Becca lagged behind, taking in the large open foyer, wincing at the brightness as the sun reflected off the snow and ears ringing from the sound of her own heels clicking on the hard tile. Michael took point, heading straight for the receptionist housed behind a long sheet of bulletproof glass that spanned the twenty or so feet open to viewing as people walked up.

Even knowing their every move was being monitored on camera and by a dozen or so curious eyes, Becca caught her eyes straying to where the cut of Michael's trousers fit snug on his waist then draped over his firm backside. Taking a hurried step, she brought herself up even with him, matching his long strides. Inwardly she chastised herself for being unable to control her hormones. What was she, a teenager?

As soon as her eyes were off Michael's ass, they caught the receptionist's locked onto Michael's gorgeous blues. Becca knew they would be that deep blue they went to when he was totally focused. She could almost read the woman's mind. It was exactly where Becca's had been about ten seconds ago. Her lips tightened and her hands balled into fists.

The sound of Michael's throat clearing brought her back to her senses, or rather *from* her senses. A quick pass of his hand, it would look accidental to any onlooker, brought a sense of calm back to her being. That he'd had to rein her in made her burn in another way and he brushed her forearm again. This time, he left his fingers on her for a count of two. He was warning her.

Becca swallowed her wounded pride and averted her eyes from the woman who was not respectfully doing the same. Becca busied herself with scanning the desks and occupants she could see in the front office. Any who met her gaze looked away. Only one held it. A young cop in his mid-twenties, not much older than her. Unblinking, he tipped his head and watched her come to a halt next to Michael.

"Good morning," Flirty McFlirtypants, or Pam, according to the name plaque on her white formica desk, greeted Michael warmly.

"Hi Pam," he let his timbre change, drawing her in. It would help their cause to butter up the gatekeeper although it set Becca's teeth on edge. "We're hoping to talk to the chief of police. We were sent over to help out with a case. Someone from our office should have called."

Apparently Michael's influence was working too well. Pam was entranced. Simpleton.

"Pam?" He backed off of his influence, stripping it from his tone. "Would you call the chief, please?"

Movement at the white steel door over to the left of the glass wall caught their eye and Becca shifted with Michael. They wheeled to face the person coming out.

Lean, white haired and mustached, the man who approached was garbed casually in navy pants, a tweed jacket, and open necked tan shirt. At no more than five-foot-eight and still fit despite his maturity and surely sedentary job, the man had a presence Becca sensed as soon as he came through the door. "Never mind, Pam," he waved off his useless employee. "I got it." Striding forward, he held out a hand first to Michael. Old-fashioned, she was used to it. "Chief Kowski, I was expecting you."

The smaller man was just to Michael's shoulder but when it was her turn to clasp hands, she felt the strength in his grip.

"I have to say I'm surprised the military is interested in this one." His bushy brows wrinkled. "Somebody come back from the war with troubles?"

"Possibly, sir." Michael offered him a grim nod. "This one must have caught someone's eye at the top. We're here to offer our services."

Experience wizened brown eyes scanned first Michael, then Becca. "The call I got was more than an offer, son." He lifted a brow skeptically. "But right now, I'm beyond a pissing match. We want to catch this son of a bitch, and if you two can help, I'm all for it."

"Us too." Becca tried to be friendly.

Another long appraising glance, this time of her, and Chief Kowski touched the badge he wore at his waist. "Come on. We might as well get started. My town's on eggshells and the guys are getting itchy. We're worried something's gonna blow. Soon."

Chapter 8

"Here." A stranger's voice startled Becca from her stupor and her elbow scooted off the edge of the dark wood veneer desk. Catching her body before she fell out of her chair and made a complete ass of herself, she half turned to see who had entered the office. The way the computer was positioned in the corner of the "L" shaped desk, her right side was to the door, which had been mostly closed. The helpful officer hovered in the doorway and had pushed the door halfway open. The same dark haired detective that caught her eye hours ago when they'd come in was standing in her doorway holding a Styrofoam cup; coffee by the smell.

His cheeks colored and he stepped forward to set the cup on the edge of the desk before retreating to the relative safety of the doorway. "Sorry, I didn't mean to startle you." He pointed toward the desk out front where he'd been when she first noticed him.

Chief Kowski had given Becca an office on the outer wall with a door versus one of the desks out in the open, offering privacy while she searched through endless unrelated reports of violent crimes throughout the entire state. Thus far, she'd yet to find anything even remotely like the string of murders at least in the last ten years. She hoped Michael was having more luck combing through the boxes of evidence taken at the crime scenes and detectives' notes in his office three doors down in the corner.

Remembering herself, she cracked a smile. Crack was right, her lips were dry and she licked them before trying again. "Thanks, that was nice of you."

Dark brown, near black eyes twinkled back. "I could hear you snoring all the way out there. I figured you might need a little caffeine boost. A small offering of inter-department goodwill."

Her cheeks colored. "Is it that obvious?" She flicked a finger at her monitor and reached with her other hand toward the steaming cup. It smelled good. Something else did too, his cologne. It was a combo of sweet and fresh. Maybe Armani. "Officer?"

"Detective Salvo." He lifted the corner of his black sport coat to flash her his badge. "I know I can't handle being at my desk for more than a few minutes." He jutted his chin at the offending box. "You've been staring at that thing for the better part of two hours." Genuine concern leaked through his professional mask. "You look kinda tired."

She recognized the name from the case files. This young man, not much older than her, was the lead detective on a high profile case. That was odd.

Surely the department had someone older who was itching to have one like this on his resume, the chief even. Becca leaned back in her chair, holding the steaming cup in both hands. It was cool in the office and being immobile had slowed her circulation to a trickle. She didn't want to give the curious young detective anything more than she had to. He seemed willing to handle both sides of the conversation so she let him, giving him only a friendly smile meant to encourage.

"So you and your partner are here from…?"

"We were asked to help out. We have some experience with these types of cases." She let him draw his own conclusions.

"What, vets with PTSD who come back and cut up the locals?"

"Do you think it's a vet come home?"

"No. We checked out all the local boys already. Everybody with a record, felony and military, has been cleared. Anybody who could handle a knife like that." Detective Salvo straightened his tie. "It would take a freakin' ninja to sneak up on some of these victims. Whoever did it had to be sly enough to use that knife without them getting a sound out. He took his time too, judging from the amount of blood at the scene." Somber, he smoothed a hand over his lower face. "Bill Tyler, the farmer," he clarified needlessly for her sake, "was in 'Nam and about as paranoid as they come. His wife was in the house not twenty yards away. She didn't hear a thing, not until she heard a woman screaming. Same as all the others, it was all over by then. Who knows how far away the screams came from. Sound travels in the country, especially in the winter, and we haven't been able to trace them back to any specific locations."

Unfamiliar with snow and any differences in acoustics it lent, Becca was curious. "Sound travels differently in the winter?"

"Not from a snow state?" He smirked, liking having one up on her.

She smiled warmly back. "Nope, California born and raised."

Shaking his head and grinning, he launched into an explanation for her benefit. "No leaves, no grass. All the soft surfaces that would normally absorb sound are hard. They carry a lot farther. And out where Tyler's farm is they're way off the beaten path. No cars or anything for that good old background hum we get used to in the city."

Becca considered altering her image of the staggering zombie-like vampire to one of a much more frightening, and stealthier, version. "That's a lot like the desert so it's not an *entirely* foreign concept to me." She dropped her chin to give him a look of mock disdain. "Do you have a theory?"

He slid a tanned hand up the doorjamb, taking a step further in, his expression going dark. "Oh sure, I have a few. But are you sure you want to hear 'em? After all, a small town detective's opinion isn't worth much. Not to one of you big city Feds." The first undercurrent of distrust rippled into the room. "You guys are so much smarter than us out here I figured I'd just wait at my desk until you asked me to drive you somewhere. Maybe a crime scene or something?"

Uncooperative didn't bother Becca. It annoyed her, but it didn't get under her skin like it did other people. She'd forgotten what it felt like though, her old partner Danny was a pro at soothing pissed off sailors and marines. A pain went through her chest when she thought of him, burned to death in the middle of the desert. And Michele, his widow, who would forever wonder what really killed her husband miles from the base where he should have been working. The explanation of a "training accident" rang hollow to everyone with half a clue.

Seeing the shadow fall over her face, Detective Salvo's demeanor changed abruptly. "I'm sorry, that was an asshole thing to say. I don't know why I did." He took a step further, resting a hand on the desktop. "We've never had a big enough case come through to bring the Feds but I know other guys in Madison who did and they said once the Feds are in, locals are left holding their hats and if anything goes wrong, we get the blame."

"We're not like that, Detective. You have my word." Becca assured him, hoping she could keep that mostly true. He seemed sharp and was going about the investigation the right way from what she'd read in his files. His cooperation and knowledge of local details could help them tremendously. "Although I *would* like to see those crime scenes if you don't mind, and you do know the roads better." She smiled warmly. "That wouldn't be an asshole thing of me to ask, would it?"

His answer froze in his throat when he heard the cold voice from the doorway he'd just vacated.

"Yes Detective, if you wouldn't mind acting as tour guide." Michael eyed him coldly. "I'd like to get out of the office for a little while." His dark gaze turned to Becca, ignoring the hostile stare of the young detective. "You, Captain Sauter?"

"Sure." She set down the cup, reluctant to lose its warmth. "If it wouldn't be too much trouble, Detective, I think visiting the crime scenes would be very helpful."

Recognizing the vibe in the office as having officially changed to unwelcoming, Detective Salvo gave each a slight nod, his gaze remaining on Michael as he brushed past him to exit. "I'll go tell the chief."

***

Michael stepped in and took a seat at one of the black fabric chairs in front of her borrowed desk. Becca tipped her head and aimed a severe look his way. "Well, that wasn't very nice."

He didn't even try to pretend his abruptness had been accidental. The vampire inside him clamored for release, demanding to follow the overly friendly detective and squeeze the life out of him. *Mine*, it hissed. Shrugging, he kept his voice low. "I stopped over to give you a break. Have you found anything? Signs of where this thing came from?" He indicated the computer with a hand.

Leaning back in her chair again, Becca yawned and ran a hand over her eyes. "Nothing. This thing came out of nowhere." She raised both hands and clasped them over her head, stretching her stiff back.

Pulling his eyes from the purple shadows showing under her freckles, Michael nodded. "I was afraid of that."

"Tell me you found something in the files." Her shoulders sagged for a minute before she sat up enough to grab her coffee.

It was difficult to hide his frustration. Michael was distracted by Becca's declining condition. When he'd heard her heartbeat accelerating he'd barely kept his pace human as he came to evict the forward young detective who had upset her. He couldn't step on too many toes without jeopardizing the cooperation they needed for the investigation. Still, Becca was suffering in ways he didn't understand and there was nothing he could do about it. The nagging worry that somehow giving her an unprecedented amount of blood had caused her harm gained momentum. He needed to bring Black into the loop. His fear of losing her outweighed his concern that Black would wield it over her, or him.

"Michael?" She was looking at him. "Want to let me in on whatever you're thinking?"

"Is that decaf?" He nodded at the cup in her hand. "You should watch how much caffeine you take, it isn't good for you."

She screwed up her face. "Of all the things I do and see in a day, I don't fear my coffee."

Letting go of the argument for the time being, he filled her in on what he'd seen in the boxes upon boxes of evidence collected at the scenes. "There wasn't anything new in the files." Reluctantly, he added, "I think the detective is right, it's time to visit the crime scenes. We might notice something they haven't. Something that will point to a location."

"I was thinking about that. If something's controlling it and we know it's here because it's only attacking locally, and Ryan and Gabrielle didn't find anything last night, do you think it's living indoors?" She tossed back the last of her hot beverage, lifting an eyebrow at him, waiting for him to comment. The corner of her mouth lifted when he didn't. "I'm thinking whatever is using this thing is hiding it as well."

"That's a good guess." He was fascinated by her deductions once again.

"So what are we looking for? Is there a specific 'type' of thing that would be using it? Any precedent we can use to go on?" She yawned again.

"We're going to drop you at the motel. I'm going to look at the crime scenes with the detective while you get some rest." Michael knew she wouldn't agree. He was right.

Her features clouded, eyes flicking up to the open room full of River Falls' finest behind him. He could guess they were being watched from the way she carefully controlled her anger. "We have a killer out there only we can understand, only we can stop. I'm not going back to take a nap while you take a civilian into danger."

"He's not a civilian, he's a police officer. They're trained."

A rough laugh erupted from her mouth. "Yeah, not for this."

His eyes narrowed. Her stubbornness was not what he loved about her. That word stopped him. He couldn't think like that. Creatures like him didn't get to be in love. Having her in his arms, even briefly, had been a blessed reprieve from his isolation and its time was coming to a close.

The detective reappeared before they could go any further into their discussion. A brief rap of knuckles on wood announced him, although both already knew he was there. "Ready to roll?" he asked tightly, possibly sensing the tension between them. "We're gonna be hard pressed to see 'em all before we run out of daylight."

Chapter 9

They were on the second to last crime scene when dusk began to cast long shadows across the snow. The bearing of the towering trees shifted from sentinel to stockade, silently threatening to reach down and touch one of them as they wandered about the quiet yard.

Susan Borchert had been a forty-two year old mother of three coming home from working the second shift when the windigo struck. Her husband found her upon waking to strange screams around one o'clock and finding her not in their bed.

It had been two and a half weeks since the murder and fresh snow covered all traces of what had transpired there. The detective had called ahead to ask permission of the grieving widower to view the scene. He took the kids out to dinner and the site was theirs for an hour.

Nothing unusual jumped out at Becca. She would have noticed too. Her senses were so hyper alert her skin was tingling. Snow covered everything, changes in its elevation marking where the body had lain and where she assumed someone had shoveled the soiled snow away before more of the white stuff came to take its place. A path had been shoveled from the detached brown garage leading to the back porch of the matching house. Burlap wrapped shrubs and straw covered gardens stood on either side of the walkway. Susan had been an avid gardener by the number of such spots on the property. Becca thought of her father, Ed.

Ed Sauter and Susan Borchert would have had much to talk about. Ed's years in the Marines had given him a need for routine and precision. After retiring he'd been able to fill that need with cultivating an enviable garden. It was hard not to imagine what it would have done to her mother to find her husband butchered in their yard, feet from the safety of their home. Her stomach turned and her eyes stung.

Sensing her upset, Michael crossed the yard to stand beside her, offering her what comfort he could. Detective Salvo caught the gesture and glanced up so he limited his contact to a hand on her shoulder. It wouldn't do them any good to be seen as intimate in front of the hostile allies. It would only give them cause to question their professionalism.

"The detective says the husband asked the police to keep the sirens quiet while he got the kids handed off to his sister through the front door. He's the only one who saw her," he told her in a low voice.

"I know, but it's just so pointless." When she forced her eyes from the depression visible in the snow where the evidence had all been dug up, tears glittered on her long brown lashes. "This thing is pure evil." She sniffed. Her mind's eye painted the sterile white with the puddles and splashes of red in the file.

Hard expression softening at her distress, Michael rubbed a thumb over her shoulder and appeared torn between keeping their relationship quiet and giving her the consolation she so desperately needed.

"I'm fine." She sniffed again, blinking away the offending wetness behind her lids and wiping the few strays away with the sleeve of her black coat. Seeing that he wasn't convinced, she forced her lips into a quick grin and took a step away.

"Hey, you guys see what you needed?" Salvo's impatient voice cut across the quiet of the late afternoon.

"I think so." Becca watched Michael close himself off before he turned to face the interloper.

The sound of an engine brought all three heads around to see a late model silver Impala charging up the drive to stop in front of the garage. Detective Salvo muttered something that sounded tired and unhappy before striding past them to head off the gray-haired man stalking angrily toward them. Michael and Becca looked on curiously.

"Mr. Nowak, we were just leaving." Salvo waved a hand in a friendly gesture.

"What the hell are you people doing here? You've been here enough already." The large man was not so easily appeased. "You shouldn't be wasting your time here, you should be out catching the animal that killed my daughter."

"We are, Mr. Nowak," Salvo held up both palms in a peaceful gesture. "These two are from a special task force assigned to help us do just that." An expectant look over his shoulder told them this was the story and not to argue, even if they wouldn't tell him where they were really from.

Not surprisingly, the victim's father turned his anger on them. "What do you think you're gonna see here that this guy didn't, huh?" He gestured heatedly toward Salvo standing patiently by. Hands loosely in his pocket and a carefully measured amount of cool on his face said he'd endured this sort of thing before. "My grandkids haven't been able to sleep or play outside since it happened. Between the newspapers and the cops, this place is crawling with people day and night, rehashing the details when they should be out looking for new clues before someone else dies." His fury mostly burned out, the grieving man finished with a quivering chin.

That he didn't know about the last kill was a blessing. It didn't look like his nerves could take any more strain. The details from the last one had been easy to keep from the media due to the nature of the scene. Although the windigo killed and took the heart, the victim was left in the road. A driver coming around the curve ran over the already damaged body, leaving the driver a basket case and unable to see any telling details. The sheer horror and carnage prevented him from seeing that the chest cavity had been ripped apart before his wheels crushed it. Police told him the victim suffered a heart attack while walking alongside the road and hadn't felt anything when he'd been struck.

"Mr. Nowak," Becca stepped forward. "I'd like to extend my deepest sympathies to your family. We are going to do everything in our power to catch this guy." She smelled the adrenaline on the man's skin through his padded flannel shirt and canvas jacket. He was a big man, at least thirty pounds too many had settled on his middle. That he kept coming at her warned Becca he was going to use all that to try to intimidate her. Spots in her vision told her she was right.

It wasn't unusual given her age and youthful appearance that, if anything, made her appear even younger. Settling her weight evenly on the balls of her feet, she got ready for whatever he was preparing to do. Her eyes darted sideways to

Michael to see his jaw was set but he wasn't going to interfere unless absolutely necessary. It bothered him with her, but he let his people fight their own battles whenever possible. He knew Becca could handle this, even if he didn't like it.

Nowak didn't stop until he was inches from her, his meaty hand curled into a fist with one sausage shaped finger pointed straight at her nose. "You listen to me, little girl. You're gonna catch this fucker and you're gonna string him up by his balls. Then I'm gonna gut him and see how *he* likes it."

Spittle landed on her lip and she kept herself from flinching or wiping at it. This man lost his daughter. He was angry and he was scared. She understood and wasn't going to let him get himself landed in jail because of it. One move and he was likely to explode. She let him vent, knowing Danny would have been better at handling this. "I understand how you feel, Mr. Nowak."

Clear blue eyes ignited under bushy blonde and gray brows. His thin lips pulled back to expose large, square tobacco stained teeth. "You come here from some big office where you look at a hundred cases like this one a week, cases that deal with someone *else's* daughters and husbands. And you're gonna tell me you understand how I feel? Do you have any idea what it's like to know someone you love died scared and in pain?" His voice cracked, the corners of his mouth trembled.

Deliberately, Becca nodded her head. "I do know how that feels, sir." She blinked slowly. "My former partner died on a case a lot like this one not too long ago." Then she let some of her own heat bleed into her eyes. "I caught that bastard for him just like I'm going to catch this one for you. And for Susan."

For a tense couple of seconds they gauged each other, then Mr. Nowak blinked and took a step backward. Wiping at his nose with the back of a hand, he offered it to her solemnly and she took it. "I'm holding you to that."

"Me too."

****

On the ride back to the station Michael sat shotgun and Becca slumped in the back with her head resting on the window. His eyes continued to catch her in the rearview when he thought his passenger wasn't looking. After it became obvious that the girl was asleep, Detective Salvo attempted to discuss the scene he'd just witnessed.

"So, uh, Captain Rossi," the chief had told him their ranks at the same time he'd informed him he would be cooperating with them fully or his ass would be in the filing room for the next month. "When did you get partnered up with Captain Sauter?" He got the impression he should refrain from using first names with this guy. He was kind of a jackass and more than a little territorial about her. Not old enough to be a fatherly kind of protective, the detective figured if he hadn't closed the deal yet with his young partner, he wanted to. Too bad, she was cute and he liked the tight look of her body. He bet she ran. She kind of seemed like the type. She seemed kind of sweet too.

Cutting his eyes sideways, he saw Rossi staring out the window at the bleak winter scenery flashing past on the curving road. It was icy in patches where snow had blown over the asphalt and been packed down so he had to cut his speed by half. He'd passed another green mile marker by the time the man answered.

"Captain Sauter and I were assigned to each other almost three months ago." He continued staring straight ahead. "She wasn't responsible for her partner's death."

That he knew where any cop's mind would go wasn't surprising. When it came to loyalty and responsibility, partners were *it* in a cop's world. Someone who had gotten theirs killed would be a pariah in any station. "Are you saying that because it's true or because you don't want anybody leaving her swinging if the shit comes down?" The chief could do what he wanted. Salvo wasn't trusting his back to this girl until he knew what happened to the last guy who did.

Dark eyes swung around and Salvo felt the temperature in the car drop about twenty degrees. "There was nothing anyone could have done to save him. That same night Becca nearly died saving the rest of our unit. If anyone 'leaves her swinging,' they will answer to me."

"I can't." The feminine monotone broke the uncomfortable silence, adding a new layer of awkward to the dynamic. "Wait, what are you doing?"

The girl started thrashing in the back seat, her feet kicking the back of his seat. Alarmed, Salvo checked his rearview mirror again and saw the girl had gone completely white and broken out in a sweat. Her eyes were rolled up in her head. "Shit, she's not having a fit or something, is she?" He started to slow down, pulling over as he checked Rossi for a reaction. What he saw wasn't what he expected.

Jaw clenched tight enough to shatter his teeth, the guy was whiter than usual. Weird since he was Italian like him except they were polar opposites on skin tone. That wasn't what struck him as freaky. It was the way he was watching her. He'd turned around and was staring at her intently, listening like she was some sort of oracle. It was like he was committing everything she said to memory. Did he find her nightmares that fascinating? What kind of weirdo was this guy?

The car came to a halt on the side of the road and Rossi was out his door and into the back before Salvo looked up from putting it in Park. That guy was fast. He'd gotten in back with the girl but on the other side and, as much as he looked like he wanted to, he didn't touch her.

Salvo didn't like the way the girl's face was contorted. She was seriously scared. "Shouldn't we wake her up?"

The captain's focus remained trained on the girl. "No, we can't interrupt," he said softly, offering no further explanation.

"Hey man, my grandmother was into that whole bad juju thing and she figured you couldn't wake somebody up without their soul getting lost or whatever, but that's bullshit. The girl's having a nightmare, it's pretty shitty to let her be that freaked out." He twisted in his seat and extended a hand toward her knee.

Rossi's hand caught his mid-reach. "Don't touch her," he growled.

"Please," she pleaded in a whisper, "don't make me do this." Tears ran down her face. "I can't."

Detective Salvo was pissed. "Dude if you won't wake her up, I will." He tried freeing his arm to no avail. The guy was about the same size and build but his hand was like a steel clamp and just as warm. There was no moving it. "Let me go." These people were weirding him out. He was going to be asking the chief again where they were from. And when they were going back.

With a whimper, the girl's body went limp and his hand was released. Making no sound at all, Captain Rossi slid over until he was almost on top of the little thing and he wrapped an arm under her shoulders, tucking her in against his side. Her head flopped onto his chest.

Yep, he was totally into this girl. Part of Salvo was disappointed. He'd hoped she was a free agent. She was cute and there was something about her, that quiet confidence that usually had him chasing older women. The way this one carried herself said she'd seen some shit and she could handle it. That and the tight little ass in those snug pants turned him on.

"Is she okay?" Salvo glanced back at them again, not liking the whiteness of the girl's skin or the dark shade of her partner's glare he turned his way.

"Drive us to our motel," he ordered.

"What about your car? It's at the station." Did this girl have some sort of medical condition? "Why's she so pale? Is she sick?" he wondered aloud. "Maybe we should take her to the hospital."

"Screw the car, get us to the motel now," Rossi barked. "She'll be fine."

Glancing up again at the strain in the man's voice, he was sure there was something more to this nightmare the captain wasn't sharing. "Alright." Irritated, Salvo turned himself back around and put it in drive. The motel was closer anyway and he was going to be more than okay with getting rid of these two. Then he was going to see what he could dig up on the mysterious Captains Rossi and Sauter. He was positive they weren't Feds. At least not the normal kind. He had a quick mental listen to the X-Files theme music. "Shit," he muttered under his breath.

Chapter 10

She was still sleeping when a gentle knock rattled the metal door. Michael hurried to unlock it and step outside, holding it mostly closed behind him.

"Is she okay?" Ryan's concern was written plainly on his face. "It's been hours."

Taking one hand off the door handle to rub his knuckles over his jaw. "No, she hasn't moved."

Putting a hand on Michael's arm, Ryan gave him a quick pat. "Sorry Mike. What do you need us to do?"

Glad to have something else to talk about, Michael focused on the other issue he'd encountered when he called Ryan to tell him they were back and what state Becca was in. "Have you heard from Gabrielle?"

It was Ryan's turn to be the stressed out boyfriend. "No. She just up and disappeared after I came to bed." He rolled his huge shoulders looking oddly helpless. "I don't know what's going on. All night she was fine until we cut through that farmer's place. Then, she just sort of stopped and changed to human. We never do that when we're tracking." He reinforced his statement with a direct stare. "Seriously, I mean most of the time she's kinda sad to change back when it's time to come home. This time though," his big head wagged from side to side. "It was like she was so shaken up she couldn't hold to her wolf form. And then, when I tried to talk to her, she ignored me. It was eerie, she completely zoned me out. She just followed the trail back into a section of woods for about a mile. I changed so I could talk to her and then as soon as I did, she changed back until I got the message and left her alone. She went back to human and I stayed wolf. Figured if I was furry I could protect her better if anything happened. Funny thing was, *I* didn't smell anything different at the farmer's place than anywhere else. I have no idea what spooked her."

Michael heard his pain and offered him a tight smile. "You know her Ryan, she needs her space."

"This is more than space." He crossed his thick arms in front of him. "She's avoiding me. Something shook her up man, and now she's gone."

"I can help you look for her."

Ryan held up a hand. "Hey, don't worry about it. I'm sure she'll come back when she's ready." He aimed his chin toward the door behind Michael. "Besides, *she* needs you in there when she wakes up." He backed up. "I'm going out to look for her now that the sun's going down and I can do it my way. I'll check in when I get back."

"Right." Michael nodded, tight lipped. "Give a shout if you need me, I'll hear you."

"Thanks." Ryan backed away and jogged into the woods. Seconds later a cinnamon-colored wolf trotted out and looked both ways before crossing the road to disappear into the trees beyond. He would howl if he needed help. Michael could hear it from miles away.

Stepping back into their room, he breathed a sigh from habit, not need. His unit was under fire from within and he didn't know how to fix it. The admiral would want an update and he couldn't put it off any longer.

Easing his phone from his pocket, he stood at the edge of the bed to gaze down at his Becca.

"Michael."

The admiral's cool voice rankled him instantly. "Sir, we have some problems."

No hesitation, not even a break in his serenity. What all had the man seen in his centuries, maybe millennia? "Such as?"

He started with the least worrisome first. "Gabrielle, Sir, she's disappeared. Ryan's out looking for her."

"Disappeared how, Michael?"

"She's wandered off, Sir. Ryan said they were out trying to follow the scent of the windego to find its den when she came across something that distracted her. She wouldn't talk about it and now she's gone off. He's out looking for her now."

"Is that all? I can't help but notice you sound rather upset. Given there is no lost love between Gabrielle and yourself, I must assume it involves our human?"

If they'd been in the same room Michael's expression would have drawn the admiral's wrath for sure. *He* wasn't allowed to call her *ours*. "Sir, Becca had what I believe was a vision on the ride back from a tour of the crime scenes today. She hasn't woken up." His struggle to keep his distress from his voice wasn't enough.

"Would this have anything to do with her recent weakness?" Black floored Michael with his insight.

To admit Becca was weak and possibly unable to do her job might devalue her in the admiral's eyes and that didn't bode well for her longevity. "Sir?"

The admiral chuckled. "Did you think you could hide her deterioration from me? She is not the first human who has received a heavy infusion of vampire blood in history. Although she is the first I have seen harbor the side effects for this long. Most likely that is because of her unusual genetic twist."

"You mean the fact that she's a witch?" Michael referred to Black's archaic title for her prescient abilities. He avoided commenting on Black's damning testament of her decline.

But the admiral was in the mood to discuss it. "Honestly Michael, did you think you could keep such an enormous donation a secret? I can nearly feel her body vibrating when she enters the room."

"If you know she's having trouble, why are you intent upon making her stretch her ability so soon? You know it's draining when she jumps." He was dangerously close to questioning Admiral Black. Binding aside, that usually drew a painful punishment for his insubordination.

Black's tone lost some of its airiness. "I had hoped that if things were dire you might see fit to turn her. *I* would have done it by now if I were able."

Michael was speechless. Black's one attempt at binding Becca to him by giving her his blood had nearly killed her. They were incompatible, a rarity Michael had only heard of before, never seen. It made him question the type of vampire the admiral was, or if it was his ancient blood and its potency her body found objectionable. Regardless, for whatever reason, Black wanted Becca a vampire and Michael didn't. Nor did Becca.

"You knew this day would come, Michael." Serenity once again flowed through his words.

"No," he choked out, "I didn't. I thought after Kenneth you realized prescient humans couldn't be vampires. They go mad with the change."

Kenneth had been the last member they'd tried to bring into the unit before Becca. Kenneth was turned shortly before the admiral found him. Turning had sharpened his senses and honed his sight until all he could see was death and bloodshed, mostly at his own hands. He'd been unable to function and the admiral "put him out to pasture" to adjust to the severity of his new nature, intending to try to indoctrinate him after he'd settled in a few decades.

The admiral dropped his voice. "And you don't think what you did to her is any different?"

Horrified, Michael sank down on the bed behind him, his eyes never leaving the pale face that hadn't so much as moved in over an hour. "I didn't think…" he whispered.

"Of course not." Admiral Black almost sounded sympathetic. "Your concern was to save her life and you did. What you couldn't know was that the amount of blood she ingested allowed her to see as we do, smell and hear like us. More than merely enhancing as a typical infusion does, every emotion is tenfold what she's used to. The growing strength of her ability is adding to the strain on her already taxed system. It is not a level of functioning that is feasible for a human body to endure long term."

Michael knew he should have gone to the admiral when he'd noticed the side effects weren't fading. Only he'd been so fearful that Black would capitalize on the power Michael's blood would have over her until it wore off, he'd kept them separate except for necessary meetings. Mostly he'd run interference and limited their contact, hoping she would be back to normal before Black caught on. It had been foolish and he realized that in retrospect. Black could outmaneuver him any day and he of all people should know better. It didn't matter what he did, Black would always know. Again, he felt the mantle of his failure to protect Becca settle around his shoulders.

"Why isn't it wearing off, Sir?" His forehead rested in his palm, defeat staining every word. "Why is she still like me? Have I saved her life only to doom her to madness?"

"She is more like us than even I realized, Michael." Black's tone was thoughtful. For the moment he wasn't jockeying for control or pitting one against another. He was a mentor advising his protégé, nothing more.

These moments were rare and Michael used this one to learn what he could to help his lover. "Did the blood enhance her abilities or are they getting stronger naturally? Is *that* what's hurting her? Was this inevitable?"

"She is preternatural, a being that walks between what we are and pure humans. There are many levels of preternatural, and from what I have seen she is a strong one. I have not seen her equal in a millennium." No small amount of satisfaction oozed through the admiral's words. Obviously he was proud to have added Becca to his ranks. "Her value to us is incomparable."

"Then we need to figure out how to fix her, not drive her over the edge by turning her into one of us." Michael became more resolute.

As did Black. "That is why she needs to be immortal. Once she is gone, we will not be able to replace her."

His words gave Michael pause. Becca was mortal. She was a human living and working alongside dangerous creatures, charged with the task of hunting down other dangerous creatures that were a danger to humans. That she would come to harm seemed inevitable. Then he remembered Kenneth's descriptions of the torment of his madness and shook his head. "No Sir. If she were turned, *then* we would lose her. What makes her what she is, is the fact that she's *not* one of us."

Black's words were icy. "Do you think you can stop what is already happening by hiding your head in the sand?"

Just then, Becca took a deep, shaking breath like a diver emerging from the depths of a pool. Her eyelids fluttered.

"Sir, she's waking," Michael murmured into the phone.

"Call me as soon as she interprets the vision."

"Yes, Sir."

No need for instructions after so many years together, Black and Michael both hit a button and screens went black. Michael's phone went in his pocket and he slid down to his knees to kneel at her bedside and take her hand in his.

"Michael? How long was I out?" Her voice was scratchy and hoarse from disuse.

Kissing her hand, he set it down to retrieve a glass of water for her. In less than a minute, he had returned. "Can you sit up?" He positioned himself to assist if she needed him.

She nodded and together they had her upright and drinking in short order. Michael sat on the edge of her bed. After a few sips, she groaned. "That vision, it was in the car with Detective Salvo, wasn't it?"

"Don't worry about him," Michael assured her. "He thought it was a nightmare, nothing more."

"Are you sure?" Becca wouldn't want anyone to be witness to her sight. Surely she'd talked during it, she would assume she had. "I mean, what if he figures it out?"

Michael lifted one shoulder casually. "Then I'm fully prepared to kill him."

Becca looked like she believed him. The warning was there; his eyes were dark, he could feel it, and he wrestled to hide his upset. His conversation with Black continued to run through his head while he tried to work through it and find a different solution for her.

"That's not funny." She reached for his hand again and squeezed it when he gave it to her. She was weak. "He's probably telling everyone what a case of nerves I am." She rolled her eyes, revealing several broken blood vessels. "He's kind of got a point there."

"It's my fault." Michael's eyes closed, he was unable to look at her when he told her what he'd done. He'd come close to doing the thing she'd asked him not to. "After the fire demon, when I gave you my blood, I had to give you a lot." He could feel her eyes on him; he wished he could find some release from the pain he felt tearing his mind apart and release her from the curse he'd laid upon her with his blood. Her destruction had been his doing. Deep down he'd known it would be that way from the beginning. *Humans are fragile.* God, it had been his mantra that kept him loyal to them while maintaining a safe distance since he'd returned from the War where he'd been turned. And now, because he'd been weak and had fallen in love with one, he had destroyed her. He would have wept if he were able. Bowing his head, he rested his forehead on her hand. Her warmth seeped into his cold flesh and he welcomed its familiarity. It had been too long since he'd eaten, though the thought of having to consume blood while he was here with her awakened an entirely new wave of disgust with himself.

"Your blood saved me, Michael." She put her small hand on his cheek and he turned away. "Why are you so upset?"

He couldn't look at her. "I gave you too much. The heightened senses and your ability's increasing strength, it's taking too much from you." Rolling his head on her flesh, he whispered, "I'm sorry."

Her voice shook. "All we have to do is wait for the effects to fade. They should be fading soon, right?"

"Not with you, Becca." Opening his eyes, he raised his head and her hand fell away, taking its warmth with it. It would help to see the hatred sure to be there. Then he could force himself to keep away and avoid hurting her anymore. Only there wasn't hate, just fear. It was his undoing.

"Why? What's wrong with me?" Tears had started to mark her white cheeks with wet trails. Her other hand lifted from his and he no longer touched her.

He shook his head, frowning. "There's nothing wrong with you." He'd hoped to tell her in a less damaging way that she was even more different than she knew. They had not yet informed her of the level to which her prescience altered her. "It's just that…" He stopped. He watched the pulse in her neck picking up until it was flying. "Becca please, your heart shouldn't be racing like this. Can you try to calm down?"

Fear quickly turned to anger. "Can you ask me a dumber question? You're telling me I'm falling apart because of the blood that saved my life is too strong for me and from the way you're acting, it's about to get worse. And you want me to do some deep breathing?"

Her cheeks were coloring and he smelled the beginnings of sweat starting to break out on her body as the stress and adrenaline combined to bring her precariously close to passing out. From the way her eyes were glazing, he could guess she was having trouble seeing. Whether that was from her eyesight growing spotty with warning or a lack of oxygen pushing her to faint, he couldn't tell.

That made his decision. At least if he told her everything at once she could pass out and reset herself. He might be able to bring her pulse down if he stroked her. His touch soothed her for some odd reason. Not that the mysterious phenomena would continue much after what he would tell her this night. "Becca, you aren't purely human and the blood of a supernatural creature lasts longer in you. I'm sorry, I didn't know." He watched her mouth form a small "o" and her chest heaved. "It wasn't until Admiral Black told me what was happening that I understood what I'd done." He shook his head again. "I'm sorry, I should have talked to him sooner. I thought I was doing you a favor by keeping it from him."

"What?" Her eyes flew to his. "You kept something from him? I thought you couldn't?"

Everything in the room stopped for Michael. "Why would you say that?" His eyes darkened, tightening at the corners. "What do you know about that?" The vampire was creeping up his spine, listening.

Becca's chest rose and fell in rapid succession. Her eyes were wild. "The power he has over you. I felt it. When I was in your head I couldn't hear your thoughts or anything, but I could feel it when you tried to argue with him. It hurt." A shaking hand went to her temple. "Your head got tight and your guts twisted up. Like how it feels when I'm getting a warning that we're in danger, like you're going to be sick."

Furious to have his weakness exposed, Michael temporarily lost himself. He forgot himself and he forgot his guilt. The vampire already perched on his back launched itself into the forefront and he felt his control falter. He tasted blood as his fangs tore their way through his gums and his eyes went black. The room fell away and there was only her as his eyes zeroed in. "No one knows that," he whispered darkly. "It's too dangerous for Black *and* for me.

And now *you* know. A witch with a vampire's blood driving her mad." His words hung in the air.

"A witch?" There couldn't have been any blood in her face. Her lips were turning a dusky hue. "I'm a witch and now you're going to what, kill me because I know a secret I haven't told a soul for months?" Her eyes were completely glassy, not even focusing on him anymore. "Even you?"

That she thought him capable of killing her and was nearly blind as she faced him, gave him the strength to wrestle the vampire back. *I love her.* He reminded it.

Hissing, it dug its claws in and refused to budge. *She knows.* It clung to its position stubbornly. Self-preservation was its only concern.

His hand went to his forehead and he bit his bottom lip. Warm blood dripped down his chin.

Becca, temporarily focused, went green. "Michael, please. I know you will never hurt me. Do you remember when I told you I knew that? I still believe it. The good in you is stronger than anything else. Even Black's hold on you." She bravely put it right there in front of him again. "He can't make you hurt me and I know that."

Needing to touch her, to feel the warmth of her skin as she spoke of her undying faith he snatched at her arms, pulling her to her knees on the mattress. She swayed but held her ground, eyes trying to roll back into her head as her consciousness struggled to fall away. "How do you know that I'm stronger than the beast inside me?" he ground out between clenched teeth. "How can you be sure I won't lose control of it or that Black won't order me to kill you? What if I can't say no?" The strain was impossible to keep out of his voice.

Her body went rigid under his hands and she stopped wavering. For a few seconds she controlled herself enough to look him steadily in the eye. "Because I love you and I know you love me too. And that's stronger than anything that asshole can try to put between us."

The vampire stopped, as did the man. "Love?" A poleax would have been less effective than her declaration. His hands fell to his sides.

One of her knees buckled and she fell forward, Michael catching her against his chest. "I love you Michael. I have since the beginning, even if it took a little while for me to figure it out." Her eyes closed. Her breathing was ragged; his hands on, then off, were stressing her system even more than the conversation.

"What about Black? What he can make me do?" He gave voice to his greatest fear in front of her since they were laying it all on the line. "How can you not think I'm a coward when I have no power against him?"

Her hand touched his chest, resting where his heart used to beat. "You are the bravest soul I've ever known," she whispered hoarsely. "As much as you know what he's going to do to you for disagreeing, what he was going to do to you for saving me, you still did it." She knew Black's punishment methods. She'd borne witness to them firsthand when Michael had suffered because he'd disobeyed that first night after Black's effort to bind her had nearly killed her. He hadn't realized she knew the cause of that night's penance. The revelation shocked him almost as much as her own bravery that same night when she'd told Black to stop. "You're a good man, Michael. You're stronger than the beast. Both of them."

And with that he felt her go limp in his arms as the strain proved too much for her weakening human body. Her body touching his was already bringing her heart rate down and soon she was breathing evenly. Gently, he cradled her against his chest and laid her back in the bed where he held her, clinging to her nearly as tight as the glimmer of hope she'd lit within him. She believed in him and he wanted to prove her faith wasn't false. To hell with what Black had done to him. Becca was his real tether and one that he would hold onto with both hands. For her, he would be his own man again, or die trying.

Chapter 11

Becca wasn't alone when she opened her eyes in the room just starting to glow with dawn's first rays. Nor was she damaged in any way. As a matter of fact, she felt good. For the first time in a long time she felt rested. Not entirely back to herself, but better than she had been in weeks. She shifted to stretch and was stopped by a hand wrapped around her middle.

"Good morning." Michael tugged her back against him so that their bodies were pressed together along her entire length.

"Mmm." She stretched her legs then scooted back into position. "Good morning."

"How are you feeling?" He sounded uncertain. "Last night was," he paused, "cathartic."

Happy fluttering tickled her belly. "I take it that's a good thing?" She ran a hand up and down his forearm.

"I had an idea last night after you fell asleep."

She made a noise. "Fainted, again, you mean."

"Whatever you want to call it, after you were out and I touched you your vitals settled."

Her cheeks were hot. "You have that effect on me." Licking her dry lips, she went on. "Sometimes just being around you does it."

Michael took a moment to respond. "I'd noticed it before but it didn't come to me until last night after we'd talked everything out." He paused, shifting beside her. "That was when I realized we might have the answer for your condition."

Condition? He was being so clinical. Had he not heard her when she'd told him she loved him? Realization hit, nearly taking her breath with it. He didn't feel the same. Becca went quiet, waiting.

"If your senses are having trouble handling overstimulation then we can reduce the stimulation and its effects until the blood's effects start to fade. It'll take a while because of what you are, but they will fade." He actually sounded embarrassed. "With trying to maintain a professional distance and sleeping separately when we were at the estate we were underutilizing our best resource to combat your weakness," he said, touching her shoulder and slipping his hand down it, "our own bodies."

"Dialysis through the skin, huh?" His logical approach and cool manner cut her to her very center. While it made perfect sense, it did nothing for the fact that her heart was under his heel. She swallowed her disappointment. "That's pretty drastic."

"Drastic situations call for drastic measures." He let his head fall back behind hers, making it clear he wasn't planning on going anywhere. They lay like that for a while, neither one speaking until Becca had to get up to use the bathroom. When she poked her head back out, he looked expectant and she frowned.

"I think I should take a shower and change." She smoothed the massively rumpled shirt she'd slept in. "We have lots to do today." That and she wanted to be alone. She'd told him she loved him for the first time, and a second, and he'd said nothing. No, that wasn't true. He'd told her she was a witch and she would be reliant upon him to keep her from running down until she could finally manage her own condition.

In the light of day it all seemed ridiculous and she could feel the hulking thing creeping into the room with her, the polka-dotted elephant neither one was apparently going to talk about. He wasn't being distant; quite the opposite, but that didn't matter considering he'd explained how he understood she needed him. Physically. That and he might be acting kind out of pity for the girl who'd fallen for her commanding officer, the thing she'd sworn she wouldn't do when she'd first caught herself stepping out over that particular abyss. Nothing was said on the subject. He lay watching her, a glint in his eye she knew far too well. Part of her, an insistent part, yearned to satisfy itself with him. The rational part of her brain told the horny part to cool it. No one was going for more sex if that was all this was to him. That had been enough for her in the past, but not anymore. Not with him. After love was on the table, unless he returned it she wouldn't take his scraps. No, sex wasn't enough anymore.

Instead of going to the bed where he lounged, tempting in a white tee and jeans, she went to her suitcase sitting open on the dark blue berber carpet. She'd hung her nicer things but the underclothes were all in there. There was something gross about putting her underwear in a drawer where other people put who knew what. Clothes picked out, Becca had an oddly self-conscious moment and carried them bundled against her chest into the bathroom. Once inside, she closed the door and sat down on the toilet lid, face sunk in her clothes. Had she been presumptuous in thinking he might love her? Maybe she'd been wrong. That she could have mistaken the motivation behind the lengths he'd gone to in order to save her didn't seem right. Of course he loved her. Didn't he? She didn't think she could be so wrong. Maybe he wasn't the type to tell her, his actions had spoken loud enough in the past that should be enough, she consoled herself. And yet it didn't help. She'd always thought the first time she told someone she loved him, he would say it back.

Clean, dressed, and presentable Becca came out to find she was alone. It wasn't unusual for any one of them to have to take care of something. The timing was suspect, but that he was gone wasn't. Not at first. Often, Michael had to call Black for updates. That froze her feet where they were. Would he tell Black? No, she tried to brush it away as paranoia. He wouldn't tell Black anything that would give him more of a hold over her, or him. That was why he hadn't wanted to know how the jumping thing worked.

But he knew that now, didn't he? She'd told him what she felt in his body when she jumped. Maybe he was off telling Black right now. He'd love *that,* she thought bitterly. Making the best of her time, she went in and threw her hair up in a perfunctory ponytail. When she'd finished with some light makeup and he still wasn't back, Becca went next door and knocked.

"Hey sexy." Ryan ran a hand through his sleep tousled hair and grinned at her.

"It isn't too early, is it?" She worried she'd woken him and glanced back over her shoulder to see that the sun was indeed fully up over the one level restaurant across the street though it hadn't cleared the treetops next to it. She turned back. "Were you out all night?"

He yawned, flashing mildly pronounced canines and scratched his chest through his white undershirt. "No, not really. Where's Mike?" His eyes searched beyond her.

Unable to stop herself she winced, then shrugged and averted her eyes. It wouldn't help matters to have him making fun of her for letting her heart get involved where it was never meant to be.

Ryan regarded her quietly and stepped back. "Come on in. I was about to get dressed and head over to the restaurant for breakfast. Have you eaten?"

She shook her head and he waved her in. Taking in the chaotic swirl of blankets Becca knew that she had, in fact, woken the poor man. She cast him a disapproving glare for lying, which he caught and sent right back, squinting at her until she cracked a smile.

His green eyes lit with some of their usual spark and he gave her a lopsided grin. "I'll just be a minute." He dashed around the room in a random pattern until he held a pair of jeans and clean underwear. Making a quick diversion into the bathroom where Becca heard the sounds of rustling fabrics, Ryan popped out in jeans with nothing else covering the rest of him.

It was impossible not to admire what he had going on. Tight, tan, and bigger than most men, Becca had a passing urge to hang off one of his huge arms. So much skin exposed got her body thinking things her mind wouldn't allow.

Ryan had to walk past her to get a shirt out of his bag and when he did his head spun toward her. He took a minute to dig a gray long sleeved henley out and pull it over his head, giving Becca a full view of rippling muscles and an amazingly broad back. Gulping, she looked away and cursed the blood mix yet again.

He turned and leaned back against the wall, crossing his arms over his chest. "You know I'm flattered Becca, but we can't. Even if Gabs and I *are* in a weird place."

Jaw dropping, Becca realized he had sensed her body's reaction and her face flamed. "Oh my God, Ryan. No. I'm not here to try to do *that*. I mean, I get what you picked up," her face had to be tomato red, "but it isn't what I want to do. It's the whole vamp blood thing. I'm really sorry, I can't control it." She blathered on, digging herself an even deeper hole until she finally gave up and snapped her mouth shut.

Several very long heartbeats of silence later, Ryan's face split into a wide smile and he laughed. "So what you're saying is that you're turned on right now, but you don't want to be? I can live with that."

Becca couldn't laugh. She wanted to hit him for mocking her. "It's not funny, Ryan." She wished he'd stop.

That only made him laugh harder. "Are you kidding? That's hilarious!" He roared, stopping and making a serious face for a moment. "You know it's totally okay if you just want me for my body." Then he broke out again sparing her from having to even make an attempt at an answer.

Humiliated, Becca turned on her heel and stalked toward the door. Ryan appeared beside her, the wolves were nearly as fast as the vampires, as her hand closed on the handle.

"I'm sorry, I shouldn't be making fun of you like that." There was genuine remorse in his voice. "Your timing just couldn't be more perfect."

Becca looked up to see his face, to gauge whether he was serious or not. What she saw there caught her unawares. "Ryan, are you okay?" Her mortification took a back seat to the troubled expression he wore.

Those big shoulders rolled and he frowned. "I don't know, all these ladies wanting me for my body with no strings should have me dancing a jig. Only I'm not." He let his eyes catch hers, failing to hide the sadness there. "I guess I wouldn't want a chickish guy like me either if I was a girl."

The turn in topics had Becca in a very awkward position. "You mean that's what's got you two in a funny place? You're more into it than her?" Maybe she was wrong; Ryan would understand *exactly* what she was going through.

His lack of a response told her she was on the right track.

"We talked about this, didn't we? That she's just not the warm fuzzy type?" Becca wasn't sure if she was talking Ryan through his troubles or hers.

"I'm not whining about her not telling me all of her deepest darkest or saying I want to talk about feelings all the time." He gave her a look letting her know he wasn't *that* bad.

If he didn't look so hang dog, she would have laughed. The thought of Ryan talking feelings deep into the night was almost as funny as thinking of Michael doing it. That sobered her.

"All I'm saying is that she sees this as a long term hookup. That's it. I mean it was hot and fun and everything at first, but come on," passion leaked into his plea, "we've been at it for years. And it's not like we're doing it with anybody else." He grabbed a handful of his own hair and tugged. "It's exclusive casual sex and it's not enough." Ryan finished with a frustrated growl.

Giving up on playing it safe, hoping that if she could help him then at least *one* of them would be satisfied, Becca turned around and leaned her back on the door. "Have you tried talking to her?"

He started to open his mouth and she cut him off.

"Seriously talking, like we are right now? Not the usual 'haha' Ryan speak we all know and love." She gave him a serious look, demanding a serious answer. If he wanted to do this now, she was going to make him do this. Funny how brave she was when it wasn't her heart in the scope.

Ryan looked like a kid who'd gotten his hand caught forging a hall pass. "Well, not seriously. We've joked about it."

"*We've* joked about it or *you've* joked about it?" she countered.

His expression began to close off. "I don't want to talk about this anymore."

Forcing air through pursed lips, Becca spun and opened the door. "I'm done with this, at least until I get some food in my stomach." She walked out, throwing a, "you coming?" over her shoulder.

She was halfway through the parking lot before a door slammed shut and she heard the heavy thudding stomp of his boots behind her and she smiled. She didn't want to eat alone and she enjoyed the big lug's company.

Chapter 12

A belly full of toast and coffee had given Becca far more patience and when only a few crumbs remained on her plate she leaned forward, cupping her coffee between her palms.

"I think you should talk to her," she reopened the conversation.

Ryan, having finished his eggs, hash browns, and toast, started on his pancakes. He paused in his attack to take a swig of his milk and answered over the edge of the glass. "I tried."

"No you didn't. You said so yourself, you joked around about it."

"She knows me, that's how I talk about things."

"Then you're not really in love with her. Not if you aren't willing to tell her for real." Becca reflected on the irony. She'd had to be almost passed out and blind to admit it. Who was she to make rules about the right way to profess one's love?

Ryan dropped his fork with a clatter and the tables immediately around them grew uncomfortably quiet. He took one breath, then two before he looked up.

She saw heat in his eyes that didn't bode well for her and she wondered if she'd crossed the line. Spot-free vision allowed Becca the courage to stand firm and she refused to back down. "I mean it. If you love her, tell her." The voice in her head poked her to take her own advice and she poked back that their situation was different, and she *had*, nosy little voice.

There was no warning because Ryan's attack wasn't physical. Glowering, he leaned over his plate and spoke quietly through locked teeth. "How about you? You willing to practice what you preach?"

Seeing where this was going, Becca put her cup down and sat up straight.

He saw that he'd struck a nerve and instantly dropped the anger, switching to his usual flippant attitude. "You tell Mike you love him, and I'll tell Gabs straight up."

"I already did." She pushed out her chin, hoping if she fessed up he wouldn't ask too many questions.

He wasn't fooled. Smiling confidently, he leaned back. "And?"

"And what? I told him," she snapped. "That's what we're talking about, isn't it?"

"And what did he say?"

The smug way he was looking at her had Becca's paranoia on the subject flying into overdrive. Would Michael have told Ryan anything? She thought about keeping her mouth shut. "Nothing," she mumbled.

His brows shot up. Thankfully he didn't laugh. "Nothing?"

"No, nothing. I think I fainted before he had a chance to comment." Her cheeks burned. Again.

Ryan's guffaw drew more stares. Becca wished the floor would open up and she could politely roll in before she had to speak to anyone else.

"You two look like you're having fun."

Becca's back went ramrod straight and Ryan wiped at his eyes. "Hey Mike. Where were you this morning? You missed breakfast." He raised an eyebrow as Michael slid into the booth next to him, eyes trained across the table. "I take that back, it looks like you just finished."

She gave him a long look, taking in the pinked up skin and knew that if she touched him he would feel warm. Cutting her eyes to Ryan, she willed him to keep his trap shut or she would throw him under the bus as soon as she found Gabrielle.

"So, what did I miss?" Michael fiddled with a fork resting on the paper placemat in front of him.

"Nothing," Becca said quickly.

Winking, Ryan grinned. "Becca's giving me love advice."

In her mind's eye, Becca saw her fist landing in his mouth. "You were the one asking for it, Ryan."

Eyes going from one to the other, Michael sought to figure out what had transpired. It was obvious it was only entertaining to one party. Becca was sure she didn't look nearly as amused as Ryan. An elderly woman sitting on the outside of the table across from them shifted her purse to the inside. Apparently, in her head, an altercation might lead to a purse snatching.

"Well why don't you go use some of it? Gabs's back."

All mirth evaporated and Ryan shifted nervously in his seat. "Guess I'd better go see what's up then, huh?"

Nodding, Michael's expression was troubled. "She looked tired, she must have been running all night. She barely looked at me when I said hello." He slid out of his seat to make room for Ryan's exit.

Getting to his feet so fast he banged the table, spilling half her coffee, Ryan said his good byes and hustled out the door.

"Don't worry, I'll get it," Michael joked, reaching for the check.

Becca threw her napkin at the light brown pool spreading on the table. "I'll catch it. You didn't eat." Becca snatched the white register tape from his hand, eager for something else to talk about.

"Okay, I'll let you expense it just this once. But next time it's mine." He offered her a small smile.

Becca walked the check up to pay at the register, leaving the tip with the hostess when Michael joined her at the front.

As they were walking across the parking lot, Michael broke the silence. "Can I ask what sort of advice you were giving Ryan?"

"He wanted a woman's opinion so I gave him one." Becca's answer was short. He was acting like nothing had changed.

"Huh."

Wanting to confront him, afraid of what he'd say, Becca kept walking. How was love a great thing? This was excruciating. Wrestling a drunk with a knife or fending off a shifter's teeth beat this situation hands down.

He let her pass him and every step she took she waited for his hand on her arm or shoulder, even a word to stop her. There was nothing. She stopped at the door to their room and glanced his direction. "What was our plan for today? Are we heading back to the station?" Her hand touched the key in her pocket and she pulled it out.

"I thought you could tell me what you saw yesterday. It *was* a vision, wasn't it?" he asked her quietly.

Dropping her eyes to the key sliding into the lock, Becca blinked away the hurt she felt. It was her fault for dropping the bomb. She was the one who'd brought up the "L" word, not him. He liked her and she knew that. It wasn't right for her to change things now that she'd thrown out the game changer. Swallowing, she straightened, though she couldn't turn and face him. "I, I'm not sure what I saw. Give me some time to figure it out?" That wasn't out of the ordinary for her to give it a day or two to sort out before she advised them what she'd seen. In fact, she was putting off discussing her most recent vision. There were some aspects of it she was having a hard time explaining. Like why it felt so different. It was like she was someone else, only she wasn't. The hands she'd looked at had been female, not male so it wasn't like she'd jumped into one of the others. The whole thing confounded her. In light of the whole vampire blood messing with her sight and body, she didn't want to tell him until she figured it out. If she gave him yet another thing to worry about her for, she thought she'd scream. She hoped he wouldn't push.

He was quiet and she glanced up. He was shaking his head. "The chief has his people doing some sort of mandatory state required training this morning. He was thinking he'd like us there no earlier than one."

It was barely nine.

"Okay. Do you mind if I go for a run then? I'm feeling stronger this morning and it'd be nice to stretch my legs." She stressed how well she was feeling. Freeing him from his obligation to her for the time being.

"Mind if I go with you?"

"Sure. I mean, no. That's fine. Let me get changed." She took in his jeans and blue shirt under a darker blue hoodie. Not that he would sweat or anything, but he might want to change and look the part. "Are you going like that?"

Hands in his pockets, he shrugged. "Yeah, I'll wait out here."

They parted ways awkwardly and Becca ended up taking much longer than necessary to get into her running clothes. At least with running early mornings and evenings in the desert, she had the right gear. Thick black leggings, pink wicking shirt, fitted black zip up jacket and shoes and she was ready. The thin pair of gloves she'd tucked away evaded her, making her delay even longer.

He smiled when she emerged ten minutes later. "I thought I was going to have to send in a search party."

Offering a quick, polite laugh, she made a few last adjustments to her wardrobe and thought about her iPod sitting on the bed. It would be rude to carry it but it would keep her from having to talk too. And she had the feeling that was exactly what Michael had in mind. They'd never had a "feelings talk" but it looked like she might have started something. She pondered the benefits of rolling an ankle and having to go to the hospital. She flashed him a tight smile resembling more of a grimace, and bolted.

Endurance and speed were more "enhancements" she'd gotten from him and she used both to their maximum. Not that she could have outrun Michael, but it let her get out of talking by keeping up a punishing pace any human would have had trouble holding for more than a sprint.

They'd started out on the main county road the motel fronted on and curved onto dirt the first chance they got. Becca, a California girl, thought it would be quieter without the traffic. She hadn't realized the problem with running on a side road in the winter. Ice.

And so it was that after only four miles, nothing for a vampire and his "juiced" girlfriend, she had to pull up or risk breaking her neck. Hands on her hips, she walked in small circles and panted through her nose and out her mouth, making small clouds of smoke as she caught her breath. Michael had no such needs and merely came to a halt, hands in the pockets of his hoodie. Becca could feel the tension tying her shoulders to her neck and bringing them into a painfully tight triangle of angst.

Tilting her head back, she took in the pines towering over them on either side of the narrow path. This particular area had been planted in rows, extending outward in long, dizzying straight lines as far as she could see. The snow covering was thin there, she could tell the depth from a set of rabbit tracks crossing in front of her. A few more steps would take her inside the shadowy forest. Her feet carried her without a second thought.

What little road noise there had been died when she entered the woods. Fallen needles covered with puffy snow cushioned her steps and marked each footfall with a soft "hush." Her memories went back to her cypress copse at Miramar. It was her favorite place on the base where she'd lived for several years. It was also the place where she first met Admiral Black and the wolves, changing her life's course forever. The knot in her back began to let go and she rolled her neck, helping it along. Another deep breath brought in the crisp, pine scent with only a hint of the musty earth stirred by their passing.

The mature thing to do was to face Michael and talk through what he would have said last night if she hadn't fainted at the crucial moment. Or hearing him tell her it hadn't been that for him. That it had been fun at first and now was an obligation they would have to continue with if for no other reason than to prevent her from burning out.

Picking up speed, she took off through the narrow opening between the trunks. Ducking low boughs and hopping over small depressions where roots had shifted the ground soon took all of her focus and her problems became an afterthought. She failed to notice when Michael came abreast of her and caught her arm, slowing to bring them both to a walk.

Puffing, she gave up trying to avoid him and stood waiting, like a sullen teenager. She wasn't going to talk first this time. In her head, she already had. And now, she was terrified at the power she'd given him over her.

Chapter 13

Ryan entered their room quietly, not exactly sneaking, but damn close. Gabrielle was in the shower. He could smell the wet, pungent tang of sweat and earth combined with a trace of blood emanating from the pile of clothes by the bed where she'd stripped. She'd been in human form again last night while he'd favored the wolf. Better to protect her if they ran into the windigo or whatever it was working for. She had only changed for a few moments to hunt. The blood wasn't hers. He could smell the difference even dried.

Their continued silence pained him deeply. Becca was right, he did love her and he was too big a coward to admit it to her. He stood outside the bathroom, knuckles resting on the closed door while he listened to her in the shower. The flick of the shampoo bottle's lid echoed off the white tile walls. Closing his eyes, he pictured her as she washed her hair. He could smell the familiar scents of the soaps and products she'd brought from home. His fingers rubbed together, feeling the phantoms of her honey blonde strands between them.

The water turned off and Ryan backed away. He didn't know much about being in love, but it didn't seem like a good idea to get caught stalking a girl. "Hey Gab," he called out to let her know he was in there.

"Hey," she called back after a long pause.

It was doubtful she would go to wolf form here in the tiny motel room. That would be more than ridiculous, it would be blatant. No, it was more likely she would try to seduce him or sleep to keep from talking.

Sure enough, when the door opened to reveal a towel wrapped Gabrielle, she yawned. "I need a few hours. You?" Her eyes barely skimmed over him, she wasn't interested in his answer.

Ryan, however, was studying her features and frame closely. Dark, puffy circles beneath her amber eyes were easily visible from across the room as was the slump to her normally proud shoulders. Even the sway was gone from her shuffling walk. He clenched his hands into tight fists and crossed his arms to keep from going to her and folding her into his body, protecting her from whatever was haunting her. The voice inside his head told him this was really not the time, yet Becca's words had goaded him into a now or never mentality. He took a deep breath and let part of it escape in a hiss. "Can you wait? I wanted to talk to you about something."

Falling sideways onto the bed without pulling back the covers, Gabrielle eyed him warily and headed him off. "I know I've been distracted the past few days but I'm trying to work something out." She managed a tired smile. "I promise we can talk about whatever you want, soon, if you could just give me a few more days to get some answers for myself." She offered him a timid smile. "I'll be in a better place to talk then, I promise."

The edge of panic he saw behind her fatigue dissolved his nerve on sight. He couldn't confess his love after her request, and she didn't look like she was in any shape to handle an emotional outpouring anyway. Silently cursing his timing, he smiled and crossed the room.

She pushed up expectantly and he kissed her gently on the lips before reaching behind her to pull back the covers.

"Get some rest, we've got nothing going until tonight."

All too willing, she laid down at his gentle guidance. "Are you sure? If you need to tell me something, you can."

Leaning down to pull the blankets over her and kiss her again, Ryan gave her a small smile. "No, it can wait."

"Thanks Ryan," she mumbled, already heading off to sleep.

He sat on the edge of the bed once she was down and tortured himself by listening to the restless tossing and muttering that began shortly after her breathing regulated. There it was, the name she spoke only rarely at home. He'd heard it at least ten times yesterday after she'd gone to sleep. She'd cried out so loud the one time she'd actually roused him from a dead sleep in a panic, thinking someone was in the room.

"No Luc, please." Her whimper tore out his heart, the tears he saw wetting her cheeks stomped on it until there was nothing left.

Chapter 14

Michael's hand on her arm held her firmly in place while Becca stared at her feet. Her erratic behavior since breakfast was maddening. If she wasn't going to talk to him soon he was going to have to get it out of Ryan. He had a slight speed advantage over the wolf, but that didn't mean the fight wouldn't hurt like hell.

"You can't keep avoiding me," he growled.

"What?" Large, tear filled eyes flew up to his face.

The distress so plainly written on her face tore at him and his vampire flared within him. "What did Ryan say to you? I'll tear him apart."

"You're mad at *Ryan*?" She took a step back, jerking her arm loose. "Ryan has *nothing* to do with this."

"Then what has you so upset?" He watched her features twist into a scowl. "Is it the vision you had yesterday? You can talk it through with me, we can try to understand it together." They'd talked through a few confusing ones in the past. He was willing to help her again if she would let him. There was a slight hesitation before she answered and Michael knew there was something there, though that wasn't what she wanted to fight about.

Becca ducked her head, hiding her eyes. "I said some things last night." Her voice was choked. "I was upset and freaking out and then you called me a, *that*. And then I said some stuff I shouldn't have. Stuff I didn't mean." She rushed through the words. "I wanted to tell you it's okay if we need to…" Her voice broke before she could finish.

The metallic taste of blood littered his tongue and filled his nose as his fangs pierced his lower lip. "What did you say that you didn't mean Becca?" Her acceptance of him, her knowledge of Black's hold and her professed love regardless had liberated him from the prison that had held him hostage for decades. If not for the mission they were on he would have holed up in their room for days showing her how he felt in return. Was she saying that her declarations, any of them, had been untrue? His nature threatened to take him to a dark place. A place where he would lose all hints of his humanity, at least for a short while. The damage she would take would be much more than the occasional love nip she'd suffered. *Not her.* He warned the vampire. *Never her.*

She heard the change in his tone and shrank back, her eyes beginning to dart. Her sight was warning her of danger; he recognized the signs. It sobered him at once and inwardly he roared in frustration. *He* was the danger and he knew it. Michael fought back his beast with a Herculean effort.

145

Reaching for her again, he hid his agony at her flinch. "Becca," he let his hand fall and called softly to her.

Again she let her eyes seek his, studying them to gauge his beast. When she took a half step toward him, he knew that he had won for the present. The vampire would let the man rule this time. Tentatively, he reached out again. She allowed it and his hand slid under her arm to wrap around her waist. Fangs were willed back and a quick flick of the tongue sealed the holes in his lip.

"Becca, you're special to me," He watched her breath catch, preparing herself. "You affected me the first time I saw you." Michael's own chest hurt, phantom pains of what it would be like to feel his heart stop, he was sure. He started again. "What you said last night." He paused when he saw her flush, fearful she would repeat those fateful words and he would lose all hope again. Girding himself to face a more frightening enemy than any he'd opposed in battle, her disapproval, Michael stepped closer and took strength in her nearness. "You can't know what that meant to me." Even saying the words took all of his will, to admit his weakness to this woman who meant more than she could comprehend. "I've feared the day you might see the admiral's influence. Even more, I've feared that you wouldn't. That you would think me a coward for not standing against him." Blue eyes searched hers desperately. Any care he had for hiding his emotions was gone. Here he was, vulnerable at her feet, jugular exposed. From habit, he swallowed and licked his lips. "That you would love me, knowing that I'm his," he shook his head still disbelieving, "you've given back my life. How could I not love you for that alone?"

Anxiously he waited for her response. Carefully studying her expression as it went from pained to jubilant. "You do?"

Michael, capable of figuring out the most intricate of double crosses, privy to ploys for power at the highest levels, and witness to some of the worst manipulations the admiral had maneuvered, realized how dense he'd been. His jaw dropped. "You thought I didn't? That's what was upsetting you?" Relief that it was so simple poured through him and Michael's chest rumbled with laughter.

Pulling back, Becca hit him on the pectoral. "Don't laugh at me. It's not every day I put that out there." Her lip was sticking out in an adorable pout. "I didn't know what was supposed to happen after I said it." The corner of her mouth twisted. "I guess fainting wasn't really in the plan, either."

The desire to consume her built and Michael had to settle for pulling her in to wrap himself around her and cover her mouth with his. Needing to do much more than taste her, he groaned when her lips opened to his tongue. She whimpered, stretching his already strained tethers on his nature. Reason tried to surface. They were visible from the road should anyone look. It was winter and she would be cold with her back on the snow. With his periphery, he scanned for a thicker cluster of trees where he could legitimize what he wanted to do to her as being out of sight and maybe give them a vertical surface since the horizontal was frozen. Becca pushed her body into him and his responded.

Her hand had snuck lower and was working to take away the last of his restraint when his phone rang. Neither stopped. Seconds later, hers echoed from the inside pocket in her running jacket. Reluctantly, he pulled away and was pleased to see his frustration mirrored in her flushed cheeks and heavy lids. For a second he was tempted to crush the phones and take her right there. She was all too willing by the look of her and the way her hand lingered on his hip.

"Rossi." His phone was in his hand before he could think too hard about it.

Becca was fishing hers out, answering a moment later. "Captain Sauter."

Michael's hearing picked up both voices. His eyes narrowed when he caught Salvo's voice in Becca's ear. Their police chief had called him.

"We've got another body." He sighed, heavy with the burden of his office.

"Where?" Becca and Michael asked simultaneously.

He felt his passion receding as sense of duty took precedence.

"It's not far from you. You at the motel?" The sound of his hand running across his face was audible before it muffled his words. "Detective Salvo's already on his way to the scene. He can pick you up on the way."

"We were out for a run. We can be back in a few minutes." He bristled at the voice on the other phone asking Becca if she needed to shower first when she told him of their run. It wasn't okay for the prick to even have a mental glimpse of her naked. Logic told him the man was being polite.

Chief Kowski sighed again. "Great, I'll let Detective Salvo know."

Michael informed him tightly. "Captain Sauter can tell him. He's on the phone with her now."

She smiled and the love he saw in her eyes instantly put him at ease. "We'll be ready in about twenty." Nodding, she said a quick good bye and hung up.

The chief grumbled something about Salvo being on top of things and he was gone.

"We'd better get back," she suggested.

Michael nodded, refraining from touching her. Duty wouldn't keep him from having her if they started again. She bit her lip, clearly thinking the same thing.

"We should go." The first step was hard, the rest got easier and soon they were running. Becca was going to need a shower at the speeds they were going. Michael averted his thoughts and kept his eyes to the ice patches in front of him, cold thoughts not nearly as effective as a cold shower.

Chapter 15

Detective Salvo was knocking on their door as Becca emerged with a still damp ponytail and clad in jeans and light green sweater.

"I wish we could wear our fatigues," she told him, leaning over to grab her boots where she'd left them by the foot of the bed. "Out here, who knows if we're going to be in the woods or crawling around a field. It would be nice to feel prepared."

Grinning, Michael crossed the room to answer the door. "Get used to them, don't you? Imagine spending a lifetime or two in them."

She laughed her agreement as he opened the door.

"Come in. Becca's just finishing getting ready." Michael stepped back to allow him entry.

That he was so blatantly showing the detective their joint sleeping arrangements, only one bed clearly having been used, had her smiling at her boots while she laced them. Michael was obviously making his claim known, the hell with their professionalism. Surprisingly, it didn't bother her. Either way, there wasn't time for worrying about it and it would have been rude to slam the door in his face. What was, was.

"Uncle Sam's tightening his belt too, huh?" he joked uncomfortably, keeping his eyes from touching Becca. "Can't spring for two rooms?"

"Oh, they paid for two rooms," Michael told him. "We aren't here alone."

Detective Salvo glanced over at Becca then and opened his mouth to speak just as the door rattled again. Boots tied, Becca stood as Michael opened the door and huge shoulders blocked the light right on cue.

"Detective, meet Captains Ryan Hallbeck and Gabrielle Brion." He waved them in, Gabrielle invisible behind Ryan's hulking form.

Michael filed through the tight quarters to Becca's side by the farther bed, leaving the other three to hover by the door. Ryan and Gabrielle idled, relaxing by the door while Detective Salvo maneuvered his back to the wall. His eyes raced from one side to the other where he was flanked by two pairs of what he believed to be federal agents infringing upon his investigation. His reaction was understandable.

"What the hell?" he fumed. "Where did these two come from and why didn't I know about them?"

Ryan grinned. "We handle the behind the scenes stuff." He nodded his head at his unit members across the room. "The whole 'office niceties' thing isn't our deal."

Gabrielle stood quietly beside him. Becca couldn't help noticing how tired and distracted she looked. They'd been running hard the past two nights. She felt a guilty nudge at having slept so well last night. While she'd been snuggled up in a warm bed, they'd been out running half the state by the look of Gabrielle's pasty complexion. A tiny scrape marred her cheek, though that would be gone the next time she changed forms. Changing helped them to heal faster.

Furious dark eyes glared at Michael and Becca. "So what, while we work our asses off you bring in your own team to run your own investigation?" Singling Becca out, he knifed a thumb at the newcomers. "When were you going to tell me? Were you planning on sharing any of this?"

Unmoved by the detective's outburst, Michael met his gaze evenly. "These two have been trained for jungle fighting, guerilla warfare, and any other secret-type shit normal police don't handle." He raised his voice over Salvo's forthcoming objection. "No offense, those are merely the facts. They go to ground, they see what they can track, and then we see if we can find where the killer's holing up. The fewer who see them, the better." Seeing the detective wasn't going to immediately hit the roof, he lowered his voice. "Meanwhile, the rest of us work together to follow the clues and see if we can find him that way."

The room was quiet while the detective absorbed all that. Showing a level head unusual for someone his age, Salvo gave a single bob of his head and thumbed at the other two. "As long as they share, I'm cool." His demeanor had eased, though not the heat coming off of him.

Becca could sense that he was not as okay as he said, but if he was willing to accept and work with this new dynamic, then how could they complain if he was a little pissed off? As far as he could tell, she'd done exactly what she'd said she wouldn't. "Absolutely, Detective." She smiled.

He cut her a look that told her how much he valued her input at that point.

"Well, now that we're all friends," Ryan ran a big hand over his shirtfront, "let's go check out a fresh crime scene." He turned and walked out, waving over his head at the room he was leaving behind. "We'll be waiting in the truck."

Wordless, Gabrielle gave a last searching look and nodded, bidding her adieu as well. She closed the door softly behind her.

"Maybe he's right, niceties aren't their thing," Salvo said to the door. Then, shaking himself, he stepped away from the wall and moved toward the door. "You two ready? We got a scene to get to."

****

It wasn't a surprise that the scene hadn't been discovered right away. The young man had been out walking his dog in the early hours of the morning when he'd been attacked. The remains of the dog were strewn all over. Its black, fur-covered parts were thrown in a hateful pique as far as forty yards from its human companion. A section of intestine hung from a low hanging, leaf barren branch. Trees lined the small clearing only a few yards from the road, wheat colored grass hip high on the tallest of the men stood between the road and the clearing. Blood and meat covered snow had been trampled in the area immediately surrounding the bodies while only a few feet away, unmarred snow led to the bases of the naked mature tree line. Those trees marked the beginnings of a wild area that would have been impassable in the height of summer. At present, they hunkered and watched stoically over the tragedy at their feet while a storm brewed above.

Becca held her finger under her nose and stifled the urge to retch. The stench of opened stomach and bowel was overpowering and her eyes watered.

"Breathe through your sleeve," Michael, one of the few who could understand what her powerful nose was picking up, whispered as he stepped away from her to explore the scene. If this was hard for her, it had to be terrible for the other members of her unit. Their sense of smell was even stronger than hers.

Brown canvas-jacketed sheriffs and blue parka-clad local police were working to process the scene. Darkening skies, heavy with snow-filled clouds, urged them to be quick. One young officer leaned against a tree trunk on the perimeter heaving out his breakfast, a camera hung by its strap from the hand not propping him up.

Unashamed to have anyone else think she was near vomiting herself, Becca pulled her hand inside her wool sleeve and held the end to her nose and mouth, trunk-like. Several gulps of warm air allowed her head to clear. Blinking away the reactionary dampness that had formed in her eyes when she was gagging, Becca pretended to be searching the ground for tracks and other clues while she watched the scene out of the corner of her eye. Her skin itched from the tension coming off the blue and brown coats littering the scene.

Ryan took long strides past her, heading straight for the bodies. Circling first the human, then the dog, he came in close. Odd considering the attention everyone was paying to the human. Sensing her gaze, he looked up and winked.

That was the moment Gabrielle happened to stop beside her. "They're all stomping around the human, the dog is relatively untainted." She informed her flatly. "Better scents there."

Although she knew what the woman meant, Becca would have strongly disagreed with the quality of the sniffs surrounding the dog's various parts.

"Is everything okay Gabrielle?" Becca kept her eyes forward, watching Salvo talking to a few of his brethren gathered across the bodies from them. Sensing her eyes on him, Salvo turned and his expression softened. Several glanced up and followed his gaze to land on Becca. One elbowed Salvo in the ribs and he grunted something below her audible range. Redirecting, she went back to watching Ryan. Salvo shifted to see what had caught her eye. Following once again, the rest of their eyes turned to take in Ryan hunkered over the dog. Becca watched a sheriff pale and turned, catching Ryan putting a finger in dark snow and pulling it out to smell it. She fought a smile, knowing if they hadn't been watching, he might have licked it. The sheriff put a hand over his mouth and his eyes went wide. Becca didn't have to look back to know that he had just put that finger in his mouth.

"We've put in a lot of miles since we got here." Gabrielle sighed. "It's tiring running all over the countryside following a smell that's everywhere." She nodded her head back toward where Ryan was standing and sniffing at the branches. "He's distracted, because of me."

Becca was seriously trying hard not to laugh at the one sheriff who was supposed to be lamenting the new guys with Salvo and company while he was completely distracted by Ryan's unconventional scene exploration. She couldn't help sniggering imagining what the young man would do if he saw Ryan do the half-wolf thing where only his head changed. He'd probably shit.

Hearing Gabrielle's measured air intake beside her, Becca worried she'd mistaken the laughter as being directed at her. "Oh Gabrielle, I'm sorry. I was just…"

"Forget it," she said absently.

Catching the odd tone in her voice, Becca's head whipped around to check on the woman beside her. Only Becca could see that she'd already lost her, her eyes were focused on something in the distance, something out past where the trees started. Quick, so she didn't miss it, Becca turned and followed her gaze. There was nothing.

"I'll catch you later." Gabrielle started walking, her eyes never wavering from some fixed point only she could see.

Becca was used to the woman being distant. This was checked out. "Um, okay." She watched her go, making note of the direction before taking off to find Michael.

He was crouched beside the chest cavity of the human's body. The forensics team was packing up and the other cops were comparing notes off to the side so he was alone. Becca hurried over and leaned in, speaking quietly in his ear.

Startled, his eyes shot up, searching a moment before landing on the woman in question currently maneuvering her way past the cars and heading into the trees.

"I'm worried about her and I think Ryan could use a break from the stress." She glanced down and pointedly ignored the worried look he gave her, nodding instead toward the group of uniforms hovering uncomfortably a short distance away. "I'm going to follow, but I don't want them out there just in case I run across anything. Distract them for a minute?"

Watching her, knowing he couldn't make a scene without drawing unwanted attention, Michael gave her a deliberate nod. "Careful. This thing is close, can you smell it?"

Lowering her sleeve, she took a deep sniff of the human. Too deep. The iron and bile scents of blood and guts filled her nose. There was a hint of something else she caught on the back of her tongue and, cautiously, she took several smaller sniffs. Underneath the overpowering immediate whiffs lay the faint sweet smell of decay. "I smell it. Is that the thing?" She didn't use its name even though no one was near enough to have heard.

He gave a tiny head tip in Gabrielle's direction. "You smell that out there, get the hell out. No questions. Don't try to handle this thing on your own." The severity of his expression allowed for no arguments. "Do you have your gun?"

"Loaded with the good stuff." She patted the holster under her arm where she carried her 9mm loaded with pure silver, guaranteed to kill any supernatural creature they might encounter. "Buy me some time?"

"Alright. I'll follow as soon as I can run these guys out." He straightened up and marched over to Salvo's group, putting on his darkest glare.

Becca was glad it wasn't aimed at her and felt a twinge of guilt for sending him over, tempering it with the knowledge of what might happen if one followed her into a windigo's den or worse.

"Who the *hell's* in charge of this scene?" he shouted. "This damned place is a zoo. There are footprints and puke everywhere. Is there any evidence that *hasn't* been contaminated?"

Smiling at his ability to play the role of massive jackass all too well, Becca walked past staring straight ahead. When she'd met Michael she thought he was hot, but an ass. She was more than happy to have discovered how wrong she was. Handy the local officers didn't know that. She moved like she was going to the car and, after checking that no one was watching her, zipped back up to the trees and cut in where she'd lost sight of Gabrielle.

At first she followed the footprints, then when they looped back, she feared she'd been ditched. It didn't make sense that Gabrielle would want to lead her in circles, or even that she'd seen her. Why would she want to hide her tracks? Was she hiding something else? Kneeling down in the snow, she saw that some of the tracks had a fresh dusting of snow in them.

"She's been here before," she breathed aloud, tracing the outline of a heel with her fingers. "But why?"

Becca, after some quick discerning, sorted the old from the new and backtracked to find where she'd gotten confused. The tracks crossed themselves repeatedly. Gabrielle wasn't leading her anywhere, she was searching for something. Deliberately and tediously, she followed each boot-shaped indent. It wasn't easy. Even with the lack of leaves, the density of the trees and fallen debris hidden by snow and snarled where patches were packed down with the weight of fallen matter and the white stuff made for slower and more difficult going as she progressed. Then, mercifully, it opened up in a few spots. Several times she lost Gabrielle's tracks in the leaf litter and had to resort to following the direction and, staying true, recovered them. "What are you looking for?" she muttered, taking a moment to catch her breath. What might not have been a brisk pace for the wolf was punishing for the already taxed human. The freshness she'd woken with that had sent her out for a run this morning was gone now, replaced by a weariness she felt in her bones.

After over an hour of spine straining crouching and ducking limbs, her back smarting from a few new scrapes and her lungs threatening to explode, Becca saw movement up ahead. Instinctively she dropped into a crouch behind a log and branch combo that provided some amount of cover if she stayed low.

Gabrielle was alternating between slow steps and halts. Her eyes were aimed at something up ahead, her focus disturbingly fixed.

Her quads were burning and her panting was like a freight train ringing off the frozen surfaces. The detective was right, sound did carry in the winter. Becca tried adjusting to give her upper thighs a break and Gabrielle's head whipped around, her nostrils quivering. Becca stopped breathing and her lungs burned, her entire being froze. For several painful moments, she stared at the exact spot where Becca crouched. Neither moved. At last, Gabrielle seemed satisfied that what she smelled was of no consequence and snapped instantly back into her entranced state. About ready to believe her teammate was hallucinating, following some unknown ghost, Becca had to cover her mouth to stop the sound that wanted to come out when a pale glow in front of Gabrielle illuminated the outline of a tree trunk up ahead.

"Wait!" She reached out a hand and darted forward. "Don't go."

The glow moved ahead, matching the blonde's speed, keeping the distance between them even. She caught her foot in a tangle of underbrush covered by snow and went down on her knees. Becca used the noise of Gabrielle's fall and subsequent recovery to cover her rapid surge forward. The burst drained her yet she pushed on. She wanted to see what it was Gabrielle was following. Was it the windigo? But if it was, why was Gabrielle pleading with it instead of fighting it?

Chapter 16

"Well, that's the last of them," Ryan chuckled. "I gotta hand it to you Mike, you sure know how to clear a room, or scene. Whatever."

"Yeah, I have special skills." Michael watched the dark sedan pull away, a few loose stones thrown by its tires coming dangerously close to him. He refused to budge, seeing Salvo watching in his rearview mirror. Tempting fate, he raised a hand and heard the engine roar in response.

Ryan laughed beside him. "I think you made an enemy." He ruffed his hair then smoothed it. "You want to tell me why you sent Becca after Gabs instead of me? She's not as fast and if they find this thing, I'd be better suited. No offense."

"None taken." Michael frowned and kicked one of the stones that had nearly hit him. "You've been out with her the last two nights. We thought you could use a change. Plus, you were the one who was being so obvious. It's not like you could have snuck away with that kid locked in on you." Michael snorted. "I thought he was going to puke when you licked that blood off your finger."

"That dog must have really gotten a hold of it. The spatter in the snow looked like it was femoral." His tongue traced the inside of his lower teeth, his jaw hanging partway open to pull air over the scent receptors. He was recalling the elements he'd tasted in the windigo's blood.

"So," Michael crossed his arms over his chest, "what did you get? Thoughts on where it's been hanging out?"

"Yeah." He slapped his hands together. "It's a combo of minerals I smelled the first night here." Ryan rubbed a palm on his thigh. "I've smelled it on Gabs both mornings she's come in." Pained, he made fists and turned to face Michael straight on. "She had to see it. I mean it's only in a few places out here. If she's been hitting those spots, she had to cross paths with it. Why didn't she tell us?"

"No clue Ryan. Let's see if we can find out though." He aimed for the hole in the trees where Becca disappeared. The need to follow and make sure she was okay was making him twitchy. It would feel good to let loose and run. Glancing up, he watched the clouds rolling in and smelled snow.

The advantage they had over Becca was that their senses were stronger even than hers, and the sources were doubled. Being mindful of where their feet fell, careful not to make too much noise, they followed. Both men were focused on catching up to their team, each for a different female reason.

Gabrielle's progress had brought her to a place on the far side of a tall, triangle-shaped pile of pale brown limestone. Becca continued to duck and dodge, weaving her way between trees and stones as the terrain grew more rocky. She stumbled repeatedly. Scrapes burned on her knees and the bruising beginning on her shins was going to hurt before it cleared up by tomorrow. A tic on the positive side for having Michael's blood in her: quick heal time. The glow continued to pull them along, further into the wood, which had changed from birch to oak. That meant they were moving to higher ground, away from the reedy wetland that had been hanging them up. They walked until the upper canopy of dead leaves, those not due to fall until the spring growth pushed them out, worked with the coming snow storm to block out the light. Soon it was dim as dusk in spite of it being just past the noon hour.

There was something Becca wanted to try but she needed to be still in order to do so. It wouldn't be a good idea to jump and be distracted in one head, while the other body was weaving between trees and marching over dense knots of brush. As if to prove her point, her toe caught a large stick and she had to jerk her foot twice to loose her lace from a chunk of bark.

The glow stopped moving and Gabrielle, completely engrossed in her dance with it, halted as well. Sensitive to every crunch, Becca wished she could be walking on the rocks like Gabrielle instead of shadowing her from the trees. At least her head wouldn't feel like it had been plucked bare by the countless tree fingers hanging down.

"Finally," she breathed raggedly. Ignoring the nervous energy racing up and down her exhausted body, Becca concentrated on the tall blonde balanced precariously atop a large boulder. If she could only see what Gabrielle did, she could help or at least understand what had cast such an enchantment on the seemingly untouchable woman.

The blonde hovered in a half crouch, her hands out to her sides, balancing. Her lips moved only Becca was too far to hear. Choosing to stay and focus on jumping, she gave up on hearing what was being said. She'd get both if her attempt was successful. Briefly, she considered that she might be too tired to be successful, then shooed the thought away. Black wanted her to do this, she *needed* to do this, so here she was and she was going to jump. Eyes narrowing to keep from blinking, Becca slowed her breathing and brought calm to her being. When she was ready, really only a minute or so later, she reached.

When she did, several things happened right on top of each other. The twitching she'd willed away returned with a vengeance and her skin was alive with thousands of needles pricking her flesh. Her teeth ground together and she doubled her efforts, forcing her mind to neglect the body she needed to leave in favor of the one she was hoping to get into.

It was no use. Try as she might to push her way in, there was no opening. No thinning of the barrier that separated their minds provided the opportunity she required to jump in. *Becca pushed harder, throwing herself out recklessly and felt something warm latch onto her psyche. There was a feeling of being yanked sideways, and then of being trapped. In a flash she was blind as spots gave way to a sheet of blinding light. The thing that had latched onto the part of her reaching out to Gabrielle tightened its grip and her body caught fire. Every fiber of her being, inside and out, was alight with pain. Without being bidden, images of the fire demon popped into her consciousness and terror paralyzed her mind and body. Her skin was once again being charred and her mind screamed out while her body began to shut down.*

****

"No, come back!" Gabrielle shouted desperately as the glow disappeared. Snapped out of her trance with a rude shove, she felt the tether that had pulled her along let go. The backlash of its release upset her balance and she fell. Waking suddenly, she tore her fingers and ripped off a nail clinging to the boulder she found herself perched on.

The same disorientation she'd experienced coming off her tracking shifts the previous nights left her shaky and weak. If she changed to her wolf form she could be strong, but that same pull that had called to her had urged her to stay human. It blocked her will to call her beast and share its strength, leaving in its place a human; weak, confused, and bleeding. Tears of unknown origin wet her cheeks. She touched her face, leaving red streaks as she wondered what had possessed her to depart the crime scene. The last she could remember, she'd been talking to Becca. Now she was here. And why did she feel like someone kicked her in the stomach? Without understanding why, she hid her face in her hands and gave in to the overwhelming grief threatening to tear her apart.

****

Becca fell to her knees, blissful oblivion closing in and taking with it any conscious thoughts she might have had. It didn't register when she struck her head on the rocky ground nor did she notice when warm blood began leaking out onto the snow. Images of the cabin where she'd faced down the demon, the images that had haunted her dreams for weeks, flooded her mind, numbing it. The smell that wafted to her on the air made her gag. Her mouth opened in a terrified scream, only nothing came out.

Neither woman noticed when a third figure emerged from the woods where the glow had disappeared. The creature scuffed a bare foot against the ice-crusted rock it crested to come into the opening. Taller than a normal human male, the creature had to weigh less than a young girl. Skeletal limbs covered in sagging gray flesh protruded from a rail thin body barely covered by the filthy rags that draped it. Too short pants exposed bony ankles and threadbare patches in several places offered glances of more sickly physique underneath. Long, shaggy hair hung in mud-fused clumps leaving little of the dull brown color showing through. The mop of dirt and debris also served to cover the majority of the creature's face. Aimed down at the sobbing form ahead, it kept its features hidden. The sickening sweet smell of rot perfumed the crisp air around it.

****

"You smell that?" Ryan was in the lead when he picked up the new scent. "There are two somethings we're following."

"Just figured that one out." Michael grunted. The vampire was shrieking for him to run, to fly to Becca. A windigo was challenge enough. The second creature was something else. It smelled of something old, nothing he had encountered before, he was sure of it. He knew it had to be the thing using the windigo, which made it something to be feared. And he'd let Becca go after it? That had been careless on his part. But working with her these past few months he'd learned once she got it in her head to do something, there was no stopping her. He hoped she'd caught Gabrielle and they faced it together or that he and Ryan would get there before there was a confrontation. Exchanging a glance, both men doubled their pace. Stealth was compromised only a shade as they flew through the woods.

What felt like hours could have only been minutes. Michael and Ryan held back very little as they leapt fallen trees and ran over the tricky footing as only the supernatural can. To a normal human it would appear they floated without care over the ground when in actuality, their hyperawareness allowed them to scout the ground just as carefully as any pedestrian without slowing. Combined with their sense of urgency, they all but flew.

The two of them stayed to the woods, following the rocky opening in the trees. Cover was essential for them to maintain the element of surprise as best they could. The clouds had opened, large fluffy flakes falling slowly at first, then much heavier as they ran. Soon it was a near whiteout where the rocks impeded tree growth, only slightly better in the leaf barren woods. And so it was purely sense of smell that led them to where their quarry had come to a stop.

Chapter 17

The smell of decay hit him full in the nose and Michael skidded to a halt, putting a hand out unnecessarily to signal Ryan to do the same. He'd caught the same scent. Both fell into a crouch and Michael squinted into the white mess, scanning for signs of movement.

"Holy fuck," Ryan breathed from beside him. "Found it."

Michael followed the track of his unit member's gaze to behold the skeleton hovering on the rock, a living creature straight out of a nightmare. The wind had picked up with the storm and whipped the dark tattered clothing about the bony gray creature's filthy head. He registered that the lump in front of it was alive and not a part of the rock. She was curled into a ball and a howling sob rolled out just as the creature lowered itself to touch her.

Ryan's snarl cut through the wind and the creature's face came up. It was cut short as he beheld the thing exactly as horrible as Michael had described it. The gray flesh hung loosely over hollow cheeks and empty black eyes. Sagging lips did nothing to hide the fangs that were as long as a man's ring finger and nearly reached the bottom of its chin.

Seeing the stronger being that was Gabrielle incapacitated had Michael in a frenzy. Casting his eyes wildly about, he searched the area for Becca. There was no sign on the rocks or in the woods. And to further inflame his frustration, the wind gusted again, filling his nose with aged death and taking with it any chance of finding Becca that way. A second growl erupted from his shoulder mate and Michael quit any semblance of secrecy.

"Becca!" he yelled.

No answer.

Narrowing his eyes, he rose and rushed forward. There was no making this thing speak; it was unable due to the level of physical deterioration. Death was its only future. Michael and Ryan matched strides to be the deliverers of its sentence.

Two legs turned to four as Ryan changed on the fly, clothing bursting into pieces to litter the forest floor. Together they broke from the trees and hopped from rock to rock, splitting to flank the thing. Michael sunk lower, gathering himself to leap, knowing Ryan would be doing the same.

The vampire snarled as he took the head and the wolf's teeth snapped on bone where he clamped onto the femur. The thing's body went down, legless and headless but not destroyed. Michael had educated Ryan on the destruction of this specific creature during their pursuit. The body was torn limb from limb into tiny pieces without a word being spoken between them. No blood in the body, it was set into a dry pile of crumbling bones that Michael easily set ablaze using its clothing as tinder, burning the parts so that no amount of magic could ever reassemble it.

That done the men split, their goals no longer common. Ryan's soft reassurances echoed in his ears as Michael began circling the perimeter, scanning the fresh white blanket covering the ground and blinding shower of large wet flakes obscuring even his vision.

"Becca," he called again, stopping to listen for a response possibly too weak to hear over the sound of his boots crunching in the snow. He was circling back around the rock, peering into the woods when the wind dropped for a few seconds and he caught a whiff of blood. Fresh blood. Head shooting up, eyes searching, he caught one more sniff before the wind picked up again. It was enough. It was Becca's blood and it called to him.

Long strides carried him to where she lay on the other side of a cluster of trees and heavy brush that blocked her from him until he was almost on top of her. The blood had stopped, but he saw with a stomach dropping realization that it had come from her head. She'd hit it on the rock sticking out of the ground not a foot away. White flakes were working to cover the dark stain his eyes didn't need to tell him was there. His nose gave him all of the information he needed. She was hurt, thankfully not severely though the temperatures were not doing her any favors. Her skin was turning blue from cold, not blood loss. She hadn't lost enough to cause her a shortage and her heart was strong. Racing in fact. On his knees next to her small, prone body, Michael smelled fear. And gently, he wiped away the snow that covered her face to reveal her features frozen in a mask of abject terror that sent a stabbing pain through him.

"Becca, honey, I'm here. Becca wake up, it's all right." He comforted her as he picked her up and cradled her close. "Ryan," he called over his shoulder and turned to see that he had Gabrielle up and on her feet. She was shaking her head and wiping at her face but seemed okay, if a little bloody. "I'll meet you at the truck." Without waiting for an answer, he took off.

It was a much faster return than the hike out due to the simple fact that nothing held him back and he had motive for getting her into a warm truck ASAP. Back at the truck, he held her one-handed while he fished the keys from his pocket.

"Hold on Becca, just give me a minute and I'll get you warm."

She made a little sound and Michael checked his grip, loosening his arms immediately. He looked down to see her eyes still terrified and struggled to keep hold of her, fighting back his nature demanding he go back and reassemble the ashes so he could tear the creature apart again. He reminded himself not to lose control or squeeze her too tight again.

He found the keys and got her inside the back to lay her down, letting her go long enough to start the truck, put the heat up to full blast, and get in back with her. Resting her head on his lap was the only way for both of them to fit. Stroking her hair, he lifted it to see that the cut was minor and the bump had been kept down by the cold. She'd have a nasty bruise though it would disappear relatively quickly.

The damage wasn't severe enough to have caused the mental paralysis she was suffering. As far as he knew, a windigo wasn't one to possess or manipulate one's mind. That begged the question: what was working with the windigo? It had to be powerful to take down Gabs and Becca. Impatient for her to wake up, he rubbed her shoulder vigorously.

"Becca, come on. Wake up, honey." He watched her face. Color was slowly bleeding back into her lips and cheeks, her eyes relaxed finally and drifted closed. "You're almost there, honey." Michael smiled to himself. If someone had told him twenty years ago that he would be in love with a human, that she would love him back, he would have killed the person for being a dumbass. A cruel dumbass.

She sighed and her lids fluttered open. The big hazel eyes that stared up at him were quiet. Becca was in there again. He felt his lips pull back into a smile. Blinking, she twisted her lips in return. "Hey."

"Hey. How are you feeling?"

Touching her head, she tried to sit up and fell back. "I've got a hell of a headache. Why?" Her hand found the bump and she grinned, "Oh."

"Do you remember what happened?" Michael touched the side of her face, noting the exhaustion lining her features and frowning at the way her eye twitched when he asked. "I'm sorry, we need to know."

She shook her head. "Not really, just bits and pieces." Offering an unconvincing closed mouth smile, she tried to sit up again. "Could you?"

"Sure," he helped her up. "Okay?" His eyes searched her for signs of fainting or illness. God he was a fool for her. If something happened to her he would go back to the husk he'd been, doing whatever Black wanted without a conscience. Without a soul.

"Thanks." She smiled shyly, embarrassed to be reliant. "Um, out there, I was following Gabrielle. She was after this thing. It was glowing, only I didn't see what it was." A wrinkle formed between her brows. "I never saw it." She rolled her head lazily from side to side, too tired to give it more. "It managed to stay away from both of us."

Uncertain and unable to meet her gaze, he glanced past her out the window to see if the others were coming. Nothing. "Did you get any sort of feeling from it? A vibe or anything?"

Tipping her head, she eyed him curiously. "What do you mean 'vibe'?"

His tone changed, he looked away again. "You've been getting stronger. Uh, I thought you might have picked up on something since you're…" He stopped, hoping she would understand without him having to say the word again.

Realization dawned and Becca's expression darkened. "Since I'm a witch?"

He regarded her grimly. Personal feelings aside, he had to think of their mission. And if she had a set of barely tapped abilities that could help them, then it was his duty to push her to use them.

"Why did you call me that?" Becca didn't rant or scream. She was pragmatic about the whole thing. "Does my sight make me a witch?"

"It's an old term. We don't really have one for your type now." It was hard to keep his hands to himself. He wanted so badly to stroke her face, to bring her comfort and not make her feel like he was using her to forward Black's agenda.

She managed a weak smirk. "My type. It's okay." She held up a hand when he started to object. "I'm not offended." She frowned in thought, "I'm just, I don't know. Witch is so not how I thought of myself." Then, running a hand along the side of her head, she winced and probed more tenderly. "I'm getting stronger?" She gave him a look, her disbelief obvious. "You think so?"

Michael glossed over the physical weakness Becca was suffering. "I don't know if it's how much you've been working with it or the blood, but you've been powerful with your abilities." He watched her face fall at his mention of her blood ingestion. "I didn't mean to bring that up. I know you don't like to think about drinking blood."

They'd avoided speaking about the whole thing in much detail. She took on a decidedly green hue whenever they got too far down the line. Truth be told, he'd used her aversion to keep her from asking too much. Michael didn't want her to know. He didn't want her to know how close her blood consumption had brought her to being like him; how close he'd come once to doing the unthinkable. All it would have taken was a bite from him.

He'd refrained from turning her into a vampire, even when it would have made her healing faster and less uncertain. God knew there had been moments during those three days when they'd been shut in his room together with only Ryan allowed near the door with blood deliveries. There had been moments when he thought he would lose her, when he thought he had. The temptation to turn her had been unbearable. The only thing that prevented him from being selfish, from turning her even if it meant she would hate him forever but he would know she still lived, was the fact that *she* didn't want it. How could he say that he loved her if he ignored that? How could he turn her into a thing he hated. Doomed her to serving the admiral for an eternity?

And so, he had pumped himself and her full of enough blood to fill two live humans. That amount was beyond what any other had taken in without being bitten and turned. Mixed with her not quite human nature and they had virgin territory.

Her heart was picking up again. "Michael," she put a hand on his where it lay in his lap, "it's time you told me what happened." Her pulse slowed, her reaching for him was subconscious. His vampire gloated.

His eyes searched hers. He kept his features decidedly even. A half a century of wearing a mask served him well. "They had given up on you in the hospital; there wasn't anything they could do for you." A picture of her burned body superimposed itself over the one in front of him. "I took you out of there and brought you back to the estate. I knew how to heal you, and I did."

"I knew all that." She squeezed his fingers, encouraging. "What I want to know is how much?" Her throat worked convulsively. "How much blood did I drink?" Touching him was the only thing keeping her from panicking, he could sense that she was on the edge.

"A lot," he told her flatly. "Why does it matter?"

"Because I want to know. If I'm stuck like this, if it never wears off, how close am I to being like you? To being a vampire?" She touched her temple and flinched.

Michael worried she had a concussion and turned to the side, hiding the flare of his nostrils as he sniffed again to rule out internal bleeding.

On cue, the door opened and Ryan threw himself in behind the wheel with an angry grunt. Gabrielle was slower, yet equally furious as she climbed into the passenger seat and crossed her arms. The brief illumination of the dome light before the door closed showed eyes red from crying and a face covered in red, bloody streaks.

The four rode back to the motel in silence, all lost in their own thoughts. None of them noticed the figure that stepped out from the trees into the clearing as they pulled away.

The man-shaped being stood still and unseen, his form all but hidden by the long, dark coat he wore. Thin lips pulled back, a full set of pointed teeth shone in the faint dirty orange glow radiating from his flesh. Grinning wickedly, he roughed his black leather-clad palms together. These four were strong, their emotions raw. They were perfect. The blonde one had already given him enough to secure his place on this plane, he no longer needed the windigo to lure them to him. Having tasted two of them, he could find them again.

Chapter 18

Gabrielle wanted to stay under the hot water forever. She sat down, hugging her knees to her chest and let the water run over her shoulders while she stared at the gray water-stained ring halfway up the edge of the tub. If it were any other day she would have refused to even touch the dirty tub. This wasn't any other day.

Since that first night in the woods, when she'd cut across the trail, nothing had been right. The rotting smell had been vampire all right. Different than Michael and Admiral Black but definitely vampire, there had been enough of them over the years of all different varieties for her to recognize it. She was becoming a connoisseur. Soon she'd be able to pick the region where they originated by the particular smell of dirt and minerals permeating their bodies. A sommelier of the undead, was that a thing?

No, this one's smell was different, earthy and powerful. There was no smell of decay like that thing she saw in the woods that night; no rot, only earth and energy. Then there was the fact that it controlled her, took her over. It drew her for hours through woods, mud and over rocks, leading her on some chase she could never remember when she woke in a different part of town, filthy and exhausted. Always with a sense of loss and grief strong enough to send her running back to the motel, to check on Ryan, fearing the worst. Fearing she'd lost another one. And now she was seeing things. Well, not *things*. *Him*. She was seeing glimpses of a ghost from her past. Out of the corner of her eye, on the edge of a crowd, turning a corner on the street, he was there for only a second. But when she followed, he was gone. She hadn't gone out since that first morning, avoiding the inescapable sighting. Avoiding facing the guilt head on. She knew she deserved it, except she wasn't strong enough to face his ghost and hear him condemn her. And she couldn't handle Ryan hearing it. Loyalty was everything to him. What would he think of her leaving her unit alone and vulnerable? Of letting them die while she lived?

Ryan. He meant more to her than she thought, more than she was intending when she'd started things with him. Waking with that sense of loss brought to mind the heartrending pain she'd felt when she lost the last man she allowed herself to love. Never again, she had vowed that day in Northern Africa after she buried her entire unit with her own hands. And now, despite her efforts to avoid it, it had happened. The fear of his loss had her pulling away as fast as she could. She couldn't survive pain like that again.

Knuckles on the white pre-fab door had her on her feet at once. "Gabs?"

Swallowing first, she breathed once, then twice. He already thought she was losing it. So did she. Better to be thought a cold bitch than seen as weak. She had to do this. It was the only way for her. "Yes." It was a challenge, not a question.

"Uh, Michael called. He wanted us to meet for dinner. To talk about today."

The hesitation in his voice, his inability to hide his hurt was hard to ignore. Calling forth the last she'd seen of her lost love, the mound of sand she'd shoveled atop the shallow graves she'd dug with her own hands in the Algerian desert helped her to find strength where she thought she had none. "Fine. Give me a few minutes."

Long pause. He was deciding whether or not to say something. Probably wanting to talk about the state she'd been in when she passed out on that rock and he found her. Nerves jolted her stomach and she doubted she would eat this night. Footsteps moved away on the thin carpet over concrete and she felt her shoulders fall.

"It's for the best," she muttered to herself, not believing a word. Some day she would have the satisfaction of destroying the creature who had taken her unit and her lover that day and only then could she ask forgiveness of their ghosts. Until then, she had no right to happiness, to Ryan.

****

"Shouldn't we call him?" Becca smoothed the black fabric ending at her knee while she sat on the edge of the bed, waiting. "I mean, you did yell at him in front of his peers. Shouldn't we be doing some damage control?"

A growl rolled out of the bathroom where Michael was finishing getting ready. His hair took longer than hers did. Becca snorted at her lover's one vanity. She either threw hers in a ponytail when it was still wet or brushed it out and let it air dry. Michael's, however, was thick and took longer to dry, plus he had to use gel to get it just right. The effect was drop dead sexy waves that fell in all the right spots. She was pondering teasing him when he stepped out, the look in his eye sending thoughts of teasing and smoothing Detective Salvo's feelings into retreat. The black shirt was open at the neck, revealing the divot at the base of his pale throat that led to his smooth chest. Tucked into black trousers that accented his lean waist and finished with freshly shined Italian shoes and topped with a pewter belt buckle, he looked delicious. His lips curved when he saw the way she sucked in her breath and followed him with her eyes.

Becca sat up straighter, she knew they needed to be outside to meet the others soon. Running her hand over her skirt again, she considered staying in. No deal. They had to meet with the others, brainstorm, and then get back so Michael could have his evening rundown with Admiral Black. It was a necessity of this life. Not one of the perks, but this life had brought her Michael, and for that gift she could handle some inconvenient check-ins from the road.

Michael's long strides brought him to within inches of where she sat. She slid her fingers under her legs lest they take on a will of their own and start something.

"Now that he's had time to cool down he'll figure out what I did." He slipped his hands into his pockets and looked down at her, shirtsleeves rolled up partway exposed his lean forearms.

She stared up at him, watching a wave of hair fall forward over his forehead. Her teeth clenched her lower lip. "He who?"

"Detective Salvo," Michael said softly, the blue in his eyes giving way to the growing black pupils. "He's smart. He'll figure out I was distracting him. He and his fellow officers will have a bitch fest about us over a few beers tonight."

The sheer presence of Michael was enough to get her started. Throw in the fact that he was *trying* to tempt her and that her blood reacted to his nearness and Becca was fighting a losing battle. "And you're okay with that? With them thinking you're an ass when it suits you?" She started to think of positions that wouldn't mess up her hair too badly. Feeling her give up the fight, her body heated up another notch. It knew what was in store and the craving was beyond fighting.

"Yes. I want him to know that he's outranked." A hint of fang showed when he ran his tongue over his lip. "Especially when I see him going after something of mine."

Becca stood up, bringing her face even with his chest. Her hand reached out to touch his firm skin, starting at his abs and running up to his chest. Pushing off, she tilted her head up to see him. Flecks of blue were less visible as the black bled over and the vampire inside him fought to be free. She knew that meant fast and hard, their usual flavor. Her pulse quickened in anticipation. "Yours?" There was a hint of a challenge to her tone. Screw her hair, she'd do it again gladly.

His growl rolled out and arms of iron trapped her against his chest. When his lips met hers they were insistent. Nerves had been strained all day. Both wanted a release. Becca's tongue traced his lip and she flicked it against his fangs, being careful not to prick herself. A drop of blood would throw him over the edge the state he was in and then they'd never make dinner. Though as her blood pressure came up, Becca cared less and less about dinner or who might be waiting for them.

Need to dominate rose in Michael; his arms shook with the effort to maintain some control and Becca's body hummed with anticipation. Knowing how to slake his thirst fast, she pushed against his chest and gained some space. Enough to grab his shirt and maneuver him around to sit in her recently vacated spot on the bed. Hands sliding down, she picked up the hem of her skirt and pulled it up around her waist. One knee went up next to his leg on the bed.

Michael's dexterous fingers trailed their way down her back to slip into her black thong. One hand roughly pulled the lace aside while the other continued to round the curve to slip first one, then two fingers inside her. Aching for him, she moaned and pulled the other leg up until she was on her knees, straddling him.

He left his fingers dip inside then come out to wet her nub, which he proceeded to roll around and flick alternately, sending shivers running up and down her legs. Becca's thighs began to shake as she worked with him to keep the rhythm. Michael left his fingers to work her into a frenzy while his other hand cupped her small breast.

Lowering her face, Becca caught his mouth eagerly. Her hands fumbled to open his pants. Lifting his hips, he helped her shove them out of the way. Once he was freed, her hands moved south. She cupped his balls, squeezing until he growled while she used her body to stroke him.

His hold on himself was tremulous at best. She felt his struggle as he grazed his teeth along the side of her neck. He'd only really bitten her once and had been ashamed to lose control. Becca had her own view on the subject. She didn't want him to bite her necessarily, but knowing that for him to do so meant she'd driven him out of his mind with desire posed a personal challenge. She could feel that he was close and she wanted the victory.

Making a little mewling noise in her throat, she put her hands on his shoulders and pulled herself harder against him. Opening and closing her knees a few inches while shimmying her hips let her stroke his cock while her fingernails raised goose bumps on his low back and flanks. Light touches made him wild and she used that knowledge against him.

Roaring back the passion that had to be screaming to get out, Michael gripped her hips with both hands and pulled her off. It took only a few seconds to reverse positions so that she was lying down and he hovered over her, his feet on the ground. He slid himself inside her in one deliciously slow, controlled motion. Becca's breath went out with a whoosh and a groan. Shuddering, she grabbed his upper arms while Michael pulled out and slammed in a little harder. She could feel a new tension building, the ringing in her ears starting almost immediately.

Within a few strokes Michael was pushing hard and Becca was on the edge. Hands releasing her hips to raise her shirt so he could hold her breasts while he pounded into her, marking her as his, Michael gritted his teeth and she clenched around him, her legs behind his back holding him captive. She needed him to lose control. She needed to know he was hers as much as she was his. That her body's reliance upon him wasn't just one sided. His tongue ran up the side of her neck to her ear and she felt the tip of a fang just before he raised his chest off her and double-timed his thrusts until she didn't even know what was happening anymore.

When she came, it was one orgasm flowing into the next, all focus lost in her bliss. Before she floated back down, his last desperate thrust marked his release and he leaned forward to kiss her neck. Sensitive all over, Becca shivered. His chest rumbled against hers with soft, dark laughter. She was too dizzy to make a smartass comment about how pleased he was with himself. He should be, she thought. He'd earned it.

Chapter 19

Dinner was at the mom and pop joint across the lot from the motel. Fine dining had its place, but no one was too worried about it that particular night.

Gabrielle was distracted, Ryan wouldn't stop fiddling with his fork, Becca was having a little trouble sitting and Michael kept reaching into his pocket to check his phone. It was getting late and Black would call soon if he didn't hear from Michael. They all knew it was better to be the caller, not the callee.

After waters were brought and burgers ordered all around, Becca broke the tense silence with a hand slap to the cream formica table top. Everyone in the booth as well as a few around them looked over.

Cheeks coloring, she plowed ahead with a voice low enough only they could hear. "We came here to talk through what we know, so let's do it and be done." When it was obvious no one else was intending to speak, she leaned in. "Fine, if no one else wants to go first."

Her gaze swept around the table and she felt her mouth pull into a smile when she met Michael's beside her. Hearing the exasperated sighs sure to come from the other two in her head, she aimed her eyes straight at her fingers then to the wolves alternately. Wisely, she kept from making eye contact with Michael for the time being.

"Gabrielle, I followed you," Becca waited for the explosion, "from the crime scene."

Instead, the woman who should have been at the very least glaring hard enough to incinerate, only rolled her shoulders. "I figured that out, so?"

Faced with the intimidation factor ratcheted up a notch, Becca started to lose her nerve. "Uh, there was this glowing thing you were following. I didn't get close enough to see it. What was it?"

All eyes were on Gabrielle who sat slumped in her seat and shrugged again. "I don't know." She glanced up at Ryan, then caught herself and focused instead on the ice cubes floating in her glass. "I've been following something for the past few nights, but until you said you saw light," she frowned, "I haven't known what it was. Just that I had to follow it and I had to be human to follow it."

"Why did you have to be human?" Becca asked the obvious.

Still staring at her ice cubes, Gabrielle mumbled, "It told me to."

Ryan's response cut Becca's off. "You mean whatever you keep following is telling you what to do and where to go and you didn't think to say anything?"

Distinctly uncomfortable, Gabrielle gave her eyes to Becca. Apparently she was the least threatening. She tried not to be overly offended. It sort of worked.

"I was going to. I was working it out in my head." Confusion painted her perfect features for the first time in Becca's memory. "What was I supposed to do, tell you how I keep waking up in different places and have no idea how I got there?" Some dark emotion passed over her face and she stopped talking.

Becca jumped in. "Wait, you mean you blacked it out?" She wasn't sure she believed such a thing was possible for the unflappable Gabrielle. She'd thought *her* blackout had been due to her failed attempt at jumping into her head.

Her blonde brow lifted and she tilted her head, an oddly canine gesture. "Do you mean to say you remember *everything* that happened out there?" Her scrutiny was all at once intensely focused.

There was no way she could know what Becca had been doing when she'd, what, been hijacked? What *had* happened out there? After she tried to jump she'd lost herself in her memories. Eyes going wide, her mouth opened but nothing came out. Self-conscious the others were paying way too much attention, she snapped it shut without speaking. Michael went quiet beside her and Ryan was getting twitchier by the second. Did he know what Gabrielle was seeing? Becca wasn't close enough to ask.

A reprieve came in the form of the short woman carrying a tray of burgers and fries. "Anything else?" she asked, her exhausted slouch begging them not to answer.

Politely, Michael shook his head and gave her a brief smile. "No, thank you."

Just for a moment she perked under his attentiveness, shooting the women at the table a wary glance. Off balance already, Becca clenched her fists on her thighs. Reason told her there was no threat, but, like in the police station, she felt her body tense up, readying for action. Michael's hand touched hers under the table and she relaxed.

The waitress, seeing this wasn't a free agent, gave them all a quick smile and moved on. The thick rubber soles of her black lace-ups squelched away.

"We killed the freaky ass vampire." Ryan popped a fry in his mouth and reached for the ketchup. His mild tone belied the angry, jerking motions of his hands. "Are you thinking you were following something else? That something else out there is powerful enough to induce hallucinations and blackouts and we missed it?"

Shaking her head slowly with her hands folded in her lap, Gabrielle pursed her lips. "No. I mean, I don't know."

"I doubt whatever thing was using the vampire hobo to draw you out would let us take its killer puppet out without so much as a peep. Unless it knew it couldn't handle us." Ryan's bravado wasn't entirely false; he and Michael made a formidable team.

A new sort of emotion, desperation, flavored Gabrielle's words. "You weren't there. You weren't close enough to be under whatever sort of spell or influence or whatever," she said to Ryan as she leaned over the table, bringing her face closer to Becca's, her eyes trained solely on her. "I felt it and it was very powerful. So did you. Didn't you blank out?"

The last thing Becca wanted to do was to tell them she'd tried to jump into one of their heads. They had just started to accept her when she'd discovered that little gem. The only reason anyone didn't demand she be kicked out of Black's special paranormal hunting unit was because they thought she could only jump into Michael. Ryan was yet unknown, even to him. Although if Black had his way she'd be his little trained spider monkey, jumping whenever the mood suited him. She had to come up with some reason why it had taken her memory as well.

Michael caught her eye. The knowing she saw there, mixed with the tension around his mouth, told her a lot. He knew what she'd been doing. He knew she had been close enough to be affected just as strongly as the one standing right there. That he wasn't saying anything implied he might continue to keep her secret from the others. The little voice in her head reminded her he couldn't keep it from *some*one. At least this time, that didn't matter. They had to tell him anyway.

"Maybe it's a proximity thing. I was close by the time you stopped. Obviously it was close enough." Becca took a bite of her burger, chewing slowly.

"Have you," Gabrielle hadn't blinked, she was getting creepy, "*seen* anything weird since?"

Breaking off, unable to handle such anxiety from the unflappable woman, Becca shook her head quickly.

Laying his hand down on the table, Michael claimed the conversation though he took his time in answering. Thoughtfully, he pushed the fries decorating his plate into two sections, flanking the giant homestyle burger. "Gabs, I think it's best for you to take some time, for now."

When she didn't argue at being sidelined, Becca felt a twinge of fear. Whatever this thing was, it had her spooked. And anything that could get under *her* skin scared the hell out of Becca.

"We need to get back into the computers at the station," Michael went on, giving her a quick glance to tell her she was the other part of "we" again.

"What do you think that will tell you?" Ryan asked around a mouthful of meat and bun. "You had hours to dig through what they had yesterday and didn't find anything."

Dark waves dipped slowly in acknowledgement. "Yes, but we were only looking for violent crimes. Now I want to open up the search." His eyes flicked toward their subdued unit member. "Not just radius, I want to see their reports on any sort of oddities. People report it when they see bizarre things. Bizarre isn't acceptable to the human mind."

"Yeah, but will they report it?" Becca was human and agreed with his sentiment. However, she saw a hole in his reasoning. "Wouldn't they be worried to admit they saw," she avoided looking at Gabrielle now sinking into herself, "things? Or that they blacked out? It's a relatively small town and word gets around when you're waking up in weird places, blacking out when you're sober or seeing the walking dead."

"In some cases that's true." Michael tipped his head her direction without making eye contact. "But I guarantee, if this is affecting the populace, there have been at least a few people who have come forward."

Nothing more was said on the subject and their meal was quietly consumed. Michael left his alone and Gabrielle barely touched hers. Only Ryan and Becca ate. Hers, she had to admit, was more to give her something to distract her than out of hunger.

Becca trailed Michael back to their room, not looking forward to the inevitable confrontation. Cool façade aside, she wasn't good at personal confrontations and usually tried to avoid them. Last in, she pushed the door shut and slid the chain lock into place. Leaning against the door, she waited.

Nothing happened. She wasn't sure what she was expecting. He knew she was supposed to master her new skill. Her facing Black as a failure was a terrifying prospect for both of them. She'd seen how he punished defiance. A human couldn't survive that kind of beating.

So, if he knew this had to happen, why was she dreading it so much? Sighing, she studied the outline of his back. He faced away from her, the muscles in his shoulder shifting against his shirt as he twirled the phone in his pocket. The call to Black had to happen soon. He was putting it off. Again, why?

A man used to being closed off for decades didn't share easily and Becca understood that. She never demanded more than he gave. Yet the recent development of this nervous fidget he had of playing with his phone told her he was newly anxious about something. Most likely it related to her. She presented the unique challenge of forcing him to maintain a secret from the one person he couldn't.

At last he broke the silence. His quiet words forced her to lean forward to hear. "Did it work?"

Becca shook her head at his back. "No."

"Do you remember what happened?"

The image of Gabrielle's desperate face flashed and she blinked. "No, I tried to reach her and after that…" She stopped herself from telling him what she *had* seen. "I don't remember."

"Your time is running out. He only gave you two weeks," he reminded her softly.

"I know." Becca glanced down at her feet, wondering if she might be as lucky as the elusive Kenneth. The one Black let go. Would he be as understanding if she couldn't master her ability? Would he give her more time?

Michael's phone clicked against his nail. Lifting her eyes, she watched the side of his pocket flare and go in, flare and go in. The spinning went faster as his agitation grew.

All of a sudden it was too much. "Just tell him, Michael. He's going to find out anyway. I can't do it."

His hand went silent and his body stilled in that vampire way that unnerved the living. "He's not going to accept that."

"Maybe he'll give me more time," Becca said softly.

Voice rough, Michael refused to turn around and face her. He was going to hide his difficulty with this as best he could in this tiny room. "He can't."

"What do you mean he can't?" Intrigued, Becca willed him to turn around and face her.

"There's something specific…" He started to raise his voice but stopped dead. Nearly turning around, he showed her half a face contorted in frustration and something else. Was this something Black had forbidden him to speak to her about? Knowing she was right, she could almost feel the tightening in his head and twisting in his stomach.

Becca wasn't sure what Black wanted her for or what would happen if she failed. All she knew was that he was in pain and it hurt her. Pushing off from the door, she approached him slowly and leaned against his back, her cheek resting lightly on the soft fabric of his shirt. "It's okay, you don't have to tell me. I know you would if you were able."

"It's okay that I can't even speak unless he allows it?" Michael snorted. "What kind of man am I? I should have turned around that day at the hospital." He referred to the first time he'd found her for Black. "If I'd told him no he would have gotten over it. You would have never gotten pulled into this life. You would be free of him."

"You're forgetting something." She could feel his muscles stiffening with his frustration at being unable to shield her from Black's wrath should she failed to perform. He'd been trying to protect her from that since the beginning. "He has you." She raised her voice, going over the objection she felt coming. "As long as you're here, I'm here." She slid her arms around his waist. "I can deal with anything he dishes out as long as I have you to come home to." Saying the words aloud was as hard as admitting she loved him and this time she didn't have a chance of passing out to keep her from his rejection. There it was again, twice in as many days she'd put her heart out for him to squash should he choose. For a long, agonizing moment he didn't move or speak.

Then, turning around, he gathered her to him tight enough to make her squeak. "You're a fool, Becca."

Each word pierced her heart with a separate barb and, wounded, she attempted to draw away from him. His grip on her prevented it. "I wish I could stop you from loving me. It gives him the hold over you I never wanted to be a part of. He'll use you up, it's what he does."

Tears burned in her eyes as Becca listened to the damning words, knowing they were true.

One of his hands let her go to pull her chin up and she opened her eyes wide, attempting to keep the pooling tears from falling.

Eyes dark as a starless midnight, Michael was gazing down at her. "And I despise myself for wanting it. I've failed you Becca, and part of me isn't the least bit sorry because it means I get to keep you with me." His teeth gritted together in his self-hatred. "God help me, I've pulled you into hell right alongside me."

Reaching up on her tiptoes, Becca pressed her lips to his gently. "I get a say too and I say I don't care. We're both here and there's no changing that now." She shrugged and offered him a small smile. "He wanted me before he knew I could jump. All I have to do is show him I'm indispensible," she joked. "So let's show him I've got something no one else does, even if it isn't everything he wants." Though in her mind, she worried she wouldn't be able and Black would begin searching for her replacement. She still had a week and a half to either figure out how to jump into strangers or wow Black with something other than a human security system. She was going to make it work or die trying. A little voice told her what it thought the outcome would be and she shut it up with a mental slap.

Chapter 20

Evening came fast in the winter. They only had a good hour or so before it was completely dark. Chief Kowski was curt when Michael called him, refusing to meet him at the station or give him access to the system until morning. Detective Salvo had obviously spoken to him.

Sitting on the edge of the bed, spinning the black device in his hands post phone call, Michael stood suddenly. "Want to go do some recon in town?"

Itchy to get out of the tiny room, Becca stopped her pacing. "I'll get my coat." She wasn't privy to what Michael had told Black of their day's adventure in the woods or her continued failure to do as he'd requested. The strain was making her crazy.

Town was a small affair consisting of a five-block radius of the usual mish mash of boutique stores, several bars, a post office, and coffee shop. Black iron streetlights reminiscent of Victorian era gas lamps were already on, their yellow-orange halogen glow tinting the thickening fog. The snow had stopped falling and the plows were busily pushing it to the sides of the streets and walks. Large chunks of blue salt dotted the wet concrete and asphalt alike. Moisture still hung in the air, its damp chill going bone deep.

Gabrielle stayed behind, leaving the rest of them to head into town together. There was no reason for Ryan to go out tracking with the windigo gone and the other thing yet unknown. They were as likely to find something in town as out.

"You okay, Ryan?" Becca got out on the passenger side and closed her door to put a hand on his blue, parka-covered arm.

The brief glimpse she caught before he slapped a fake toothy grin on his face answered more honestly than he did. "Fine. Looking forward to painting this town tonight. You?"

Plastering on a meant to be obviously fake smile, Becca bobbed her head enthusiastically. "Excellent." Then, let her face fall again. "Now, you want to be honest with me?"

"What do *you* think?" His hand tightened on the top of the door and he stepped out and around, poised to close it. "My girlfriend who isn't my girlfriend is under the influence of some sort of glow worm and seeing what I assume is her ex every time she turns around. When she sleeps she calls out *his* name." Catching himself, he slammed his mouth shut. He hadn't meant to say so much. He slammed the door and roughed up his hair, blowing out a big puff of air. "Just, let's not talk about it. Okay?"

Raised voices a block up the street interrupted anything else that might have been said. Several young men were hovering outside the door of a drinking establishment from which it sounded like they had been recently ejected. Michael, standing by the front bumper, crossed the wide main street at a casual jog and proceeded toward them. Without need to discuss, Ryan and Becca followed, flanking Michael on either side. Salt crunched underfoot and their breath added to the fog surrounding them.

Whether it was the potential for a new confrontation or the near miss she'd just had, Becca couldn't be sure but something had her skin tingling. It felt like hundreds of tiny little sugar ants were marching up and down her limbs and holding a dance party between her shoulder blades. Closing the distance, none needed their sensitive hearing to catch the streams of obscenities and threats coming from the five men standing on the sidewalk.

The large man who had a lot in common with a snowman, giant ball of belly topped with an overly large, hairless bowling ball of a head, was reaching behind himself to grab the silver handle on the black steel door. Popping it open, he called inside after someone by the name of "T." At no time did he break eye contact with the leader of the unrulies.

The head unruly drunkard was about the same age as the rest, early twenties. All of them were pretty much carbon copies of one another. Heavy cream stitching on their jeans marked them as "the" jeans of the hour among the fashionable and the track jacket/ hoodies they all sported from various American and Western European sports clubs identified them as upper middle class. Not the usual thugs. That and a complete lack of ink or silver on their visible body parts said they should be the customers a club *wanted*, not the ones that would end up on the curb.

Curiosity peaked, Becca sped up, drawing even with Michael. He reached out and took her hand, holding her back with him. Ryan held his speed in check as well and they paused at the corner opposite the crowd, mingling with a few other pedestrians drawn to gawk at the altercation.

"I'm not going to tell you again," Snowman was saying, becoming painfully aware of the unwanted audience that was gathering. His bosses wouldn't be happy. "We reserve the right to kick out anyone we see as a problem, and threatening other customers is a problem. Now do yourselves a favor and go home and sleep it off before I call the cops."

Unruly Number One shook his shoulder length Barbie blonde hair back and puffed up his chest, a move made significantly less manly when the breeze tossed a chunk of hair into the side of his mouth and he had to scoop it out before shooting back his witty retort. "Fuck you!"

Another unruly, who had apparently smuggled out a beer, raised it next to his head, clearly getting ready to throw it.

"Hey buddy, look out!" one of the gawkers shouted helpfully.

Snowman's eyes went to the intended assaulter and narrowed. His body language and size should have been enough to back down any of the five unlikely rioters as should the mysterious "T's" sudden appearance through the door. Taller than Snowman by a half a foot and with the only round parts on him being his biceps and likewise bald head, the united front was enough to send most packing.

It wasn't this time. Instead, the five only seemed to grow more agitated. Voices broke out in unison, their words lost in the cacophony. The bottle was thrown and sent Snowman reeling backward into the building, a red streak mixing with the sweat pouring down his face and into the collar of his black shirt. T waded in a few steps before Snowman rallied, their fists flying, and the brawl was on.

Regardless of the warning that the police *would* be called, sirens sounded within seconds of things getting physical. Apparently they'd read this one right from the beginning and had planned ahead. An ambulance showed up as well, in anticipation of blood. Someone inside was wise.

Once the men had been cleared off the gawkers dispersed, leaving Black's soldiers alone with T at the door. Only minor abrasions marred his dark skin so he remained on guard, waiting for his compatriot before going back in. Snowman was sitting in the ambulance arguing that he didn't need stitches; a butterfly bandage would be fine. They compromised with a liquid stitch the medic wasn't happy to apply before leaving.

"You could have a concussion," he argued.

Snowman waved him off, not sharing his concern for his own welfare.

Taking the opportunity, Michael stepped off the curb and headed straight for the big man. Becca and Ryan let him go alone. One was less threatening than three. Catching the movement, he turned and scowled, warning Michael he wasn't in a mood for bystander gossip.

Michael was undeterred. Lifting his chin, he approached with his hands in his pockets and his shoulders pulled up toward his ears, feigning a chill. It would be believable in this weather. Covered as he was in jeans and a wool coat, even with the collar flipped up, it wouldn't have been enough to keep a human warm in the wind that occasionally gusted and swirled random flakes around them.

"Hey Buddy, you gotta go to the main entrance around the corner," T informed him brusquely, pointing with a thumb. Giant pipes flexed as he crossed his arms over his barrel chest, bringing his goose bumps into sight. Several snowflakes landed on his dark head, sitting for a few seconds before turning into water and running down his temples.

As soon as Michael was close enough, he dropped his shoulders and looked the significantly taller man in the eye. Becca and Ryan maintained their distance to keep the other onlookers from suspecting anything unusual was happening.

"Really? Man, it's freezing out here. You sure you can't let me in?" Michael said loud enough for anyone within human earshot to pick up. Then, dropping his voice, he didn't waste a syllable. "Why were those men kicked out?"

The change in T's countenance was immediate. Face slackening, his gaze softened like he was watching something far away. "They walked in and started picking fights with other customers. One was pushy with a girl." The distracted tone of his voice was better suited to telling a boring tale to a stranger on the subway. It was entirely dispassionate.

"Have they been here before?"

"They're regulars. Usually here once a week at least."

"Do they usually get into trouble like this?"

"No, not these guys."

"Have there been other abnormally violent customers?"

The big head bobbed twice, jerky. "Yeah, for the past few weeks for sure. Not as much before that, but it's been wild since fall." Both large shoulders rolled forward then back. "It's a college town. Weird shit happens."

No need to answer, Michael shrugged and turned on his heel. The charade of begging entrance was no longer necessary and anyone still watching would assume he had been denied or changed his mind. Glancing both ways, ever the cautious human behavior model, he rejoined his party on the other curb. "Anyone care for a drink?" He knew they'd heard.

Ryan unzipped his jacket and took a step into the street. He *did not* look before crossing. Why should he? He would hear a car coming from a mile away. "Thought you'd never ask."

Waiting to follow his lead, Becca waited for a cue. Sometimes they played the couple and sometimes she had to be "single" to be approachable. When his hand slid into hers, she felt her own tension ease from where it had clamped down on her neck. Now if only she could get rid of the sensation that she had little static shocks snapping at her skin every few seconds, life would be grand. His touch wasn't helping that at all. Going one farther, Michael leaned in to kiss the side of her mouth.

"Is that how we're playing this tonight?" She looked askance as he stepped away again.

His eyes were kind. "No, just felt like doing that. You look tired, are you sure you're alright?" A thin line formed between his brows. "Are you having any other symptoms?"

The reminder of the blood complication and her witchiness brought a hint of darkness to her features. He was holding onto her because he thought he needed to, not because he wanted to. Pretending to stumble stepping off the curb, she removed her hand from his and put it in her pocket.

When he gave her a curious look, she added lamely, "It's cold."

The only answer he gave her was a furrowed brow and tight lips.

Becca blew out a big cloud of steam and walked through it, feeling Michael's untouchable nearness as an ache she couldn't ignore.

At the correct entrance, there was a normal sized fellow in a black shirt with the name of the club on it standing just inside. This wasn't New York, velvet ropes weren't necessary given the thin stream of people seeking entrance on a weeknight. And given the friendly nod they received from the man at the door, their less than club-worthy attire wasn't that unusual for this particular location either. A young woman in a short black dress took their coats once they were inside.

They fanned out automatically. Ryan sauntered casually up to the bar. With his easy, friendly nature he was the best at chatting up the bartender and crowd up there while Michael blended into the surprisingly thick throng on the dance floor. Hearing the conversations and watching dozens of interactions was his specialty. Shifting lights from above flashed and danced for a strobe effect that made the dancers appear disjointed as they moved.

Becca followed Michael's progress with her eyes, blinking from the sharp changes in light. Yet again, she wished for her sensitivity to fade. It seemed like, if anything, it was getting worse since she'd been in Wisconsin. Being here, surrounded by people, bright flashing lights and loud dance music wasn't helping either. Leaning against the outer wall, out of traffic but able to watch the entire club unobtrusively, she gulped the hot, stale air. Her lungs burned and her stomach cramped. She felt like she could burst out of her skin at any second; the itching and tingling had grown to full-blown jerks and jolts. For a second the image of one of those sci-fi movies where the people peel off their skin and out steps a demon popped into her head.

The image froze her in place and, in the next heartbeat, she saw the fire demon again. Walking toward her through the club, the dark hall lit up, framed in fire. The demon was clothed in the flesh of the human it had long ago consumed. Staggering further in, she hid herself behind a large potted plant and leaned heavily against the red painted wall. So transported was her mind, Becca swore she felt heat radiating from the painted surface. Flinching away from it, she swayed on her feet, gagging as her breath caught in her throat and tasted of smoke.

"Miss, are you okay?"

The strobe lights threw their wild flashing play of color onto the walls and floor around her, disorienting Becca completely. Closing her eyes, she rubbed them with the palms of her hands.

A hand touched her shoulder. "You don't look so good." His voice was closer, he leaned in. "Do you have someone here with you? Someone you'd like me to find? Have you taken something?"

She pictured Michael's face when he heard she was still having nightmares, only now they'd progressed to daymares. It wasn't just the modesty she feigned around the estate that had kept him out of her bed for more than a few hours at a time these last couple of months. Except when they'd been on the road and saying no would have entailed being obvious and requesting a separate room, she'd limited their sleep exposure out of shame. All of them faced horrors on each mission. They all got over them. She didn't want to admit she was the weak one who couldn't.

Chapter 21

Michael moved among the gyrating humans, taking care to sidestep several pairs and even clusters whose movement was more sex than dancing. This was not the kind of place he would take his Becca when he finally got the chance to dance with her. He wanted to feel her body against him, though if they performed some of these maneuvers he worried his desire for her would be too much. The idea of having sex with her in front of an audience was not an erotic fantasy of his. He liked sex as much as the next guy; he'd even had it in some daringly public places, but he wouldn't want anyone seeing his Becca at her most intimate. The fast, hammering music had most all of the humans sweating and dancing hard, making the minefield of flesh tough to navigate which was good, it forced his thoughts off of Becca and sex and back to his mission. The scent of pheromones choked him, the chance of distraction would have been more than a younger vampire could handle. As it was, his skin tingled and his discipline was tested as an attractive blonde woman's denim clad ass slammed into his thigh and commenced using it as a grinding post.

Twisting to see who she'd run aground on, her delicate features slack from alcohol, curved into a loose grin as she took in the sight of him. "Hey sexy," she yelled over the music as she spun the rest of her body around, her hands rubbing tantalizingly

218

up her sides. The hem of her snug, glitter-laced tee rode higher on her flat stomach and the bottom curve of a breast peeked out. "Dance with me."

"I'm looking for someone." He started to wave her off when the brunette next to her turned to see what had drawn her friend's interest. The hunger in her eyes and change in her scent left no doubt as to her intentions. The next step she took brought her leg to his, her next brought its companion to sandwich his knee between her tanned thighs. Tight black spandex rode high enough to give someone at the right angle a hell of a show as she straddled his leg.

Not to be outdone, the first woman used the beat to push herself up against his side, her fingers spreading to cover his shoulder blades and pull her front against his hip. "I'm someone." She leaned in close and flicked her tongue up his throat. He could feel her nails scraping down his back while her erect nipples poked into his chest. It was impossible not to be affected as the two women proceeded to grind and stroke him. Every nerve ending was awake, including those more sensitive than others. Willing his body to quiet, Michael was only half successful. The blonde smiled when she felt his response.

"Are you ladies here alone?" He leaned his head between theirs so they could hear, taking pause at the lack of booze or chemicals he smelled coming from their pores. He'd been sure their willingness was due to some drug. Michael knew he was physically attractive by human standards, though not typically orgy inducing.

"We're here together." The brunette stroked her friend's shoulder, letting her fingers trail down her front and circle the taught peak showing through. There was no bra to interfere and her long fingers gave it a twist to show him. "But we're willing to make room for one more."

The blonde caught her breath and arched her back. Making a little sound in her throat, she aimed a warm, heavy-lidded smile at her friend and leaned over. Their lips met and the lights flashed, offering several tongue-filled glimpses into the depth of their friendship. Breaking it off somewhat reluctantly, the blonde smiled seductively. "Don't worry, we share."

His human side was committed completely to Becca. Michael's vampire inside him, however, was less concerned with the repercussions of a one-night stand. It wanted what these girls offered. It growled and gnashed its teeth in frustration when he refused to loose it. Giving them a broad grin, he winked. "Sorry ladies, you're too fast for me." And took a step back, removing his thigh from the blonde's leg lock while shifting his shoulders sideways to slip from her friend's hands.

Both sets of glazed eyes hardened. Nails dug in and both were firmly back where they had positioned themselves originally. "We can slow down, sexy." The blonde plastered herself to his chest and crept up to his ear to assure him. "If you're nervous we can be very, very gentle." Sliding her knees apart, she allowed her body to drop and she bit her lip as she rubbed her crotch on his thigh, her hand stroking across her chest. Lowering her face, she tipped her eyes up and blinked, slow and doe eyed at him.

It would have been enough to test any man. Michael could feel his physical desire and nature both wrestling with his resolve. The brunette's hand dipped into his pants, her fingers stroking down his ass to scrape up the sensitive space between his cheeks. Instinctively, he inhaled and bit down on his fangs to keep them in. Twisting at the waist while grabbing their wrists and spinning them both, he managed to remove them again.

Not for long. Wedged between them for a third time, their nails and legs now firmly dug in and clamped around him respectively, Michael was faced with the decision of finishing the dance and biding his time for a less visible escape or making a scene by throwing the girls off of his body, which is what it would have taken with the grip the one had. "Just one dance." He shouted in their ears but straightened up before either could land the kiss they'd both been aiming at him.

Instead of getting him they were left inches from each other and, once again, their lips were on each other. The blonde's mouth ran down her friend's long neck, a hand reached out to push her hair out of the way as she let her tongue flick under her throat.

I want to taste them. The vampire was panting for the sex and blood it knew it could get from these two. Michael's body was dangerously close to reacting on its own and he pulled his mind back, forcing his eyes to scan the others on the floor around them. It struck him there was no one watching them. And why would they? As he looked closer, he could see that there were couples openly groping each other. One man had pulled his partner's scoop necked top down low enough to allow himself free access to her breasts, which he was partaking in, one each in mouth and hand. A hand slid down the front of Michael's jeans, forcing his focus back to his dance partners growing more aggressive by the second.

She cooed as she grasped his semi-erect shaft and began to stroke. "Ooh honey, you're going to be so fun." Her chest bowed into his and she rubbed her nipples on him again when she felt his body's willingness. Her other hand grabbed his ass and pressed him against her with no room for air.

Reaching in front of himself he removed the blonde's hand, using too much force to play off as casual. "We're not going there tonight." A hint of iron crept into his voice. Somehow he doubted his concerns for making a scene were all that valid anymore. Testing his theory, he trapped both the brunette's hands in one of his and put a hand on the blonde's chest. The blonde's eyes sparked, thinking he was going to be taking his liberties with her. Only he didn't. Taking care not to shove too hard, he pushed both away and stepped back. The girls pouted for only a brief moment before setting their sights on a young African American dancing with his back to them. For some reason he was shirtless and the blonde put a hand on his back, sliding it up and over his shoulder, turning him to face her. Her friend was close behind and the last Michael saw, the man's head was thrown back and happy tongues were exploring the ecstatic man's chest. He'd seen enough of what was out there and wove his way back, pondering the possibility that there was something in the music or the drinks causing the sex party behind him. The flames under his flesh were not so easily shoved aside. He had a fleeting vision of what would happen if he could get Becca in a dark hallway. It wouldn't take him long at this point.

****

"Look man, all I was doing was trying to make conversation." Ryan was standing at the bar, toe to toe, arguing with a guy a full head shorter as Michael approached. "You don't need to be an asshole about it."

The normal sized human stuck a finger in the middle of the doublewide chest in front of him and shouted up. "I saw you, dick, you were sticking your tongue in her ear."

That was when Michael noticed the leggy dark-haired woman standing in high heels and micro skirt behind the soon to be flattened man defending her honor. Her eyes were on Ryan, not her boyfriend, and the look she was pointing his way was anything but contrite. She looked like she wanted to push her knight in tiny armor aside and dangle from one of those giant arms hanging less than loose at Ryan's sides.

"My tongue?" Ryan laughed and rolled his eyes. "In case you hadn't noticed, it's loud. I was *talking* in her ear, not fucking it, you moron." Several onlookers were shifting back, giving the two men space. They could sense the oncoming storm.

"Fuck you!" the little wordsmith shouted and took a swing.

Faster by far, Ryan caught the fist easily in one of his and squeezed until his adversary's eyes bulged in pain and he fell to his knees. His hand shook from the effort it was taking not to crush the man's appendage.

Just as fast, Michael was at his friend's side before the man's knees hit the ground. Speaking softly enough no one else could hear, he cautioned him, "Time for us to leave."

Ryan turned his head and Michael could see the wolf fighting to get out behind his vibrant green eyes. "I got this," he growled around clenched teeth.

Michael didn't touch him. He only shifted so that his back was to the crouching man and he faced Ryan head on. Cautioning him again, "We both know you can snap him in half and it would be fun, but we don't have time and it'd just piss off the locals. We're here for something bigger. Save it for whatever's doing this to Gabs."

Relieved, Michael watched the green cool to the soft color Ryan sported when he was human.

Twitching his generous mouth into its typical grin, he gave his superior a nod. "We can't be pissing off the locals. You've already done enough of that for one day."

Michael felt his sexual tension threatening to spill over into violence and quickly reeled it in. No one would benefit if both of them lost it in there. The carnage would be hard to clean off his hands and his conscience. That hadn't been him for a long time.

"We're done here, shitbird." Ryan released his hand, then, leaning in, he cautioned the man still cringing on his knees and clutching his tender fist to his chest. "In the future, you might want to make sure you know who's trying to fuck who before you start making accusations." When the smaller man furiously made as if to rise, Ryan let a huge hand cover his shoulder. Losing all humor, his eyes narrowed. "I'm serious, man. If a chick's gonna step out, she ain't worth getting your face broken over."

That took the last of the fight out of the defeated man and he made no move to follow when Ryan turned his back and walked toward the entrance with Michael. Michael was watching the bigger man, wondering how much of his advice was self-reflective.

"Have you seen Becca?" Crisis averted, he was scanning the crowd.

Several inches taller, Ryan craned his neck in the dimly lit bar area then shook his head, frowning. "No." A deep furrow creased his forehead. "I haven't seen her since we split up. You?"

Growing concerned, Michael gave a quick shake of his head. "I was out there." He tipped his head absently out toward the strobe lit sex party, not breaking from his visual search of the crowd around him. "Maybe she stepped outside. It's pretty loud in here." They exchanged a look. Ryan knew Becca was having trouble with the temporary sensitivity and this was definitely not the place to be if one was easily overwhelmed.

Ryan glanced over at the gyrating forms in the distance, and took a longer second look. "Shit man, you were out in *that*?" He continued staring, running a tongue over his lower lip. "I got the raw end of this one." Then, lowering his head, he sniffed, stopped, and sniffed again. "Holy shit, Mike. What'd you do out there? I smell at least two of them on you."

"Can we worry about finding Becca, not about watching a live porn shoot?" Michael growled, irritated. "All these bodies are making it hard to smell her."

With a grimace, Ryan tore his gaze from the hot mess he was having *no* trouble smelling and let his gaze settle on Michael. The man's growing panic was easy to discern and Ryan quickly redoubled his efforts at locating their missing member. "Sorry Mike, she ain't here."

There was a minor tingle he barely felt anymore and the faint taste of iron as his fangs slid out. The vampire was willing to accept blood if sex was off the table. *It would be so easy to take one in here. No one would notice.* "This place is about to blow, we need to find her."

"We'll find her, Mike." Ryan tried to ease his mind, patting his shoulder as he did so. His eyes continued fruitlessly to scan the crowded club.

Michael's assessment was accurate and he wasn't the only one who had noticed. The man who'd greeted them at the front door rushed past them toward the bar. Both men followed him with their eyes and strained to hear.

"No more drinks, we're shutting the place down for the night. This is crazy," the must-be manager leaned over and yelled after beckoning the bartender over. "A guy just told me people are having actual sex on the dance floor." His voice went shrill and he lifted himself up on his hands on the edge of the bar, scanning the mass for evidence. "I called the cops, they're already on their way. Let's hope we can avoid a full blown riot."

The bartender braced his hands on the wooden surface between them and shouted back. "I got some seriously pissed off customers already, you cut 'em off and they're gonna start something. You sure you want to do that? Remember what happened last time."

The frazzled manager ran a hand over his chin and scanned the immediate area. Sure enough, several humans were as uptight as the little man who'd challenged Ryan. One was coming close to trading blows with another guy at a high top table near the far end of the bar. Blinking, he tightened his lips and nodded. "Fine, we'll serve them until the cops get here." He shook his head. "I got an ambulance already on the way." He threw out a harsh coughing laugh. "That'll be about every emergency vehicle we've got in this town."

"Why's a medic coming? Did I miss a fight?" The bartender glanced around as if he might see someone bleeding in the middle of the floor.

On second thought, Michael snorted, that wasn't such a far-fetched idea. Then, all of his attention zeroed in on the manager at the next thing he said.

"No, that girl that collapsed earlier. Over by the hall." He jerked a thumb at the last place Michael had seen Becca. "She went down and couldn't tell me who she was with or her name so I called 911. I'm thinking there's a batch of bad drugs going around or something." He forced another laugh. "We've got a few days before the full moon, don't we?"

Ryan fell in step behind Michael as he took off. In seconds, he had the manager spun around and tossed up against the bar.

"What the hell?" the bartender started to argue.

Ryan intervened, catching him by the shirt. "Leave it. My buddy has a few questions is all, everything's cool."

Seeing the folly in continuing to disagree, the bartender chose to listen to the large Marine's sage advice. Retreating into the safety of the bar, out of arm's reach, he cast a few more worried glances at Ryan before filling the orders of several eager patrons.

Unaffected, Michael was in the manager's face and wasted no time in pulling him under his influence. With the police on their way they couldn't be caught in here. It would be a mess and give Salvo even more reason to throw roadblocks in their way. He couldn't stop them from being here but a few disturbing the peace charges would slow them down and annoy Black. Plus, this was Becca and Michael and his vampire were both intent upon getting her back. Neither would stop until she was safely back in his care.

The manager's hopping, sketchy mind took a few extra seconds to reel in but Michael had done this before under far more stressful circumstances. Grabbing the man by the back of his neck, he brought his face directly in front of his. As soon as his eyes swept past Michael's, the vampire drew them in and the human was his.

"Where is the woman you were talking about? The one who collapsed?" he commanded him to answer.

Serenely, the manager pointed to the red wall beyond the hostess station. "I put her in the front office."

Dropping him, Michael took off with Ryan close behind. The hostesses screeched at the sight of the two men rushing past them almost too fast to register and burst through the door painted to match the black wall, marked only by the silver handle.

Inside, Michael's wild eyes scanned the closet-sized room before they settled on Becca, bent in half in a black fabric chair next to a metal and black desk. Two metal chairs lined the far wall completing the list of furnishings. A framed poster reciting, "The Customer is Always Right" sat overlarge behind the desk.

None of that mattered when Michael saw her. Ignoring the roaring in his ears, he rushed to her and was already tuned in to her heart rate and breathing before he had his hands on her body. Her pulse was erratic and her eyelids fluttered, giving occasional glimpses of whites telling him her eyes were rolled back in her head. Pain raced through his silent heart and he crouched down in front of her, gently laying a hand aside her face and turning it toward his.

"Becca? Becca we're here. What happened?"

Her mouth opened and a hoarse moaning scream escaped. He didn't have to see to know Ryan had heard the words she'd uttered as well. "It burns." The big man sucked air in through his teeth and held his breath. Michael knew what he was thinking. That she was cracking up. That she hadn't gotten over the fire demon like they'd all thought.

Only he knew what even Becca didn't want him to. How could he not? There were nights on the road when they slept together, when she would wake in a sweat refusing to say what was wrong. Or lying and telling him she was nervous about the upcoming mission or some sort of other falsehood meant to deflect his concerns.

He too had a secret he hadn't told anyone, including Becca. The demon *had* killed her. For nearly a full minute her heart stopped beating. It had been the longest minute of his existence. He'd even considered biting her, drinking *her* blood to complete the exchange that would alter her forever. Even though he knew she wouldn't want it, facing her death, he'd been willing to do anything to save her. But instead, he'd pleaded with her.

It hadn't been his proudest moment but he did it without shame. He'd begged her to come back to him. Unable to touch her burned flesh without doing more damage, his only recourse had been words and he'd fired them all at her as she lay, fading in his bed. Telling her he loved her; he needed her. That she was the only person he cared for and she'd brought him back from a mindless abyss where he'd been hiding from himself for decades. All things he would never in a hundred years admit to her if she were conscious. Though now he considered it, seeing that she'd gone to that dark place again. How had this happened when she was awake?

Tipping his head, Ryan shuffled over to the door. Still partially open, he peeked through the opening and spoke behind him. "We should go. Things are getting hot out there." The strain in his voice was clear.

Seeing that there was no bringing her back in time to run, Michael lifted her small body and held her tight against his chest. Ryan looked quick, saw that he was ready and opened the door. Michael followed close behind and they blew past the hostess stand without taking the time to recover their coats.

They were just settling into the car, Ryan in the
front, Michael and Becca in the back, when flashing
lights rounded the corner up ahead coming their
direction and colored the winter wonderland. New
falling flakes reflected the lights until the very air
was filled with nothing but red, white and blue.
Ryan waited until all of the officers were out of
their cars before starting theirs, not pulling out until
the last one entered the club. Detective Salvo
walked among them. Then, carefully, he turned the
car around in the street and headed back out of
town.

Chapter 22

Becca came back to herself, feeling the images of smoke and fire and the agony of having her clothing and hair melt with her flesh fade. Slowly her ears registered the sounds of tires on asphalt and a humming motor while her hands felt underneath her the smooth, cool leather of their rental. Sitting up already, her hand squeezed the one beside her to let him know she was conscious. Not that he needed the alert. He would have known by her breathing, as would Ryan. Opening her eyes, she figured out that they were in the back, which meant Ryan was at the wheel.

"Pretty bad, huh?" Michael asked her gently.

She could hear the carefully guarded concern and was inwardly mortified. "I don't know what happened." Becca rolled her face up, finding it easier to stare at the dark dome light above her than to look at either one of the men she'd failed by fainting while on duty. "One minute I was heading for the ladies room. The next, I was on the floor."

"You said you were burning," Ryan cast over his shoulder. Catching her eye in the rearview, he held it for a second before both turning back to the road. "We know you were thinking about the fire demon." Watching for her reaction, he flicked his eyes between the road and mirror.

Covering her face, she inhaled deeply and rubbed her gritty eyes. She swore she could sleep for a week. Not that she would close her eyes anytime soon. If she did, she was sure to have more dreams about the demon and there was no way she was going to bring that on if she could avoid it. Although if she was having waking nightmares, she was pretty much screwed anyway.

"It must have been something about that place that reminded me," she mumbled.

Neither man said anything. Becca closed her eyes to keep from catching the disappointment sure to be in both sets of eyes. Deep breaths aided her façade of calm. The seat beside her shifted slightly and Michael's cool hand slid in hers. His silent offer of support was almost too much for her and she squeezed her eyes shut to block the leakage that threatened to spill. They needed her to keep it together and do her job, not fall apart and leave them with two down. Gabrielle wasn't snapping out of it anytime soon.

When the car stopped Becca sat up, knowing they couldn't be at the motel yet.

"What's going on?" Ryan threw the car into park and turned around.

Had she not been anxious about the forced discussion, Becca would have laughed at seeing the giant man have to twist nearly in half at the waist and dip a shoulder to clear the steering wheel. As it was, she sat frozen. "I told you, I had a," she paused, "a flashback. It's fine now. I'm fine." Her stomach churned. Not only was she lying, she was terrified for her sanity. As well as for the safety of her unit. What if they'd needed her tonight? Her heart threatened to take off, and would have had Michael not been holding her hand. "Were you guys in trouble tonight?" Her words were tight. "I, I'm sorry I wasn't there for you."

Michael squeezed her hand and Ryan waved her concerns away. "It wasn't a big deal. I almost shredded a guy because his girl was into me and Mike here just about got himself raped on the dance floor." He tried to shrug but got caught on the steering wheel and had to settle for tipping his head to the side instead. "Nothing we couldn't handle."

Becca felt her mouth fall open and she gaped at them both.

Michael's face was guarded and she felt her guilt shift to anger. "When were you going to tell me about *that*?" She jerked her hand from his.

Features showing no signs of remorse, Michael eyed her steadily. "I thought I'd wait until you were conscious before I hit you with that one."

Ryan's raucous laughter filled the car.

The sudden urge to get the hell away from both of them was unstoppable and Becca leaned over, shoving her door open hard enough it snapped back and hit her knee. Grunting at the impact and throwing an obscenity in the now roaring Ryan's direction, she hobbled out of the car and struck off down the road. Mercifully, no one followed.

For the first mile, Becca fumed. The second mile she was sullen. By the beginning of the third, she'd made her peace with what had happened and had thoroughly chastised herself for being a raving bitch. Ryan said they were *both* confronted by overly passionate people and it sounded like they dealt with their situations appropriately. She had no right to be angry with either one. The only one who deserved a kick in the tail, was her. The one who had been lying to those who needed her and left them in the lurch when she should have been doing her job.

About the time she'd come back to her senses, Becca was nearly back at the motel. Up ahead, she saw a light bouncing toward her. For a second she considered that it could be one of her unit until the flashlight tipped her off. None of them needed such an apparatus on even the cloudiest of nights. Instincts and training were hard to undo and Becca felt her muscles tense in preparation should she need to defend herself. If she were any other human woman, walking in the dark alongside a country road in the middle of nowhere at this hour would have been suicide. Fortunately, she wasn't normal. Her mouth twitched at the grateful feeling that accompanied that.

It was the first time she let herself consider the upside of not just the after effects of Michael's blood inside her, but the longevity of it. The fact that she was a witch to boot. She'd taken the news better that Michael was a vampire, and Ryan and Gabrielle were werewolves. Maybe it was time she made an effort to learn more about what she was instead of trying to ignore it. It might give her some different options for managing her sight and even jumping. She could *use* her strengths instead of cursing them.

The light approached, bouncing like a flashlight being carried by someone on foot. Her brain was already calculating height and gender by the aggressive approach, level of the light, and time between bounces that hinted at stride length. By her guess, it was a man. Average size, moving steadily at an unhurried pace.

"Hello," she called out, announcing her presence right before the light hit the ground in front of her.

"Are you all right?" she tried to engage him. Certainly *he* couldn't be afraid of *her*? Women were conditioned to fear strange men, especially at night. Not the other way around.

No answer.

The light remained unmoving, illuminating the uneven surface of gravel on the shoulder and ice piled in a rising grade away from the street. Becca slowed her pace. "It's okay, I'm not going to hurt you." She spoke lightly, hoping to convey the irony she felt to the other party. "I'm unarmed." Knowing she had several advantages over the other walker, she was comfortable making the lighthearted overture.

Suddenly, without warning, the light switched off.

Becca stopped and her vision flared as if the light had gone back on right in front of her face. She was blinded once again. Crying out in surprise and pain, her hands flew to her temples in an effort to stop the sudden headache that went with the blindness.

There were no footsteps, no crunching of gravel and snow marking someone's approach. And yet there was a feeling that someone was there, hovering over her. Agony ripped through her intestines as her sight flared and, without thinking, knowing only that she needed to see what she faced, she jumped.

Her vision cleared, showing her a glowing pale rust-colored light illuminating a body curled in the fetal position on the roadside that she recognized as her. Quiet filled her mind and the feeling of disconnected nothingness struck her as she floated inside this one's head. Fires flared hot around her and at first she thought she was having a nightmare again only these fires didn't burn her. These fires were a part of her and she walked in them. At her feet, curled up and making funny sounds was a small girl lying in the road. Energy pulsed within her and she wanted to touch it; she knew that if she touched it she would consume it. Her hand reached down and the glow followed, illuminating the girl's features. The hand floated, fingers outstretched over the eerily lit face. Becca's face. The girl's eyes widened and she started to scream. One blink, then two and then she was gone, ejected roughly back into her tormented human form. Frozen, jagged rocks poked her body as she writhed.

An engine's hum filled her ears and she was back. Her vision restored, she twisted toward the sound and saw headlights glowing in the distance. Still panting and weak, nausea threatening to bend her over any second, hiding was out of the question. Coming around the bend, the headlights hit her with their full strength and, scrambling on her haunches out of the road, she turned toward the light, raising a hand to shield her eyes from their blinding beams.

The engine slowed, the car pulled over and she felt her shoulders relax when the door opened and Ryan called out, "You done with your tantrum?"

It was the second door she waited for. Keeping her eyes squinted near closed, she shuffled toward him, dragging her feet to make sure she didn't trip over the shoulder where the asphalt met the rough.

"Michael?" she called out uncertainly. "Michael, I can't see you."

Hearing her strained tone, he was at her side. "What's happened?" he asked her urgently. His hands ran over her body, searching for injuries. Any anger over her failure at the club was instantly forgotten at fear of harm.

"I don't know." She opened her eyes all the way and straightened, all hints of nausea gone at his touch. Confused, she looked up at him and felt very small. "I don't know." Pointing directly ahead of where they stood, she stammered, "There was a man. A light. I said hi and he vanished." Without knowing why she did, Becca kept her jump into the unknown private. The memory of glowing orange coming from the body she was in scaring her as much as any vision of a fire demon.

"Hallbeck." Michael was instantly Captain Rossi, taking command of the situation. "Take Becca back to the motel. Check on Gabrielle."

Years of battle had Ryan on the same wavelength without hesitation. "Yes Sir." He snapped to and his eyes sought Becca, worry springing into them, though not for her.

"Yep." She didn't have to hear his urgency. "I'm coming." Sight returned, she was able to double time it to the passenger side and hop in. Her captain was gone before she turned around.

 On the short drive back to the motel Becca filled Ryan in on what she'd seen before she fell and he slammed his palm into the steering wheel while uttering a stream of obscenities that would have done even her father, a career Marine, proud.

More than a little shaken, she frowned in genuine confusion. "I'm sure she's fine, Ryan. He was alone and I didn't smell blood or anything on him." Distracted, she offered him some limited comfort.

Spinning to face her, fury plain on his face, Ryan backed her into her window with a thud without laying a hand on her. "How are you not getting this?" he seethed. "The light is the *thing*. It's not just *some guy*, it's the thing Gabs has been following."

And I jumped into it. She repeated in her head for the hundredth time since climbing into the truck. And just like that she had the key. It was simple; all she had to do was believe she was in danger, real danger. That was what she needed to jump into someone, or some*thing*. She'd done what Admiral Black had asked her, she'd succeeded and now her place with the unit was secured. So why was she not shouting it from the rooftops? When she had the chance to tell Michael why had she been unable to say the words? Because she'd been able to go into a *demon's* mind. How did she explain that? Or the continued sense she had of not quite fitting in her skin? It was like someone had washed her skin and dried it on high while she'd been out; she didn't fit anymore. Something else was in there. Then it hit her and the icy grip that took hold of her insides confirmed it. The demon had left something behind. Some part of it was inside her. Leaning back, saying nothing, she rode the rest of the way in terrified silence.

By the time they reached the motel, Ryan's focus was entirely on what lay behind the white door his headlights shone on. Slamming her door harder than was necessary, she accepted his glare without retaliation. Unspeaking, they jogged to the door and paused only for a few seconds while Ryan used his key to let them in.

Bursting in, Ryan flicked on the light and Gabrielle shot up in bed.

"No, I can't!"

"Gabs, it's me. Is everything okay?"

Gripping her sheet to her mostly nude body, she held a hand over her eyes. "Dammit Ryan, turn that light off."

The light snapped off, leaving them all temporarily blinded in the vacuum of darkness. A few seconds and the three considered each other, two flanking the now closed door and one sitting in only a sheet.

Gabrielle spoke first. "I take it town was eventful?"

"Have you been here this whole time? Have you been sleeping since we left?" Ryan remained glued to the outer edge of the room.

Pulling out the sheet and peering down, she smiled wryly. "Ah, yeah. Unless I went off gallivanting through the woods naked." Holding a dainty, tanned ankle out for their inspection, she turned it up and down, and brought it back in. "And came back with clean feet."

Ryan's growl and cracking knuckles punctuated the following quiet.

"Hey Ryan, why don't you go next door and wait for Michael. I'll stay here." Reaching into her pants pocket, happy she hadn't left it in her coat currently back at the Wisconsin version of Studio 54, she extracted her key for him.

Apparently at a loss for how to deal with either one of them, Ryan took it and left without a word.

When he was gone, Becca crept forward and sat on the edge of the bed. "He's worried about you."

"I don't need your advice, so if that's what you're here for, you can go too."

"I'm not going to try to give you advice," Becca assured her. "Just perspective. You did it for me once, remember?"

It had been the first time Gabrielle had been decent to her, the morning after their first mission to Russia and Becca and Michael had slept together for the first time. Gabrielle overheard a phone conversation between Black and Michael and thought Michael's seduction had been orders. After telling Becca what she'd heard, the next day, she'd told her what she *saw*. That Michael hadn't been following orders, but had been acting on his own. He'd been upset at her accusation that he would bed her for Black. At the time Becca had been too hurt to see, but later she appreciated it. It was all perspective. She owed that in return.

She didn't confirm or deny. Becca took the lack of objection as exactly that. "He knows there's something going on and he's scared for you." She smiled. "Even *I* know there's something going on and I barely know you."

Gabrielle's eyes lifted, a curious expression in them. "What do you mean you barely know me? We've been around each other constantly for over two months."

"Yeah," Becca answered cautiously, "and how many times have you taken me up on my offers to run together?" She answered herself before Gabrielle could make something up. "Never. How about training? How often have you come and trained with the rest of us? Once, maybe, when Ryan made you?" Laying a hand on the blanket by her leg, Becca's tone softened. "You don't want to be best friends and that's fine. But Ryan's working hard to figure out what's happening to you and you're not giving him anything. It's counterproductive to our mission and a little cruel." She placated the little voice in her head that accused her of doing the same, telling it this was different. This was personal and had nothing to do with the rest of them. *Coward*, it shot back. *Liar.*

"What about you?" Gabrielle queried, less venomous than curious. "Michael told Ryan you had one of your visions in front of that detective and you still haven't told anybody what you saw." The way she said "vision" held more than a healthy dose of Gabrielle's patented sarcasm.

Defensive at having the tables turned, Becca bristled. "That's because I don't *know* what I saw." Pensive, she chewed her lower lip and thought back to her vision. It seemed like it happened years ago. She still had no idea what it meant. She'd assumed eventually she would see someone involved or get a feeling, but no luck so far and she was at a loss, feeling more useless by the minute. "I saw some guy I've never seen before and he was telling me I had to kill someone, only he didn't say who. All I know is it felt like it was someone personal, you know?" She picked at the ugly blue duvet. "It hurt me to hear it. At first I thought maybe it was Michael or one of you." She shook her head. "Only that doesn't feel right either. I don't know what it means."

Her confession was met with dead air. She shouldn't have been surprised. Sighing, she heaved her tired body up and turned toward the door. "I'm sure you'll be fine. I'll leave you alone." Her hand went out to grasp the doorknob.

Gabrielle's voice, unsteady and shaking, reached her before she opened it. "What did he look like? The one who asked?"

Closing her eyes, Becca recalled him in vivid detail. "He's wearing a uniform but not one I recognize. Sandy brown hair, a little lighter than mine, and brown eyes. He's got a straight nose, thin moustache like you see in old movies. There are other people there except they're in the background and I can't make them out. They feel familiar too, though."

Gabrielle asked before Becca finished, "Did he have an accent?"

"Uh, yeah. French I think."

"What do you mean, 'think'? It's an easy one to pick out."

Gabrielle's patience was obviously wearing thin and Becca was ready to be shut of her. "It was hard to make out with all the shouting and snarling." She let herself out.

Chapter 23

"I didn't find anything," Michael told them again.

Ryan wasn't content with the answer and slammed his fist into the wall. Sheetrock gave way and the cinderblock behind it cracked audibly. "How hard did you look before you came charging back to check on things *here*?"

Already at his breaking point from having been from one extreme to another and back again, Michael snapped back, "Gabs isn't the only one this thing's after. People are dead and unexplained shit is happening all over the place." Pulling his electronic tether from his pocket, Michael hit a button. "I'm not waiting until morning to see what the local files say, I'm going to check in and see if the admiral can come up with anything. Why don't you go for a walk and cool off." Seeing the big man taking his advice and heading for the door, Michael lowered his voice. "Stay close. We don't know if it'll come back and I don't want anyone going up against it alone."

He growled something in response and jerked the door shut behind him.

Letting out the breath she didn't know she'd been holding, Becca let herself fall back on the bed. "Do you want me here?" She inclined her head toward the device now at his ear.

Closing his eyes, he bobbed his head once before the other end picked up. "Admiral."

He proceeded to fill him in on their evening. Becca felt herself getting heated all over again as he glossed over the situation on the dance floor. An unbidden image of him being groped and dry humped by two other women brought her jealousy surging forth.

Sensing her reaction before he saw it, Michael assured the admiral, "Nothing happened. I didn't allow things to progress."

The admiral's eerie chuckle was even creepier over the telephone. "You may let your woman know more about the scenario *after* our call Michael. I don't care what happened with the humans unless one is dead and I have to worry about damage control."

"Yes, Sir." His eyes remained trained on Becca a long second more before breaking away.

"And you say there were unexplained incidences of violence as well?" Admiral Black prompted.

Michael confirmed that to be true.

"Was this the first such occasion?"

Michael's shoulders tightened. "No. I heard the manager and the bartender talking. This happened before. The police were involved this time. I would imagine they were last time as well. We're heading to the station in the morning. We'll search for records of any other similar occurrences in the general vicinity. I wanted to know if there was anything else we could find out in the meantime."

Black was unresponsive. Michael waited patiently. Becca practiced swallowing her tongue and reminding herself it wasn't Michael's doing. He'd said no and disengaged as soon as he could. Advantages aside, it would be great when all this vampire blood wore off and she was sane again. Relatively speaking. She still had visions of the future no one understood half the time. That couldn't ever be considered Ozzie and Harriet normal.

Finally Black's voice was back on the line. "Has Rebecca had any unusual symptoms since arriving in town?"

Their eyes met, both were equally confused. "Sir?"

"Anything unusual. Tingling, itching, general sensations of unexplained agitation?"

Her eyes went wide and Michael nodded his head. He actually looked excited. "Yes Sir. She has been unusually agitated."

"My skin's been tingly," she said softly. Her chest felt tight. Why did this have to come back to *her*, she wondered, feeling beaten. Didn't she have enough stuff she couldn't handle without being to blame for this too?

"Hmm." Black was already distracted. "I will consult with someone and call back. Stay close." He echoed Michael's words to Ryan.

Returning the phone to his pocket, Michael leaned back against the wall, facing where Becca slouched. They didn't have time to feel overly awkward. Michael's phone buzzed and was in hand in seconds.

"Sir."

"Have you heard of ley lines?"

Michael's face froze. His worried gaze shifted to Becca then back before he could shut himself down.

"I will take that as a yes," Black surmised. "Then you know what walks them and how they work."

There was no reaction on Michael's face and Becca felt her insides clenching. Predictably, the spots started to dance in front of her eyes.

"It has already found your party and most likely has detected what you are, which is why it has latched on to Gabrielle. It needs energy to survive and a werewolf has far more than any human. The witch is sensitive to them, more than you or the others. You can use her to track it, but be careful. A powerful source of energy such as this will know how to tap into each of you. It will feed from your fears and from your passions, any strong emotion. It will drain you to nothing if you let it."

"Sir, is there another way we can track it?"

"Not unless you have an experienced diviner with you. The only thing you have is the witch. Her energy is raw, but it is from the same source. She will feel its vibration when she steps across it. If she follows it to where it grows stronger, she will be able to track it and you can destroy it." Black paused and his tone changed. Was that regret? No way. "You *must* use her. The potential for loss is too great for your personal feelings to be primary. Entire cities have fallen prey to these energy suckers. Rome burned and several of America's western cities fell to lawlessness and degradation before their transgressors were stopped. You must be successful or face a potential rift that could swallow the city and all those in it."

"Yes, Sir." The call ended and Michael stared at the dim face of his phone.

Becca cleared her throat and found her voice, though it didn't sound like her. It was shaky and thick. "What is this thing?" In her head she already knew. She wanted to hear the words for some sick reason. Like hearing it out loud would make it any less painful to bear.

It didn't. The words rang out as a death knell. Hers. There was no question this time that she would fail. She'd seen what it did, felt its power. The players in her vision remained a mystery, though now she understood its message. This thing was going to ask her to kill her own.

"It's a ley line demon." Michael's confirmation was anticlimactic.

Becca made a vow to herself that she would track this thing and she would find it. But she would do it alone, far from anyone she loved and she would not allow it to use her to harm any of them. If she failed, she alone would die.

Chapter 24

The four of them gathered in the parking lot at a coffee shop not far from the police station and the main strip of the downtown area shortly before the sun rose over the tree line. The bright orange ball rose behind the evergreens, their green boughs imposed as skeletal outlines etched in black against the fiery backdrop. Becca wondered if it was a sign that this would end like the last time she'd faced a demon and everything ended up as ash.

She'd faced rogue vampires and weres and all were challenging adversaries, but nothing had been anything like the demon that had nearly killed her. The sheer power in that hellish creature continued to haunt her almost nightly. It seemed somehow right that she would face one again. Only this time she feared she might not be as strong. This time she knew what she was facing and what it was capable of, whereas her last battle had been fought in ignorance. Not for the first time, she wished she could erase the entire fire demon experience from her mind, although presently, it was for an entirely different reason. If she could face it blind again she might not freeze and get herself or one of her unit members killed, because surely that was what was destined to happen this time. Knowing what she was up against had her shaken before she even saw the thing.

"Are we clear on what we're doing?" Michael was leaning back against the hood of the car, one foot propped up behind him, hands folded over his stomach.

Everyone nodded. They'd gone through it earlier at the motel after he'd spoken to Admiral Black and they'd all gotten a few short hours of rest before heading out. Detective Salvo would be at the station within the hour at which point Michael and Becca would be allowed access to their systems. Their job was to pinpoint "hotspots" where the demon had been draining energy and use those as starting points to try to locate their demon. Whether or not it was active during the day was yet to be determined, though the admiral's source believed that ley line demons were limited to location, not hour.

Ley lines, Michael explained after a long and informative conversation with Black, were straight lines or lines making up geometric shapes along the Earth's landscape where metaphysical energy was strongest. In the ancient world, monoliths such as Stonehenge were erected along the lines to draw people to where their power would be most effective when they needed it for festivals and rituals. Becca's genetic heritage as a witch, previously unknown to her, had a special tie with the lines putting her on the same wavelength, so to speak. The admiral's working theory was that if they put her on the one that the demon was using, she would vibrate right to him. More or less.

Becca figured the demon was just as likely to find *her* since she had made a personal connection with it. Surely it would come looking for her before too long if she didn't find it first.

Ryan and Gabrielle had the more generalized task of going into town and doing some more recon work. By listening and watching they hoped to identify any spots the demon was using that maybe hadn't made the police radar. If anybody got a lead on actual real-time demon activity they were to contact the others immediately.

"Don't forget our coats," Becca reminded Ryan. "If you end up making it down to the club." She hoped they would get that far, far away from her and where the demon was sure to be before long. What better place to raise passions and then drain them? After all, wasn't that exactly what it had done the night before when Michael was attacked by horny women?

He snorted and shook his head. "We're tracking a demon and you're worried about the cold?"

Flushing, she shrugged. "My mom gave that coat to me." Her glance skimmed over Michael just in time to catch the faint smile that lifted his features, if only temporarily. Fleetingly, she wondered how many more of those smiles she would see. Angry with herself for wallowing in self-pity, she pushed those thoughts away. They were soldiers. This was what she'd signed on for. Okay, maybe demon hunting wasn't foremost in her mind when she'd enlisted in the Navy and she hadn't been given a choice in joining Admiral Black's ranks, but she was here now and this was her unit. She would fight with them for as long as she could because to quit was to leave one unguarded. Hearing herself recite her father's personal creed in her head gave her strength and Becca stood taller, taking a moment to look at each one of those who had become friends to her since meeting them. Even Gabrielle, aloof as she was the majority of the time, she would trust with her life. This time it was her turn to protect them with hers.

"All right then." Michael surveyed them one final time. "We'll meet here at fifteen hundred. Keys are in the usual place so anyone can retrieve the vehicle if need be." They always stored a copy inside the front bumper both on missions as well as home. One never knew when a change in drivers would become necessary.

Nods all around and Ryan and Gabrielle struck off to get started inside the coffee shop, a wise choice at that hour. Becca couldn't help watching their body language. Ryan's was tense, while Gabrielle's reeked of defeat, and the space between them was far more than just the hand's breadth she could see. Poor Ryan, she thought. He was like a great big heart walking around and he'd invested himself in the one person who had locked hers away. A giant sigh escaped without her notice.

"Are you scared?"

She crossed her arms and watched the two enter the coffee shop, choosing to stare at the neon outline of a coffee cup in the front window. Funny how the yellow wavy heat lines made her think of fire, not coffee. It's all where your head's at, she surmised wryly. She could probably see a snowball and think about how long it would take for a fire demon to melt it right about now. She shook her head.

"Are you up for this?"

Becca automatically took a breath and wheeled, prepared to defend herself, only to let it out slowly when she saw the sincere concern on Michael's face. He wasn't locked down. He wasn't being Captain Rossi. Sure, he was worried about their welfare and whether or not she would be able to hold up her end under pressure. There was a lot riding on her and he had to be questioning her ability to keep her head in the game after last night at the bar. But his concern in that moment was for her on a personal level. Lack of faith she could handle, even yelling she could take. This was different; this looked like love, and she wasn't sure what to do.

Sex was simple. Physical, active, always urgent between the two of them; it was as easy as breathing. This new intimacy in their relationship was the hard part and completely new. Letting him see her weak. Opening up and showing him how frightened she was when they weren't in the midst of battle or facing imminent danger was more than she'd given anyone. Confronted with such heartfelt compassion, her tough façade faltered and she felt her lip quiver.

Her voice cracked. "Yeah." She tightened her arms, hugging herself.

Pushing off effortlessly, Michael approached. There was only a hint of the oozing sensuality with which he usually came to her. This side of him was different, harder for her to accept in its realness. Sensing her discomfort, Michael stopped inches from her and put his hands in his pockets, leaving the small space between them as a buffer. "You know, after I was changed, I wasn't afraid of dying." His voice was low, meant only for her ears, though he spoke over the top of her head.

Becca felt the sting of her inadequacy once again. This unit was so strong. Her prescience served as a warning system. Her physical capabilities were limited to her borrowed strengths until they ran out. Only a very little of what was useful about her even stemmed from her natural abilities. Forcing her shoulders back, she blinked hard and tried to appear brave.

"I didn't have to be." He continued, his voice low and soothing despite the heartrending words passing through his barely moving lips. "What was there for something like me to lose? My life was gone and Black took my soul. Death would have been a welcome release from my bondage."

"Don't say that." It hurt to hear him talk that way about the worth of his existence. "You've saved countless lives. You've done so much good in this world."

The body before her remained immobile. "It wasn't until I had something to lose that I learned how to fear again. Not until I thought I'd lost you did I remember what it was like to be truly afraid." He felt her stare and let his chin drop to give her a full view of his face.

Passion brought forth his beast while work made him hide behind a stoic, unfeeling mask. Letting her see him for the man he still was altered how he looked to her. She could see the suffering in his eyes, the miseries he'd bourne in silence and servitude. He let her see the extent of the anguish his losses had caused him. In seeing the toll being a vampire had taken, he was made all the more human.

Tentative, she reached for him, fingers brushing lightly against his sleeves as she pulled his hands from his pockets. Unable to convey her feelings into words, Becca stepped into him and slowly let the side of her face lay against his chest. Equally measured, his hands let themselves be freed and wrapped around her, pulling her close.

"You're a strong woman, Becca," he murmured in her hair. "You were before you met us and your strength makes us all stronger by its addition. My CO told me when I took my first command, 'Don't ever doubt yourself, because to do that is a disservice to us all' and I want to tell you the same thing. We're a team and we make each other better. That goes for us too, we're more together than we are apart because we love each other."

Her hands slid around behind him and she pulled herself in as close as she could get, seeking the comfort of his nearness. What he'd said was true; she had been strong *before* them. However, she would have argued that she was actually a subtraction. Not only did they have to worry about protecting her due to her physical weaknesses, she provided a significant distraction to Michael. And now she was a demon magnet.

Instead of pointing any of that out, she clasped him to herself tighter yet. If he'd been human, he wouldn't have been able to breathe. He wasn't. He let her hold on as tight as she needed.

Chapter 24

Salvo was at the station, waiting for them. The receptionist was markedly cooler toward them as well. Apparently word had spread about Michael's dressing down of the cops at the crime scene. When they asked for him they weren't buzzed in, instead Salvo came out. Acting as gatekeeper on the outside of the locked doors, he crossed his arms and stared. A few hard looks were sent Becca's way, but for the most part all of his hostility was aimed at Michael.

"What department did you say you were with again?"

"We didn't," Michael responded coolly. "You never asked."

"I'm asking now." Salvo remained unruffled.

"We're with the United States Navy."

Becca found a fixed point on Salvo's blue on blue spotted tie to keep from looking like she was watching a tennis match.

"No you're not." Detective Salvo's head slowly tracked back and forth, not buying it. "After yesterday's little show I had a buddy of mine with some pretty high clearances do some digging." Widening his eyes, he let his jaw fall open sarcastically. "*And did you know what*? He didn't find any record of you in any of the agency databases."

"Did your chief receive a call from my superior yesterday informing him that we would be given full access to your systems?"

Arms coming down, Salvo took a half a step toward Michael. He didn't appreciate the reminder of who had more brass behind him. "Yeah."

Michael's nonchalance was bordering on arrogance. "Then I don't see as it matters what my business cards say."

"Do you *have* a business card?"

"No."

Rolling her eyes, Becca entered into the pissing contest. "You know, watching you two compare badges is really impressive, but we have work to do." Yet again she wished Danny were with them. This was his specialty, not hers. She'd never been much of a people person. Funny, she hadn't thought about it before, but she didn't work with *people* much anymore. If *she* was the one responsible for bridging that divide they were in trouble. Why Michael had chosen *this* case and *this* detective to lose his people skills on was beyond her, but his timing sucked.

Running low on tolerance, she looked from one man to the other. Detective Salvo was bristling and Michael had his hands in his pockets, clearly unthreatened. She refrained from throwing up her hands and walking out the door to leave them to it and concentrated on winning Salvo to their side. "Look, all games aside, Detective, we work for the United States Armed Forces in a specialized unit. Our duty is to perform specific investigations involving unusual crimes that might involve others like us." She rode the line of what was sharable, knowing he wasn't going to accept the usual smokescreen of "need to know." Let him make the connections he was comfortable with.

Brow furrowing, he gave Michael a look and shifted his focus to the smaller, non-threatening woman beside him. "You're Internal Affairs?"

"Sort of our own special version." She watched the skepticism fade from the lines in his face and felt her shoulder blades dropping back out of her skull to where they belonged. He wanted to believe her.

Dark brown eyes flicked to Michael once then focused entirely on her. "That would explain why *he's* such a prick." He pointed a long finger at her companion. "But it doesn't explain why you and your friend ran off into the woods while your dear captain here had us chasing our tails to keep us from following. Or why he had to make me look like an asshole at my own crime scene."

"You were doing a fine job without me," Michael baited him.

Speaking quickly, Becca kept the detective's attention on her. "Gabrielle saw something and I followed to provide backup." She maintained an even tone despite the image of fire that blazed through her mind. Pulse speeding up, she breathed steadily through her nose and out her mouth to slow it.

Michael shifted beside her, automatically prepared for the worst.

Ignoring the gesture, she made it clear she would not show any vulnerability in front of the detective. "We didn't want to draw resources away from the scene while it was being processed so we went alone. We didn't find anything or we certainly would have shared it with you." Her eyes dropped to look up at him through her lashes, an old habit she'd developed in disarming hostile men. Combining her femininity and unimposing stature tended to diffuse them quickly and it seemed to be a winner with this one as well. "That was your concern wasn't it? That we were leaving you out of our investigation?"

"The thought *had* crossed my mind." His tone lost some of its bitterness.

Smiling partially for his benefit and partially out of relief that he was willing to be reasonable, Becca held out a hand. "Truce?"

A faint rose color tracked across the detective's sharp, olive toned features and he took it. "Truce." Frowning, he looked at Michael who had gone into lockdown. "That go for you too? Are you going to stop getting in my way?"

"On the investigation, yes," he replied carefully.

Puzzled, Becca scrunched up her face but got no signal from him as to what he meant. He'd intimated that he thought Detective Salvo was interested in her before and she'd paid no attention. Surely that wasn't what he was still thinking. The concept of Michael Rossi being jealous of the detective was ludicrous.

Seemingly placated, Detective Salvo reached for the key card hanging from his belt and let them in with a short nod to the receptionist who stopped glaring on command.

Good girl. Thought Becca, preferring the woman's nasty looks to the wanton ones she'd aimed Michael's way on their last visit.

Detective Salvo wordlessly led the way through the low, pale, fabric-covered cubicles to the back wall of offices. Becca assumed she would go back to the same one Chief Kowski had parked her in before but he walked them right past.

She and Michael exchanged a curious glance behind his back. Salvo stopped at the corner office and rapped twice with his knuckles on the open oak door. Signaling with a finger that they should wait, he walked in and kept his back to his guests. He and the chief had a nearly private conversation. Becca picked up the majority of what he'd said, "Internal Affairs" and "I hate that guy" being the most telling things she caught. It was up to her to maintain any sort of goodwill with the police force at this point. Michael had done too much damage to overcome easily, assuming he was even interested. In her experience, cops held grudges for a long time.

"Good morning, Chief Kowski." Taking the initiative, Becca slipped in around the detective's back and moved over to allow Michael entry.

If the bland look on his face was any indication, he was about as happy to see them as Salvo. "*Captains.*" He continued to stare flatly at her.

Becca studied the lines around his pinched mouth and dark blue smudges under his eyes. Her heart skipped a beat, bringing Michael's head around. Giving him a tight shake of her head she hid with a quick duck and kept her eyes forward. "Sir, did something happen last night? Was there another murder?"

Leaning back, he folded his hands on his relatively flat stomach and rubbed it absently. "Not a murder, no."

"Then what was it?" Michael asked pointedly. "You've obviously been up all night," he lifted his chin at Detective Salvo, "and that one's in a mood."

Chief Kowski's chair made a loud bang as it flipped back to its full upright position. Hands slamming on the faux wood, he came up onto his feet in a heated rush. "So *now* we're sharing? Full disclosure?" he yelled, his face flushing. Several heads in the bullpen popped up. "Or does that just go for us bumpkins, not Feds?"

"Sir," Becca tried to soothe him.

He waved her off, not having any of it. "No, I don't think I want to hear anything else either one of you has to say. Or the rest of your damn team come to think of it. Now get out of my office!" Kowski pointed at the door.

"But sir," she tried again.

"Don't 'sir' me and you sure as shit better not try to shine that Internal Affairs baloney on me. We both know that's not true. You're some other shit." A glimmer of interest in his own train of thought sparked in his eyes, "What are you, Homeland Security? Is this some sort of chemical attack?"

Neither Michael nor Becca had to fake their shocked expressions. "What?" she asked out loud while Michael was better able to control his tongue.

"Oh don't give me that." Kowski threw his hands up in the air. "A whole town doesn't go crazy in a few months. You can't convince me it's because it's a college town, and it is *not* cabin fever. It's been a warm winter for Christ sake, nobody's shut up or cut off."

Before she could stop it, a disbelieving "Warm?" slipped through her lips.

The detective and his chief both glared at her, unamused.

Effectively cowed, she tried to appear apologetic. "Sorry."

Michael was on high alert. "Define crazy, sir."

The chief's mouth was shut. He wasn't in a giving mood.

"Would you be referring to an increase in volatility? Fights, maybe a rise in indecency?" Michael lowered his voice, forcing everyone else to be quiet to listen. It was a negotiation technique Becca learned from her father that *he'd* learned in the Marines. Michael must have taken the same class.

Anger dissipating, the chief just looked tired. "How did you know?"

He shrugged. "Remember, I was reviewing files all day yesterday. And last night, when we couldn't come back here to expand our search," the detective glowered and Michael ignored him, "we went out to take a look at things ourselves. In town."

Both Kowski and Salvo perked up at that. "There was a report of a big guy who broke a guy's hand last night at The Red Carpet." Kowski turned to his detective. "How big was that guy you met yesterday? The one that works with these two?"

"Damn big."

Letting his annoyance with the detective take a back seat, Michael angled himself to face them both.

Sensing that they had far too many ears tuned in and seeing this as going somewhere touchy, Becca moved over to close the door and leaned back against it.

Michael waited until it was just the four sets of ears before proceeding. "It's not cabin fever and it has nothing to do with an unruly student body, Chief Kowski."

The older man gently lowered himself into his seat and let his hands lay on his desk, palms flat and pressing until his fingertips went white. "Do you know what this is? Is it contagious?"

"Have you seen anything like this before?" Detective Salvo set aside their differences as well in the face of real progress. "Do you know how to stop it?"

"It's not a chemical attack and it's not contagious." Michael snuck a glance at her out of the corner of his eye, asking her to let him lead.

Not certain where or how far he was going with his explanation, Becca kept her lips firmly closed.

"We aren't sure exactly where the culprit is, but we are familiar with these types of situations." Michael went on, picking his words cautiously. "My team and I are going to be tracking the suspect as soon as we leave here."

Detective Salvo started to speak, then held his breath at Michael's upheld hand. Becca watched his face purple in barely checked anger.

"It's only been since the most recent murder that we've been able to determine anything specific about our suspect," he explained, allowing Salvo to breathe again. "Our team in California was able to make some connections with the fresh evidence and we've come up with a suspect based on their findings."

"What can *we* do?" Salvo prompted, his hands clenching and unclenching nervously. He wanted to be there when they took this guy down. "You can't expect us to just sit around doing nothing while you close in. We want a piece of this guy too."

Only this wasn't a *guy* and he couldn't be within a thousand yards when they went after it. She knew without needing to check that Michael would be of like mind. Where they differed, was that she intended for the rest of her team to be equally far away when the demon was found.

"Settle down, Detective," the chief cautioned his enthusiastic employee. "I'm sure the good captains will be sure to include us when the time comes," he leveled a gaze at Michael that had been honed by years of dealing with criminals and liars of all sorts, into a stare meant to rattle even the best, "in the interest of inter-department cooperation per post 9/11 guidelines." Those sharp blue eyes crackled with warning while the mouth curled into a peaceful smile.

Without a hitch, Michael dipped his head. After working for Black, even this human's threat was nothing. "Of course. We are here to assist in this investigation, however, it is ultimately your town and your command is primary." The men regarded each other, measuring. After what felt like a prolonged and beyond uncomfortable quiet in the office, Michael inhaled sharply and went on. "We need someone to dig through your incident logs dating back to when this started. I would like to see a map with the murders and the other incidents marked separately. That will break down our two distinctive crimes into their two patterns, which is how I believe this party sees himself. And we can predict his movements from there." He left out the part about the criminal *actually* being two separate criminals and one of them being very dead. Best to keep things simple for the humans, it would be easier to manage one missing culprit when they destroyed it versus two.

Chief Kowski shook his head. "We've tried putting men all over, but without any sort of rhyme or reason to them, I just don't have the manpower to have someone everywhere at all times. We've patrolled town heavily enough to keep the damage to a minimum. We break up the fights before they get too ugly. But there's no order or method to the killings, no patterns at all except for the fact that there aren't any patterns." The chief's shoulders slumped with the burden of his office.

"Sir, we will find our culprit," Michael told him, absolute.

Not very hopeful, the chief raised his face to look Michael in the eye, flinching as he did so when he saw something he instinctively wanted to shy away from. He refrained from answering.

"My team will take point on this." When he spoke, Michael's tone was surprisingly gentle. He was talking to the detective as a peer. "We'll be starting at the club this evening and doing a sweep through town. You can follow up with a secondary team and watch the bar where he hit last night. We have reason to believe our culprit might show up there but not until nightfall."

"But he was just there." Detective Salvo wasn't convinced. "Why would he strike the same place two nights in a row?" His brow furrowed. "He's never done that."

"And that is why we believe he will go back. Last night's prompt response time by you boys in blue kept him from getting what he wanted," Michael led him.

The chief jumped in. "What is it he wants?"

"Absolute chaos."

Chapter 25

"Do you think he'll chart out all the scenes like you asked?" Becca asked once they were outside the station and far enough away to have some privacy from official ears. "Or do you think he'll figure out you parked him out of harm's way doing busy work like some sort of rookie?"

"I think he's a good cop and he'll do what he's told as long as he believes it's the right thing." Michael stared straight ahead and stepped out into traffic without turning to look over his shoulder for oncoming.

Instinctively hunching her shoulders against phantom vehicles, like that would help her if they were hit, she made a noise. "Are you forgetting something?" She scrambled to close the small gap between them.

Cracking a reckless smile, Michael looked at her. "Super special hearing, remember?" He pointed playfully at an ear. "If there's a car, I can hear the engine. Heartbeats this close, also no problem."

"So how come I didn't get *as* super special of hearing?" Becca asked, also wondering what had him so uncharacteristically cavalier in public.

Slipping his fingers over hers, Michael directed his eyes back to the sidewalk ahead while shooting a sideways glance at her. "Because you're one step removed from the source. You're close, but not quite the same."

Becca considered what he was saying. "I suppose. I mean, when I jumped and I was in your head, it was all so much stronger, more crisp that what I get now."

Mention of jumping brought them both to a different place and a somber silence filled their bubble until Michael spoke again.

"Have you tried it since Black asked?" His voice was low, subdued.

Becca gave special attention to where she was setting her feet. Up onto the cracked sidewalk and down with the gentle incline leading away from the car and the end of the strip where surely Ryan and Gabrielle were making their way.

"Should I be tuning into the vibes or something?" Becca asked him, feeling the constant tingle on her skin growing stronger. Knowing the source of the ants marching on her skin since arriving in town opened the door, it seemed, and now she could tell where it was stronger and weaker. The tingling grew more intense as they walked down what had to be a ley line running the length of the street. Even with him touching her she could feel it, telling her it had to be strong.

"You're avoiding talking to me about this," he said evenly.

"No, I'm focusing on the mission."

Michael stopped and, hand tightening on hers, halted her as well. Becca was jerked back as she hit the end of her play. "What?"

Blue eyes narrowed. "*What*? Are you serious?" He didn't sound amused.

Her shoulders rolled. "I don't know how it works and I don't think I can do it. The only thing I can figure is the key is to have sex or share blood with someone." He couldn't know that she had indeed unlocked the key on the roadside or that the demon they hunted was to thank for it. Guilt tore at her heart. She swore to her conscience that she would come clean with him after she destroyed the demon. Providing the demon took *all* of its pieces with it, including whatever it left in her. She couldn't put him in the position of having to destroy her because she housed a piece of pure evil. It was too much to ask, and Black would. It was Michael's greatest fear and she wouldn't be responsible for bringing it to fruition. If destroying the demon didn't work, well, she would figure out a way to take herself out on her own. Michael would never have to make that call. "You can't tell me Black intends for me to fight or screw members of Congress to get a bug inside whatever committee he's stalking."

Passion and amusement warred with Michael's expression and Becca watched in fascination before he tucked it all away. Michael, the captain, was who she ended up with. Her fingers slid free from his and instantly her skin recommenced its itchy dance. The demon was close.

"You think he wants you on a committee?"

Canting her head, she watched a young couple across the street. The woman was smiling while her lover spoke in her ear and she laughed. His arm sneaked around her shoulders and brought her in for a kiss. They looked so happy and carefree. In that moment, her heart broke.

Catching the distraction, Michael swung around and watched before asking again. "Why do you think that?"

Shoving her feelings far from where anyone might see, she turned back. "Why is he stalking a committee?" Becca studied his features. There was a brief slip when he turned back to her that told her everything about his mood. The minor darkening of his eyes and tightness of his jaw told her he didn't like being ignored, while the lines around his eyes confirmed he'd at least gotten a sense of what she was watching across the street. Mentally shaking herself, she got back to business. There was no time to dally, she would have to slip away soon. She had to start looking for an opening. "It's pretty obvious, isn't it? He's cut back on our trips but not our equipment, thank God." Her finger aimed at her own chest. "This human needs grenades. Plus he's been even more interested in you and I've seen the way you look at me when you come back from one of those meetings you two have. Especially after DC. You looked sick when you came to visit me that first night back." She refrained from mentioning the knife wound he'd been trying to hide. He knew exactly what the admiral had in mind and he didn't like it. He didn't have to tell her exactly what it was but she could guess it was objectionable for personal reasons, not necessarily strategically.

He was unable to hide his shock at her insight.

Her lips twisted. "You know I specialized in investigations before I joined up with you, Michael. I see stuff."

"Apparently I've underestimated you." Concern gave way to a hint of a smile. "What else did you catch, Captain Sauter?"

Unable to refrain from playing when he was in the mood Becca smiled broadly, though her words wiped any signs of levity from his face. "I know that you're trying to keep me away from him because you know what he wants to use me for and I know that you think if you keep us apart he won't know how strong I'm getting." Reaching out, she let her fingers trail down his forearm. "And I know you're afraid that if you know what I can do, he'll make you tell him. You're afraid you're going to get me hurt or sucked in deeper."

Michael lost all the color he'd gotten from drinking the last of his traveling stash that morning.

Stepping in, she went up on her toes to kiss his cheek. "And I know I love you for all of it." She smiled.

"Why do I work so hard to keep things from you?" His eyes were dark and troubled. "It's pointless."

Nodding, keeping her concerns private, Becca agreed with him. "So stop trying to hide things from me. No secrets, remember?" She reminded him of their agreement back in the beginning. "You have to stop trying to protect me all the time; I can handle this life." Her little voice reminded her she was facing a possible suicide by demon within the next few hours and didn't plan on telling him anything. It didn't matter, he would do the same for her and that was why she couldn't let him. The good he did in his role with the admiral far outweighed anything she'd done or could do. If anyone was expendable here, it was her. And, as luck would have it, she was the one who could find this thing. Now if only she could handle killing it. She took a breath and touched his arm again, hiding her body's signs of stress in her love pets and hating herself for using him as camouflage.

Unconvinced, Michael shook his head. "I know you're capable, Becca, but sometimes Black asks things." Ducking his head, he broke from her gaze. "Things that change you."

"Michael, I want you to know that who I am will never change." Sliding her hands around his waist, she pulled herself up against him. She didn't care who saw or how that might compromise things with the locals. "And who I am will love you until forever. No matter what."

Wrapping his arms around her tight, Michael lowered his head until his lips touched her ear sticking out from under her ponytail. "I love you too, Rebecca, until forever."

A jolt surged through her body and Becca jumped, unable to hide the way the energy surge affected her. "Holy! Did you feel that?" She hopped backward and broke away from him. It was time.

Eyes wide, Michael cast around them, looking for the threat. "I felt *something*, but I'm not sure what." Spinning, he put his back to her, hand behind to keep tabs on her while he searched.

Their contact was momentarily broken while she scanned for danger as well. Without the barrier his touch provided, her flesh caught fire. Telltale spots started and Becca found it hard to breathe. "It's close." She knew the cause without any doubt and felt the power seeking her out. Whatever the demon wanted, it knew it wanted it from her, specifically her, out of all the humans in this town. Not human, a little voice whispered in her mind. Part witch, part demon. The thumping of her heart in her chest began to pull. Her feet moved, carrying her past Michael, farther toward the end of the strip and away from the center of town. At least she wouldn't have to worry about the lack of courage to go to it when the time came, it was doing it for her. No chance of chickening out. "I know where it is," she whispered, her chest feeling as though it might burst. If only she could manage to shake free of Michael, she thought with a pang. *Please don't take him too.* She pleaded in her head while her body was pulled helplessly along, muscles held tight against the rapidly building pain shooting through her.

****

Automatically trying to shield her from her obvious
pain, Michael reached out only to snatch his hand
away when he felt a stab where her flesh touched
his and watched her jump.

"No," she hissed through clenched teeth. "Whatever
it's doing, touching you makes it hurt worse."

More than any pain it caused him, he feared
harming her and left his hands to hang useless at his
sides. "What can I do?" Michael fought with
himself and his nature, both unified in their desire to
tear the throat out of the demon when they found it.

The little voice in her head screamed for him to go
away while part of her wanted to laugh. And she'd
been worried she wouldn't be able to separate from
him. All she could manage through clenched teeth
were a few words. "Go. Get. The. Others." Feet
moving stiffly, Becca was leading them awkwardly
in a definite path.

His phone was in his hand without conscious
thought. But instead of calling Ryan or Gabrielle,
Michael made another desperate call.

"Admiral, we've found it. It has taken hold of
Becca."

Chapter 26

Gabrielle sipped absently at the hole in the white plastic lid, burning her lip in the process, as she concentrated on not letting her eyes stray to the large body striding along beside her. Unlike some of her co-workers, he ran at the same temperature as her except she would have sworn he was at least twenty degrees hotter at that moment. And very hard to ignore.

Not a sound came from either of them, only the soft scuffing of shoes on pavement. The grit of salt and sand for traction ground against the occasional patch of ice missed by the plow responsible for clearing the wide sidewalks in town. Her sharp hearing picked up every syllable the mother ahead of her uttered to her inquisitive toddler, the jingling dog tags of the trotting retriever across the street and every other tiny indication of life in the bustling downtown.

Dog tags brought her mind round to Ryan again and the way his tags were always warm on her skin when they made love. Had sex, she corrected herself. They were having sex; they were not in love. Theirs were dangerous jobs and things could happen. Things *had* happened. She would not allow herself to be so stupid as to fall in love again. Going a step further, she again stopped her eyes from finding him and the tightness in her chest objected.

Ryan's feelings weren't serious either, she told herself. How could they be when she'd never had any sort of sentimental words for him? Never allowed him to say more than two kind words to her without changing the subject. The look in his green eyes that night when he'd come bursting in, clearly fearing for her safety, had nearly been her undoing. Then it had helped her to reinforce her walls.

There was nothing Ryan wouldn't do for someone he cared for and she had no doubt he would lay down his life for her if the need arose. And that was exactly what she'd been hoping to avoid. No one would die for her. She would never again have someone else's blood on her hands, least of all someone with as much to offer as Ryan. After this mission she was going to end things. She'd postponed the inevitable long enough. It was time to let him go before he had more than a few bruised feelings. He couldn't die because of her.

"Gabs."

His voice, surprisingly gentle for such a large man, made her lose a step and she glanced up out of habit. The pain in her chest ratcheted up another notch at the deep sadness she saw in his dulled eyes and lined face. Not only had she caused it, she knew it was going to be worse very soon. Her mouth opened, tongue tracing across her lower lip to wet it. "Ryan, let's not…"

Up ahead, the woman walking the toddler with endless questions stepped down onto the sloped sidewalk for wheelchairs and strollers, making ready to cross the street and Gabrielle saw the flash of light brown hair and side profile she would know anywhere. The pads of her fingers could even feel the short, coarse, darker brown hairs of his neatly trimmed moustache.

Automatically, with no ability or will to stop herself, Gabrielle made a ninety degree turn and quickened her pace, momentarily leaving Ryan behind before he caught on to her change in direction both physically and mentally.

"Gabs, wait. Where are you going?" Ryan took two long strides to catch up. Worried, he scanned the sparse sidewalks and streets for any threats of danger; any blatant signs of a seven-foot tall demon spewing fire or brimstone.

None to be seen, he grew frustrated and laid a hand on her arm. The pull from within her was stronger than his soft touch and her body moved out from under his palm.

With a growl, Ryan replaced his hand on her arm, tightening his grasp so that she stopped and waited for him to maneuver in front of her. Her progress impeded, Gabrielle became agitated and her other hand grasped at his. "Let me go, Ryan." Her stare went beyond him, losing sight of the brown haired wraith that had haunted her these last few days. "Please."

***

Her pleading should have been enough to break his hold. Normally willing to do anything to bring a smile to her face, Ryan never said no if she asked. Only that was when she didn't have a demon luring her out into the woods on a nightly basis. Nor were those occasions when she was dreaming nonstop about her ex-boyfriend. And never had he felt so close to losing her as he did that morning. He felt her slipping away from him.

"Gabrielle, stop."

Whether it was the hand or the commanding tone he took on, he didn't know. Regardless, it worked. She halted in place and remained stationary while he stepped in front of her, though after a few shorts seconds of acquiescence, she attempted to pry his hand off of hers again.

"Let me go, Ryan," she pleaded, her voice cracking.

For an instant his fingers loosened on their own before he clamped down again and locked her other wrist in his hand, taking care not to hurt her. It took a breath or two before he could push down his annoyance enough to soften his voice. They couldn't risk a domestic right there on the street; they were only a few blocks from the police station and they weren't going to be much help to their unit if they were tied up being booked for disorderly conduct.

"No, not until you tell me what the hell this is supposed to prove." Some small hint of malice crept out despite his best efforts. "I'm tired of following you around while you chase ghosts, waiting for it to be you laying there with your chest ripped open."

Gabrielle rolled her eyes. "We got the windigo, nobody else is getting their chest ripped out."

Ryan felt his fraying control let go and he leaned in close to her face so that she was all he could see and he bared his teeth, growing longer by the second. "Are you goddamn stupid?"

Amber eyes went wide but not in fear. Nostrils flaring, Gabrielle refused to give him an inch. "Actually, I think I'm one of the few keeping my head here," she hissed at him. "Michael, I'm sure relaying our commanding officer's direct orders, asked us to track this thing. I'm tracking it with whatever means available to me." Her eyes darted to the side, trying to catch sight of her ghost again before he disappeared. She took a step. "I *know* it's not real."

He caught the minor hesitation in her words and knew she was minimizing the absolute control this thing had over her. The continual tugs she was trying, testing the solidity of his hold, didn't escape his notice either. If he didn't let her go, she would become violent. But he loved her. And that superseded everything else for him at that moment. Ryan's fingers held tight and he shifted to block her. He could take a little damage.

"You think catching a demon's lackey makes *this* no big deal?" He caught sight of a middle-aged woman standing behind Gabrielle, paying way too much attention to them, and clamped his mouth shut on his canines. Inhaling through his nose and breathing out his mouth, he soothed his beast barely enough to keep it below the surface. Ryan lowered his voice. "This thing was the one calling the shots. That means it's *stronger* than the windigo and *it's* still out there. If you were thinking straight, you'd know that."

Her eyes swam with an unmistakable wetness. One Ryan had never seen there before and he felt his chest swell with hope that he was getting through.

"I am thinking straight, Ryan," she whispered, her eyes glittering. "More so than I have in a long time. I'm sorry I've let this thing with us go on so long, but it's time I made things right. It's over. Now. Let me go."

This time when she wiggled in his fingers to loosen their hold, he let them open. Gabrielle's cutting words had eviscerated him so thoroughly he lost the will to hold her back. Her wish that he remain her guard dog, trailing behind only to be called up should she need him was clear. And, as much as he hated it, he fell in step behind her. She was cruel but honest. She had never given him false hope, he'd managed to build that all by himself. But she was his fellow soldier and he loved her as a woman. For either of those reasons alone he would help her whether she wanted him or not. When combined, he knew he would die happy if he knew he had taken her place under the demon's hands.

Chapter 27

"Is she able to speak?"

"She did at first. Now she's nonresponsive."
Michael's eyes spun sideways for the millionth time
to see that Becca's glazed expression focused on
some unseen point in the distance.

"Can you tell where it is leading her?" Black, at
least, kept his head.

"No."

"Try, Michael." Black was unwilling to take his
Second's panicky answer.

Even over that great distance, the tightness in his
skull reminded Michael of his obligation to the
admiral. With great difficulty, Michael let his gaze
be torn from his love to search for road signs as
well as possible destinations. When, after a few
seconds he tried to tell Black it was no use, the
pressure in his head increased and he winced. There
was silence on the line while Black waited for him
to do as he'd been told.

Blinking his eyes, relieved when the pain dissipated
as quickly as it had come on, Michael let his
peripheral tracking follow Becca while he
maintained his close proximity. Meanwhile, he

scanned the buildings, searching for one that might suit a ley line demon's tastes. Whatever those might be.

As far as he knew the demon would remain under the surface, following the path of the lines, coming up only to feed upon the energies of its victims. Energy was its one known desire, whether that be from passion or fear didn't seem to matter to this one. With the windigo gone, it had yet to prove itself a killer, though that wasn't entirely out of the realm of possibilities. Like Black said, these sorts of demons had been known to throw entire cities into riots just to feed off of the maelstrom and, once that happened, no one could predict a human's safety.

Michael knew that Becca was strong, he'd tasted her before *and* since she'd become like him. He knew that once the demon discovered her it wouldn't let her go. Whether it decided to drain her or use her to create a riot, he didn't believe she would survive its visit. Images of the dance floor in the club the night before brought another possibility to mind and Michael felt his vampire clawing the back of his neck. He growled.

"Mind yourself, Michael," Black cautioned. "You are her survival as well as any in the town who might be caught in the middle. If you lose control, you help no one. You fail in your mission, you fail her, and you fail me."

Black's worst-case scenario trifecta worked. Michael stood straighter and walked as close as he could to Becca without their flesh touching. "Yes. Sir."

"Good." Black's satisfaction, for once, didn't seem to stem from his hold over the captain, but rather from relief. His tone softened minutely. "Now, look again. Where would a demon want to take a human to get the most energy? Somewhere he could drain her without interruption."

Sparing a quick glance at Becca's rigid frame and pale face, noticing the bruises under her eyes were growing worse with the strain, Michael gritted his teeth. Black was right, the only way to help her was to be ready when this thing showed itself. He would take great pleasure in tearing its limbs from its earthly body.

He tore his eyes from her and let his anger fuel his senses, flooding them until he was nearly overwhelmed by his surroundings. The light breeze lifted his hair, tossing it and he swore it was being plucked from his scalp. Light breaking through the patchy cloud cover burned his eyes and he blinked, lowering his lids to shield them from the glare. Garbage from dumpsters behind the local shops, wet, earthy scents from the street competed with each other to set his nostrils to tingling.

"Michael," Black cautioned him to reel himself in. Distance was nothing when one knew another's soul. The admiral could read Michael's continued struggle in his silence and used centuries of understanding motivation to help his Second. "Shut out everything but her. What is her course? Has her pace increased?" Black let him consider his answers and asked a last question. "Can you feel its energy?"

Taking a deep breath and breathing out his nose to clear the acrid scents of city from his nostrils, Michael dipped his head and felt the burning lessen. Fortunately, winter sun in this snowy state was not strong enough to harm him and he felt his body come back under his control.

"Very good, Michael," Black encouraged. "Now, what do you feel?"

Unzipping the coat he'd been wearing, Michael shrugged and let it fall from his shoulders, dipping his phone hand he let it slip off to land on the cement behind him without making a move to stop it. His sleeves, already rolled up, exposed his forearms. Skin open to the vibrations of demonic energy, Michael waited. Not for long. With his mind calm and flesh exposed, it was less than a minute before he felt the tingling once again on his arms. "I feel it," he breathed into the phone.

Black said nothing, only waited.

Several more steps and Becca stumbled at the curb. Without thinking, Michael's hand shot out and caught her elbow.

Black's stern reprimand joined Becca's outcry in Michael's ears.

"Sorry," he told them both.

"If it has possessed her, you cannot touch her without the demon knowing it. It feels any reaction her body has to yours." Black spoke evenly, glossing over the facts with no hint of emotion. "It will not risk her wasting her energy on anyone save *it*."

For a second Michael almost smiled before he remembered himself. Becca would be mortified if she'd heard Black talking about how her body reacted to Michael's touch. He knew the thrill it caused her; he felt it as well. That and he could sense her body's changes when he was near. Usually it filled him with a Neanderthal pride, knowing he had that sort of pull with her. With it causing her discomfort, he felt a sense of shame at it this time. Oddly, the fear that Black would use it to bind her to him had dissipated.

Through Michael, Black already had control of her. If he were going to use it, he would have by now. Michael finally realized that. He had been so blinded by his fear that Becca would see his bond as a weakness, he'd failed to see that Black had grown to view her as an asset and not just a disposable pawn. Feeling that knowledge filter through his brain, he was liberated temporarily until reality set in yet again.

"Sir." Michael acknowledged his superior and brought his rambling, racing thoughts back to heel. Unlike the windigo, the demon was confined to the ley lines where the earth's energy was strongest. All of the demon's activities had been isolated to this main track through town Becca now was tied to, telling him that the ley line they were following was on this street. That limited their options to this straight line only. The next question would be whether the demon would want more bodies or just Becca. At this hour, evening hotspots were out. However, they had gone past the coffee shop and bakery already; the morning gathering places. "Where are you taking her?" he wondered under his breath.

Waiting, Black let Michael study the details without interruption.

Right about then the marquis protruding over the sidewalk blocked the sun and Becca made a sharp left, stopping abruptly when she slammed into the glass door. To his horror, instead of putting out her hands to open the door or even to brace herself, she backed up a step and went forward again. The glass cracked in several places.

"Becca stop!" he shouted at her. There was no getting between her and the glass and to move her bodily would be to hurt her. Frozen, he watched her body follow instructions only she could hear.

"Where...?" Was all he heard in his ear before his hand crushed the phone and the worthless pieces rained down on the cement with empty clatters.

She made no indication she had heard him. Stepping forward again, her body whacked the glass and Michael heard it shatter. The smell of blood assailed his nostrils and his vampire raged. *I will kill it!*

Biting back the reluctance he felt, he launched himself between Becca and the breaking door before she could strike it again. Crying out in agony, she threw back her head and tensed her muscles as the demon possessing her voiced its opinion over having its vessel touched by another.

Mine. His vampire ground out in a low voice not heard by human ears in thirty years. At least not any that survived.

Becca's body jerked and her jaw fell open as the demon's control hiccupped. It was only for a second, but long enough for Michael to rip the door open, breaking its lock, and whipping her through to set her back down on her feet before she could be used as a battering ram again. Jaw clamping back shut, Becca limped forward through the sparsely lit foyer, across the dark blue carpet ornamented with kettle-sized depictions of dancing popcorn puffs and soda cups with jauntily tilted straws as the demon's control was renewed.

Below her knee, the front of her dark pants glistened as the blood leaked from a gash in her knee. The right side of her face darkened as well from the tear in her scalp just above her hairline. Michael smelled more emanating from somewhere under her coat and was more than alarmed that she would soon weaken from the blood loss. A hint of some foreign scent in her blood gave him pause, though there was no time to consider what it was. She continued to follow.

****

Ryan trailed Gabrielle, his awareness capturing the change in her stride when the demon began to guide her again. The need to take her bodily from that place, far from where anything could hurt her or force her into submission was physical and Ryan felt the seams let go as he shoved his hands deeper in his pockets.

Two men dressed in the neon-striped coveralls of road workers split to give him a wide berth when they passed him on the sidewalk. Ducking his eyes, he glowered impotently at his shoes, tracking her with his other senses. It wouldn't work for them to have the police called in now. He could imagine that detective facing off with a demon. The mental picture of his bulging eyes and wet pants brought out a nasty chuckle that sent a courier walking behind them rushing around and out in front of him like someone poked him in the ass with a hot prod.

Her light steps diverted, carrying her into the street, and Ryan looked up. A dark green minivan with one headlight was coming down the street toward her, its speed unchecked. A quick glance through the windshield revealed its dark-skinned driver's eyes were down, on a phone was Ryan's guess. Cursing, he sped up and snared her around the waist with one thick arm less than two feet before the van reached her, not setting her down again until they reached the other side. Several gasps and one stray scream, the only indicators her apparent suicide or his daring rescue were even noticed. He gave silent thanks they weren't in a busier city or it wasn't rush hour. Although that might have required fancier footwork than the simple snatch and grab he'd performed. If it hadn't been Gabs, he wouldn't have even broken a sweat. But it *was* Gabs and he feared losing her. Moisture had sprung up under his arms and was already beginning to run down his back and into his waistbands.

Feet set back on the cement, Gabrielle resumed her measured strides without pause while Ryan panted and staggered on shaking thighs before he collected himself with a quick glance around to make sure no one was following. Typical humans, they notice as soon as something upsets their routine, but would never dream of wading in to offer help or ask what happened.

Again his thoughts turned bitter as Ryan's memory briefly traipsed past his last sweating, staggering walk as a human through his own small town. A young soldier on leave, struggling to return home after being attacked by what he'd believed at the time to be a giant dog or bear. No one helped him or spoke to him, even those for whom he'd mowed lawns, pumped gas, and delivered papers as a youngster. Not a peep. They'd let him go, to spend the next month sweating, healing and seeing visions of impossible things alone in the house his family had left him. When his first change came and he felt the irresistible urge to leave his home in favor of the woods, he knew he would never see any of them again. That staggering, sickly man had been the image they would forever recall when talking about young Ryan Hallbeck who had gotten some wild hair to all of a sudden up and sell the family place, never to be heard from again.

Shaking off the familiar bitterness he never allowed himself to feel, he concentrated on the woman who needed him, even if she didn't love him. Just as he caught up to her, she turned down an alley and walked up the short set of metal steps to pull on a metal door leading into the back of some undistinguishable brick building. The screeching of a metal lock breaking reached his ears as he took the first step and he caught the door before it closed. A few seconds of blinking and his eyes adjusted. He could smell old butter and the syrupy sweetness of a soda machine. Were those popcorn *men* wearing *suits* on the carpet? "I'm not dying here," he thought as the door settled back into its frame with a scrape, leaving them in the quiet darkness.

Chapter 28

The burning in Becca's body was intense. She'd lost all sense of time and place, seeing only the flames that had haunted her for months. She felt nothing but heat all around her and the stroking of the flames as they seared her flesh. She could smell her skin cooking, hear it crackling as the ley line demon beckoned her ever onward.

"I can make it all go away," he promised, the owner of the voice in her head. "Come to me and I will take the pain. I will take the dreams and the fear from your mind."

The promises continued, all essentially the same, all desperately needed. Becca followed blindly. At some point in the endless torment she'd forgotten to suspect the voice of having anything to do with her pain. It came to represent only salvation. Blind was an appropriate term for Becca's journey. Her sight was negligible, the only way she could see was through a series of tiny holes in the center of her vision. Staring straight ahead with wide eyes, she was able to pull in enough light to make out most of what she might run into, though without control of her body she could do nothing but watch as she slogged forward. Narrow view aside, there was little she'd picked up during her walk to the theatre. Rushing flames deafened her. Her sight's cautions of danger blinded her. Her body's constant state of agonizing scorching had succeeded in removing any chance of knowing when or if Michael laid another hand on her. Michael, where had he gone? Didn't she want this?

"He's gone on without you, girl."

Alone against the fire demon. Again. Becca's mind recoiled. It was her greatest fear returned. How could Michael have left her? In her limited capacity, she was unable to comprehend more than the loss she felt tear its hole in her heart. Gone was any sense of relief that she would face the demon alone or that no harm would come to him. Grief compounded her physical and mental pain. Her feet stuttered and a moan escaped her lips.

"You are not alone. I am here," the voice soothed. "Come to me and this will all be but a memory."

Becca couldn't be alone against the demon again, her fears told her. She'd been terrified of this exact moment since facing it the first time. Even if she wanted to be selfless, with the time finally upon her, she felt terror take hold in her body. She let her feet follow the voice, wanting what it offered more than anything. Maybe it would take her fear, stand with her against the demon. Walking under the large marquis jutting over the sidewalk, she lost the light that had allowed her sight. After the first impact with the door, she backed up and tried to regain control of her body.

"It's the demon. He has put this barrier between us. Break it. Break it down with your body if you must. You will be free of all pain when you come to me but first you must reach me."

She'd felt the obstruction, her limbs so petrified by pain and fear she'd been unable to do much to protect herself when she struck it a second time. She backed up and then there was another long lick from the fire and her body convulsed. Becca lost contact with the ground somehow and was surrendered to the flame for one horrible moment. When it stopped and her body returned to her, she moved as rapidly as she could manage, intent upon finding the maker of all the promises. If there were a way of being free from this pain she would do anything to find it. Anything to be free of the fire demon's constant torment at last.

The inside of what she guessed to be a movie theatre from the reek of old snacks and popcorn was dark. The lights were off until it opened in a few hours for the staff to get ready for the matinee. Limited already, Becca was completely blind in the low light. Her steps slowed to a rushed shuffle; urgent to reach her goal yet scared she would stumble unwittingly down a stairwell.

The voice called to her from up ahead, off to one side. Her fragmented thoughts collected long enough to tell her this was the hallway leading to the theatres. She followed the call; lights above each theatre entrance offered limited glimpses of doorways that disappeared from her limited field of vision the closer she got. When she reached the end of the hall the call came again, guiding her to turn into a door on her left. A grateful whimper that this would all end soon and she walked through the door, thankfully open to her.

The floor tilted down and, after the first stumble, Becca leaned a shoulder against the carpeted wall and used it to guide her. Gradually it sloped down as well until only her elbow touched it and she searched the relative dark for a glimpse of her savior. Her eyes settled on a tall figure standing on the far side, across the red fabric seats from her. His form was hard to decipher and she widened her eyes as much as she could, making out the outlines of a long coat with lines of faint light coming from where a suit of armor would have its chinks. Her breath caught and she attempted to back up quickly, crashing into something in her hurry. She didn't have the chance to wonder how something else had gotten in there. The moment she bumped into whatever was behind her, the constant burning flames that had refused to take a backseat in her tortured mind flared and her mouth opened. If she screamed she didn't hear. All there was for her was agony.

Michael was ready for the demon when he saw Becca turn toward the last theatre door. Quickly opening the door as soon as she faced it, he avoided having her strike this one bodily and cause herself further damage. The bruising under her eyes had spread until they reached her paling cheeks, the blood loss from her lacerations wasn't helping her any though the heavy scent of popcorn was helping to mask the scent infiltrating her blood.

Walking beside her down the sloped aisle to the front of the theatre, Michael soothed his vampire, busily gnashing its teeth. *As soon as she's clear you can have it.* The scratchy cackle in his head was jubilant. He felt his lips pulling up into a cruel smile.

He hung back to use Becca's focus as a means to pinpoint the demon's location and keep surprise on his side as long as possible. The moment Becca rounded the end of the wall and he watched her eyes attempting to capture the details, he knew enough. His hands flashed, wrapped around her and yanked her back to safety on the other side of the wall. The wail that rattled her throat took a piece of him with it, knowing it was his touch that caused it. That last push was more than enough to send him flying over the top of the wall to land in a crouch facing the creature that had taken the town and members of his unit, including his love, hostage. Blood filled his mouth as his fangs broke through and Michael allowed his monster roar to the surface.

****

His scent wafted to her through the cacophony of other smells; popcorn, salt and doughy pretzel, helping her when glimpses were lost in shadow. His smell, one she'd only known as a human, came back to her in sharper detail with her more sensitive olfactories.

It hadn't been long after Luc and the rest of his squadron had been lost to a bomb in the North African deserts of Algeria near the town of Biskra that she left the service. The only reason she'd been saved was due to the fact that she'd been on a supply run outside of the camp at the time. Her role as nurse with their small crew had been considered necessary given their remote outpost and dangerous task of stopping any inroads the Muslim opposition forces were attempting to make into the larger city of Algiers against colonial French rule. Luc had asked her to stay, to spend the day with him in the bazaar. But Gabrielle was asked by the doctor heading the clinic if she could accompany him to the depot in Constantine and restock what they needed. The supply clerks never got the list right and they'd run dangerously low on several items. It took all day on the rough roads and by mid-morning, when they returned, all that remained were the smoking ruins of tents and a bomb-pitted airstrip. Together they buried the dead and left the ruins behind.

The tears she'd wept, the forgiveness she'd begged of him for leaving, digging his grave and burying him with her own hands, none of it had been enough to assuage her guilt. The next few years after she deserted her post, spent on her own, had exposed the parties responsible for her lover's death and her knowledge of medicine had allowed her to poison all but one, known simply as The Almohad, The Unitarian. The night she confronted Almohad, Gabrielle learned why he'd been so impossible to kill when he passed on his curse to her.

She had promised herself that the day would come when she would see The Almohad burn for what he'd done to her beloved. Her allegiance with Admiral Black had not yet given her that satisfaction, but she knew that it would come. Intelligence continued to circulate about a ghost among terrorist camps preaching unity in fighting a common enemy. The few glimpses the cameras had caught told her it was him. Since her joining his ranks, Black had encouraged her to use her talents to continue to take down such monsters and save the Lucs of the world. It wasn't enough. Guilt rode on her shoulders since that day with no reprieve.

A flash of Luc disappeared through a metal door painted dark blue to match with the walls at the end of the long hallway. Without hesitation, Gabrielle grabbed the silver-colored handle and heard Ryan catch the door over her head. Whispers of Becca's vision, confessed only to her, streamed through her head and she let her grief turn to anger.

"You can't come in here. This is personal," she whispered harshly, all passion gone from her eyes.

"One might argue what *we* have is personal." His expression failed to reflect the light-hearted teasing in his tone.

Her eyes remained flat. "I don't want you here, Ryan."

"It isn't him Gabs, it isn't Luc," he told her softly, reaching out to touch her arm. "Luc's dead."

Jerking her arm away quickly, her elbow hit the door with an echoing konk and she barely flinched. "Don't you think I know he's dead?" Tears welled up in her eyes and she ignored them. "That doesn't mean he isn't in there."

It took a minute for Ryan to understand what she was saying. "A ghost?"

Not blinking, she waited, wishing he would leave.

"Are you shitting me?" He took a menacing step toward her, "Does this thing have you so messed up that you think handing yourself over to a demon you think is your dead ex is a good idea? What the hell is that supposed to prove? He's dead, Gabs, not you. Not yet."

Amber eyes flashing, Gabrielle's hand hit his cheek and Ryan never made a move to stop her. "Leave it, Ryan. I have to do this." The quaver in her voice belied her sure demeanor and she set her jaw. Becca's vision said the others would be harmed; she couldn't take the chance that Ryan would be among the injured.

"Have to do what, Gabs?" His expression softened, the warmth in his eyes tugged at her. "Have to do what?" he repeated, voice cracking. "There's nothing in this world that says you need to go in there," he paused, swallowing, "and there's nothing in this world that's going to keep me from going in there with you."

"Please don't do this." Gabrielle felt her cheeks moisten as her tears spilled over. "I can't do this with you."

But Ryan had something he needed to say.
Wrapping both large hands over her upper arms, he
held her firmly enough that she couldn't easily
wriggle free without hurting her. "Gabs, you are the
singlemost frustrating, distant, cold-hearted person I
have ever had the pleasure of working with."

She heard him swallow and he glanced away, down
the hall toward the foyer, collecting his thoughts for
a moment before he returned vibrantly green eyes
back to her. Her throat worked and she closed her
eyes, more streams started down over her lower lids
and she opened them again to see him still staring.

"You are also a warm, loving person who would do
anything for your unit. And, like it or not, we would
do anything for you."

Ryan's eyes wetted and Gabrielle flared her nostrils,
taking a deep breath trying to avoid a full out
breakdown. That wasn't what she did. Not in
Black's unit. That was the safety here; cold, clear
cut cases involving bad guys she could destroy. No
confusion. This was getting confusing and she
couldn't have that. Wouldn't have that. It was
exactly what she'd been running from when she
found Black. Or he found her.

Before she could get herself under control enough
to respond, Ryan went on. "Gabs, we've been doing

this thing for two years now. You might be okay with the friends with benefits thing but I'm not."

Her eyes widened, she knew where he was going and opened her mouth to stop him.

He told her anyway. "I love you Gabs. I love you and I'm not sending you in there against who knows what without me fighting right there by your side. It's how we've always done things, just now you know I love you." The side of his mouth pulled up and he shook his ample auburn hair. "And no amount of bitching or slapping's going to change that."

Raising her hands and rolling her shoulders, Gabrielle was able to free her arms from his grip. Due in large part to the fact Ryan let her. "Ryan, I wish things could be different, I really do." Her insides were cold. Gabrielle fought the urge to shiver. "But I'm not the person you think you love."

"Don't try to tell me how I feel," he told her simply.

Forcing herself, she went on. "Things change us. *I've* changed." She willed herself to make him see her as unworthy. "I can't love you."

His white teeth flashed in amusement. "Well, I wasn't born this tall and I sure as shit didn't have a tail when I was in Boy Scouts." Smile disappearing,

Ryan leaned in close enough Gabrielle could feel his breath on her skin and hers prickled in response. "We all come from somewhere and no one ends up *here* after a stint with the Mouseketeers, Gabs. I don't care about what *was*. This is the you I know and this is the you I love."

Her eyes searched his, expecting him to go on. Holding her breath, she waited for him to throw in a "but" or somehow negate what he was telling her. It didn't come. Instead she watched his face come down and let her eyes close, breath coming faster before his lips touched hers.

To that point, theirs had been a straightforward relationship: sex on the road, not a lot of personal conversation, surprisingly few kisses. So when she closed her eyes, waiting for him to kiss her, Gabrielle was stunned to feel her stomach flutter in anticipation like it was all new. It was, she thought fleetingly, just before his warm, generous mouth pressed to hers.

Not the few hurried, need-filled kisses they'd shared during their passionate sessions, this one was more. And left her wanting more. The very things that brought Gabrielle to Ryan's bed; the lack of commitment, his impressive figure and independent spirit, all were gone. In their place was this man, declaring his love, no matter what she'd done before him, and offering forgiveness if she'd allow it. Finding herself in a foreign place, she let him set the pace. And Ryan, unhesitating, reached up to cup her face as he continued to show her how he felt. When their lips parted, she was tempted to follow their retreat and demand more. Her chest rose and fell in rapid succession and her blood rushed in her ears while she panted to catch her breath. The cloud in his darkened gaze and matching pulse told her he felt the same. Then, before anything more could be done, there was an ear splitting scream from within and the moment was gone.

Ryan's hands fell from her when Gabrielle whipped around and hauled the door open, barely waiting for the opening to be wide enough before shoving her thin frame through. *I'm too late* kept running through her mind. Just the same as he'd done hundreds of times on countless missions, Ryan followed directly behind her and they both crept wordlessly down the ramp toward the sound.

The smell served as a warning as to what they would face just before they rounded the corner. Close enough to touch, they came upon the tall figure shrouded in a long coat and shielded by shadow, his back to them, a tease of light brown hair visible in the low light. When he turned around, Gabrielle's throat closed and her nose burned. Tears sprang into her eyes as she beheld her long-dead Luc. Almond shaped brown eyes the color of warm cocoa blinked back at her. The olive skin covering the left side of his face, destroyed by bombs half a century past, had miraculously knit itself back together. His skin was smooth once more, unlike the one that so often found its way into her nightmares. She took a step, fingers seeking to prove what she saw before her. Then he smiled, and Gabrielle caught sight of a dozen yellowed spear-tipped teeth, backlit by a pale blue light that came from within.

In that moment she felt the soul-rending pain of his loss anew. Those few sightings had been enough to plant a seed. That somehow, maybe something like her change that had altered her being and delayed her aging, had seeped into the ground, bringing her Luc back to life and, after all this time, to her. But Ryan was right; Luc was gone. This *thing* had somehow found a way to pry the memory of him out of her head and use it to manipulate her. It brought her right to it and now it had used her to endanger Ryan. The small flame of what had been anger at Ryan for following, flared into a bonfire of justified rage at this thing.

"You have brought me a feast in this one. His energy is potent." He smiled Luc's smile.

"No," she declared decidedly. "Ryan is mine."

The demon's teeth were backlit again by its own internal light in what must have been an attempt at a smile. "Can you bear to watch the light fade from another's eyes knowing you could have prevented it?" it taunted, the voice asthmatic, breathless and mild. Its enthusiasm to have her or her mate, tempered by the apparent inability to breath their air.

"The only one who's dying today is you, asshole," she spat back.

Luc's eyes, commandeered by the demon, turned pitying. "What must it be like to carry such guilt?" He feigned wonder, head slowly wagging side to side for show. "You abandoned them." The demon with Luc's face dipped his chin to look her in the eye. "You left them there to die with no one to ease their suffering. They died in agony."

Her mouth opened but there was no sound.

"Do you think they called for you? You or the doctor while they lay bleeding? Limbs blown off, their bodies cut to shreds by shrapnel." Her departed's face twisted into a sneer. "Do you think I suffered?"

She continued to gape. There were no words that could make what he said less true. The full weight of her guilt crashed down and Gabrielle covered her mouth, only managing to muffle the sobs that erupted.

Ryan turned his head to see her from the corner of his eye, unwilling to take his attention from the threat within arm's reach, and his features drew together. "It's not real, Gabs."

The snarl coming from the far side of the theatre, directly across from them, stopped the demon cold and its head spun around allowing Ryan to look past it to the source.

Chapter 29

Coherent thought was impossible. Michael took a step outside himself, letting the closely guarded monster ruled only by animalistic needs have control of their shared body. Fangs out, body crouched with one hand beside him and his feet ready to jump, he opened his mouth and roared.

"Good to see you here, Mike," Ryan called across to him.

Whipping his face from the demon to the newcomers, Michael had only enough sway over his own form to turn his face from the target to his peer. Ryan gave him a brief nod. He'd been witness to what was about to happen a handful of times and knew Michael was not his friend at present. Best to keep his distance.

"Where's Becca?" Ryan called carefully, ushering the grief stricken Gabrielle off to the side, putting a few feet between her and the demon. He didn't want her getting caught in the crossfire when Mike let loose.

The demon's wheezing chuckle answered. Michael was off the wall and had the demon by the throat in time to cut off his laughter, not his pointy grin.

"You shouldn't laugh, demon," Ryan advised. "You're about two seconds from demon dust. He's gonna rip your head off."

"I don't think he will harm me." The brown eyes turned back to the big man next to Michael. "Or you either. Not so long as I hold *them*." His black-gloved hands came up to shoulder height, palms up so that they wouldn't miss him pointing at both women.

Ryan's easy manner evaporated and Michael's struggle to regain reason under threat of harm to Becca was visible. His hand never wavered from the creature's throat, its glow shone bright around his pale fingers.

The vampire gave way under Michael's fury. The only evidence it remained near the surface was the black eyes and long fangs showing prominently under his curled lip. "What hold do you have that won't go with you when we send you back?"

Panting, the demon ran its purple forked tongue over its bottom lip. "They let me in; now I have them to feed from whenever and however I please. If you destroy me, I take their minds with me."

"What do you mean 'let you in'?" Ryan let his gaze settle on Gabrielle, chewing her knuckle, her eyes glazed over with a random tear falling onto her hand now and again when they proved too much for her lids to contain. "How did you get into their heads?"

The hand on the demon's throat loosened enough to let him speak more easily. "Ah, I won't say because telling you would only spoil the fun." The brown around his pupils began to waver, the color dissolving for lack of a better word. Within seconds, the pupils went to slits and the irises flooded red. The leather encasing his hands made a chafing sound as he rubbed them together. "Then again, maybe it's better for me if you *do* know." The tongue flicked out again, hovering for just a split second in front of him, scenting. "Yours," he looked to Ryan first. "She was so beautiful. The golden fur, those long legs; you wouldn't guess how fragile she is to look at her." He made a sound low in his throat and Ryan's back straightened putting his head just below the taller demon's chin.

Michael's hand tightened again and the red, goat-slitted eyes shifted back to him. "You should be as lucky. That one," he lifted his still-human chin, "she was more than willing. All I had to do was sit back and let her come to *me*." He flashed his pointed teeth again. "It's been a while since I've seen a human who could do *that*. Did *you* know she could possess souls?" He leaned in and lowered his voice, "Has she ever possessed yours?" The forked tongue flashed again. "Mmm, now that would be interesting."

"You're lying." Michael backed him up until the shoulders hit the dark carpeted wall and the demon laughed. His words lacked conviction and they all heard it.

"It's true. You should ask her yourself." He feigned a wince. "Ooh, that's right, you can't. Unless…" The human flesh morphed into a shorter female form, perfect replicas of familiar hazel eyes gazed up adoringly at him atop a wash of light freckles. Michael, horrified, found himself staring into Becca's eyes as he choked her. "Michael, please stop. You're hurting me." It was her voice.

Reflexively, Michael let the demon go and took a step backward. His ears concentrated on the heartbeat, or lack of in the Becca creature's body. *It isn't her.* He told himself. Still, he couldn't force his hands to harm even a false image of her. That wasn't a picture he could carry in his head.

Ryan was not encumbered by the same concerns. His fist flew and the demon Becca's head rocked backward. Though instead of being cowed, the demon's response was again to laugh. Ryan's control wavered and his teeth grew, lips pulling back as he growled deep in his chest. "I'm going to stuff you back in that ley line and make sure you stay there if I have to break both your legs to do it."

The red eyes tightened at mention of his being forced back into his cage. Like a genie being stuffed back in his lamp, it was an eternity of captivity he would face once they sealed him inside. Michael knew from what he'd read and what Black had told him that the demon would weaken over time, starved of his richer sources of energy. The ley lines had lost some of their potency over the millennia, fewer people worshipping and feeding into them while the planet steadily lost giant parts of itself due to mining and drilling. Eventually the demon would become a mindless husk, cursed to wander the full range of the lines just to pull enough energy to survive. That he'd gathered enough to gain a solid form on this side had to be due to his enslavement of the windigo.

When Becca's face twisted into a snarl and spat at Ryan, Michael stayed the bigger man's hand from a second blow though he replaced his hand loosely on its neck, if nothing else than to keep its attention on him and not on those defenseless or enraged enough not to control themselves. Destroying this body could leave the demon free to possess another or take a different form. Better to have the one they could see than lose it in the streets.

Thankfully demons didn't bleed and his first punch hadn't left a mark so Becca's face remained unmarred. Turning to Michael, it sneered and spoke. "You know the changeling's plan won't work *and* you know why."

"What's he talking about?" Ryan frowned. "We can't put him back and we can't kill him?" Worried, his gaze darted to see Gabrielle still out of it on the other side of the demon. There was a hint of her he could see in her eyes, struggling to come forward. It wasn't too late to save her.

"It isn't that easy," Michael advised him.

A feminine titter escaped the thing's mouth and it ran its purple tongue over its lower lip.

The tongue, so different than Becca's small pink one, gave Michael strength. Seeing it helped him to keep in mind this was not her. He glared at the thing and continued. "We need to find where he came through in the first place. And to do that we need," he hesitated. The others weren't entirely aware of all Becca could do, but what they'd seen had made them increasingly uneasy. Hearing that she was going to continue to get stronger might shake up the cohesiveness of their unit. Then again, they would find out eventually, he told himself, justifying the breach of protocol in telling them. "And to do that, we need someone who can sense those things. We need a witch."

Ryan's eyes bulged. "A witch? Well that's just great." He threw up his hands and walked away, into the main part of the theatre. Whirling, Ryan shoved his hands into his hair. "When were you going to tell us that?"

Gabrielle gnawed at her fist, her eyes large and vacuous. The thought passed briefly through Michael's mind that she might try to eat the thing. Could the demon make her do that? The answer that came to him just as quickly made him thankful he couldn't vomit. It controlled her body and mind. It could make her do anything. Granted, he'd seen more graphic displays of cruelty, though not to someone he was close to. Not someone he'd fought side by side with. The impotent fury inside him grew yet more and his fist clenched. The demon gasped and there was a flare of sanity in Gabrielle's eyes. Loosening, he watched the haze return to her eyes and then tightened it again to see her fighting to come back.

Not entirely patiently, Michael let Ryan pace back to him before answering quietly. "We have one."

"Who?" Hands falling from his head, Ryan twisted his upper body to see the general area where he knew Michael had stashed Becca's unconscious body. He thumbed that direction and turned back. "Becca's a witch?"

"What did you think she was?" He was quickly losing the skill set that allowed him to remain calm.

The hulking man's shoulders pinched and his face flamed for a moment. "Clairvoyant," he mumbled, seeing in the light of day that his initial summary had been woefully inadequate. "Why didn't she tell me?"

"She didn't know there was a name for what she was until we were here." Michael tried not to think about that conversation and the state she'd been in. "This is all new to her, what she can do and what it means." His chest ached where his heart would be as memory of her pain and distrust of him came back to him.

The demon moaned ecstatically as their emotions escalated.

Michael pointedly ignored it and tried to temper his feelings, an impossible task at the moment. Ryan, it seemed, was having trouble effusing his usual carefree attitude. One look at Gabs' blank stare could easily explain why. They had to gain control over this situation and find a way to restore Becca at least enough to shove this hellion back down its hole. As unit leader, Michael took full responsibility and squared his shoulders. "Ryan, help Gabs take a seat over there." He pointed to the front row of upholstered chairs.

Action agreed with him and Ryan's body slipped easily into his big rolling gait within a stride. While he tended to Gabs, Michael debated leaving the demon to attempt to wake Becca. It wasn't like he was really holding the thing. As long as it had its hooks in Becca and Gabs, it was *they* who were the hostages.

The sound of the side door slamming shut reached him just before the heavy footsteps of a human intruder. His rapid breathing and muttered orders into his phone, audible to all present, announced his identity.

The demon's red eyes rolled up into its head as it continued to feed. The thing's Becca face was virtually orgasmic, then hiccupped drunkenly as a fresh surge rolled in from Michael's direction. Kicking himself, he shut himself down. They didn't *all* have to feed the thing, damn it. He was set to advise Detective Salvo to clear the premises when he rounded the corner and saw that the detective was leaned over Becca's body rubbing her arm with one hand while he loosened her shirt with the other.

His ensuing growl ripped the detective's attention immediately from the woman beside whom he knelt and landed it squarely on the captain's distorted face.

Salvo's eyes went wide right before he squinted, trying to see. It was dim in there for a human's eyes. "Captain Rossi?"

"Get out of here, Detective," he ordered, his voice low and gruff.

His eyes returned to the prone figure on the floor, Salvo's stare lingering there as well. Michael waited impatiently for the comparatively slow human to work through what he was seeing. Part of him considered the fallout of picking him up bodily and throwing him out of the theatre. It was almost enough to force the cranky vampire's tight lips into a smile. Not quite.

"What's going on here?" Salvo stage whispered. "Is the suspect in here?" He rested a hand on the slight shoulder by his knee. "Did *he* do this to her?"

For once Michael ignored the man's familiar touching on her flesh for expediency sake. "Everything's under control. We need you to leave *now*." He put a little more emphasis on the urgency for the detective's brain, woefully behind his. He wasn't long on patience.

Frustratingly dense, Salvo shook Michael's orders off. "I've called for backup. We'll have this place surrounded any minute." His fingers strayed to the open throat of Becca's shirt and pressed down, his eyes growing distant while he counted out the beats he felt there.

"It's fast, I know." Michael wanted his hands off his woman and his feet moving back the way he came but had to be careful. This was a delicate place for him. Not only was his control in jeopardy, any dustups would result in making the demon stronger. He had to get Becca's mind back so they could get rid of this thing and the stronger it was the harder her task. Then, an idea popped into his head. The vampire inside him screamed in frustration and he swore he heard the demon laugh. Taking a breath to speak, Michael ignored them both. "Detective," he spoke quietly, adding just enough influence to guarantee his orders would be followed. "I need you to take Becca outside. Get her clear of here."

Salvo's mouth dropped open and he leaned in toward Michael for only a few counts before shaking himself and blinking. Anger sprouted in his eyes and his cheeks reddened. "I would be more useful here."

The human was stronger than expected and Michael couldn't risk raising more heat from him. Desperate, he appealed to the human instead of controlling. "If she stays, she's in danger. I can't risk harm coming to her." He felt the human wavering. "Please."

Another painfully slow couple of seconds dragged by while the detective weighed decency against being on the front lines of bringing in what could be the biggest criminal his town would ever see. Michael saw his victory just before the dark head dipped once.

"Thank you." His gratitude was genuine. Risking the detective seeing more than he should, Michael crept toward her and waited a second while the human backed up a step. He leaned in, lips so close to her ears he brushed them when he spoke. "Becca, love, come back to me." And as he leaned back, he paused to press a kiss against her forehead.

He waited until he had returned to the shadows to risk eye contact again with the detective, giving him a grateful nod. Forces within him threatened to tear their way through him as he seemingly peacefully watched the human gather up *his* woman against his chest and carry her bodily from the darkened theatre.

For the first time in half a century, Michael prayed.

The demon's scream, half Becca, half demon, from behind him brought a smile to his lips. He'd been right. It wouldn't destroy something as powerful as Becca by wrecking her mind. Michael had done the right thing. Now he just had to keep it here and distract it enough that it loosened its hold.

The vampire inside him roared with pleasure that it could finally be free.

Chapter 30

Broken voices, static-filled communications over radios filled her ears. The strobing light bars illuminating the dim morning flashed against her closed lids as Becca returned to consciousness. Her fingers splayed out to feel leather and stitching under her fingers. A sniff of lemon air freshener covering the remains of what was either terrible b.o. or vomit or both hit her nostrils in a powerful wave. Becca's eyes popped open and she was sitting in the back of a squad car, door open with her feet hanging out.

Sitting up slowly, she tested both her body and mind for injury. Partially spotted vision told her she was near danger though not imminently so. Her head swiveled carefully, taking in what had to be the entire River Falls police force. Six squad cars, numerous blue uniforms stretching yellow tape and waving gathering gawkers back to establish a perimeter and the backs of two plain clothes men talking with their heads together at the hood of the car she found herself in.

Chief Kowski saw her first as she walked up beside Detective Salvo. His eyes widened a touch. "Captain Sauter, you're awake?" He sounded tired.

The detective's head whipped around and his eyes were full of concern. His hands went out as if to catch her should she fall. "Should you be up? Are you feeling alright?"

Becca offered them a quick smile meant to reassure but didn't look like it hit its mark. Unable to keep her eyes from the building they all faced, she lifted her chin toward the marquis sign and wiped at the drying blood on her forehead. It itched. "Are they in there?"

The chief gave her a grumbled "as far as we can tell," and the detective laid a hand on her shoulder. "I saw Captain Rossi in there, but he wouldn't let me in to see who else might be inside." He lowered his head to look her in the eye and, feeling his precarious state, Becca gave him her full focus for a few seconds.

Knowing they expected a report from her, Becca frowned. She'd been in a daze when she was pulled into the theatre. The demon's hold over her had broken somehow, allowing her to see for the first time where it brought her. Blinking, buying herself a few precious seconds, she decided to do something either very smart or suicidal. Her thoughts turned to Michael. Picturing him, concentrating on the feel of his skin, the smell of his body, she filled her senses with him from memory and then jumped.

In a second her vision went completely clear,
unhampered by spots or limited lighting.
Unfortunately, what she saw had her feet moving
until a hand against her chest brought her to a halt.
The duality of her split sight brought with it the
usual sense of vertigo and nausea and she took a
deep breath through her nose.

Forcing her eyes to blink, Becca turned her face to
Detective Salvo's and at least pretended to be
looking at him. "Detective, I can tell you that my
unit needs me in there. We have a highly volatile
suspect inside with.." *She trailed off while she*
watched Michael's fist ram itself into the demon's
eyes and its form go careening backward into the
black wall. Glowing eyes popped open as soon as it
hit and it lunged, hands reaching out to encircle his
neck just below her field of vision. The orange glow
flared in its eye sockets and her vision wavered just
before it dropped. Michael was on his knees. Where
were Ryan and Gabrielle? "I need to get in there to
help them."

The detective's hand didn't remove itself from her
chest and Becca's eyes narrowed. The pull to be
inside with Michael and her fellow unit members
was physical. She could feel the stress inside her
chest expanding to a painful level. If she didn't get
to follow the draw that was her duty, she feared she
would scream. Jaw clenched, she looked up at him
and let her patchy human vision take precedence.

"Salvo, I'm walking in there and helping my unit do what we do best and you're going to let me because if I don't, your town is going to be at the mercy of the worst sort of lunatic. Is that going to be your legacy? Or are we going to stop this thing and you get to be the guy who made it all happen?"

She didn't wait for either the detective or the chief to respond. As soon as the pressure on her chest lessened, she sidestepped him and started walking. A blue uniform stepped off the sidewalk and held up a hand but the chief's voice from behind her halted him.

"Let her go, Sergeant."

A little softer, lower than any but the detective beside him could hear, she caught, "God help her, let her go."

Not necessarily raised devoutly, she appreciated his crooked blessing and smiled to herself. "Not sure he's so big on watching over a *witch*, but I'll take it."

The entrance door she'd come through, cracked around where her body must have struck it on her less than graceful first entry, opened with a creak and several large triangles of glass clattered to the concrete, breaking into smaller chunks. Sidestepping them, she walked in and heard more shatter when the metal frame settled home. Built with perfect soundproofing, any noises that could have been coming out of the theatre where her friends fought for their lives were hidden. Vaguely, she recalled walking down the long hallway before she'd gone into the theatre where the demon waited.

Split vision allowed her to monitor the battle while she stopped at the end of the hall. A door on either side of her marked her two possible destinations. Walking first to the one on the right, she pressed her ear against it and heard nothing. Right as she pressed her ear to the door on the left, Gabrielle's pained cry sounded both in her head and outside.

Michael's eyes, still low enough to show he was on his knees, turned to Gabrielle who, also released from the demon's control, had changed halfway into her beast. Amber eyes atop a long snout flashed with insane animal rage as she leapt onto the back of the demon. Its hand released Michael's throat and shoved him away, her vision tipping until it was sideways on the ground. The obscenely cheerful popcorn men stretching out on the dark blue carpet in front of her smiled and danced on obliviously. *The demon didn't touch Gabrielle, it merely grinned. Its glow flared with its otherworldly strength and her body froze, dropping to the ground beside it to shudder and moan. It hadn't relinquished its control entirely.*

Not bothering to be silent, as the demon and all three of the others inside would know of her presence as soon as the door closed and the air moved around her, Becca walked in. The long walk down the side hall, too tall to see over until she reached the bottom, was torture. Inside, she was able to hear the grunts as Ryan lunged again and again at the demon only to be thrown aside. Seeing her friends repeatedly sending themselves forward to be painfully tossed around was physically agonizing to watch. This was exactly what she'd been trying to avoid. And as soon as she rounded the corner at the bottom of the wall and saw the torment live, she was overcome. Tears burned her eyes and Becca sucked in her breath.

Blood ran from Michael's ear. She could see his profile as he kept his shoulders squared to his enemy, his back to the seats behind. He gained his feet, albeit slowly, his left arm hung useless at his side, and he was favoring his ribs on that side. Ryan was running and bunching himself for another attack, he had his back to the screen and was about to take off over the metal railing that separated the short stage from general seating. One of his ears refused to stand and blood matted his fur in several spots. Gabrielle quivered at the demon's feet, her body rigid and her teeth clacking together so hard they surely were going to break. A quick scan to her left revealed an array of smashed seats. A number of sharp posts stuck up from where they were bolted into the concrete ground, glistening wetly in the dim lights. She could guess at the cause of at least some of her friends' injuries.

Turning back to the battle continuing to rage, Becca caught Ryan's massive wolf form launching itself and knocking the demon to its knees. Her jubilance at seeing him hit his mark was short lived. Ryan howled as the demon's mouth yawned unnaturally wide and those hellish teeth pierced his cinnamon fur-covered neck.

Again, she moved without thinking. As Ryan's howl died in her ears, Becca watched him fall to his paws and shake his head, backing up. The demon looked up and smiled wickedly. Michael caught it and turned to face her. His expression, one of hope mixed with dread, froze her heart in place. Its temporary lack of a beat sent pain racing down her arms. She was here, now what was she supposed to do?

Confused how *she* could fight a demon *they* were barely keeping at bay, she frowned. But before she could wonder what she was supposed to use to fight, she felt something try to shove itself into her head with the subtlety of a freight train. Screaming and clutching her head, she felt her knees buckle. The train, composed of nothing but fire and pain, continued to push, trying to make its way inside her skull. It was like being stabbed slowly with a spoon, the pressure threatening to smash as much as pierce.

"Don't let him in, Becca." Michael's voice came to her just before she heard something strike flesh and there was a moment's lessening of the pressure. "We need you to follow the line back to where he came out." The pressure returned, there was the sound of flesh being struck, and the pressure relented.

Letting her transported vision work for her, Becca closed her eyes and saw through Michael's. *He was pounding on the demon's face with rapid left- right combinations. With each strike, the pressure inside her head was disrupted. Watching, dumbstruck through several cycles, Becca was able to force breath back into her body and grow used to the pain in her head. Instead of concentrating on the feel of her physical body, she reached out to his, specifically the part where Black's hold on him was physical. If she could tap into that, Michael's need to protect her would combine with Black's and it could hold her mind tight inside his, unable to be hijacked. He would be her anchor as she tried something that was arguably insane. A tiny flicker of fear that she might not get herself back or would throw herself into the abyss that was Admiral Black's total control was minor. The danger to her unit and this town was certain, the possible link to Black not so much. That, and, she sought comfort in what she knew to be true; Michael will never hurt me. Nor would Black want her in his head, she told herself. Those factors combined equaled a rapid ejection once her job was done. She hoped.*

Stretching toward the place in his mind where she could actually feel the tight band of control Black held him with, Becca latched on with both hands and squeezed.

Michael gasped as he felt it tighten.

"Michael, look at me." She took several steps closer, speeding up when he looked her way and she was able to get a clear view of the path to him.

Out of her periphery, she caught the movement of a large and very angry Gabrielle as she shifted completely into a wolf and regained her feet. Her teeth caught the demon's thigh and her shaking it temporarily distracted the demon, the pain in Becca's head all but disappearing. Racing the last few feet, Becca was at Michael's side, being mindful not to touch any potentially broken bones. "Michael, I'm sorry but I have to ask you to use your tie to Black." No chance of managing the demon without them now, Becca would at least try to fight it as best she knew how.

His eyes registered his surprise and he cast a hurried glance over at the trio fighting less than ten feet away. At the moment, both wolves had the demon too busy to care about their conversation. "Why?" His eyes searched hers.

Resting a hand on his chest, she swallowed her reluctance to put him further in danger for her sake. Reminding herself they were soldiers and this was for more than just them, she reached up and whispered in his ear. "I want to try something but I need Black to back us up." She felt his body stiffen and her own rush of guilt for putting him in this position yet saw no other way. "I can jump into him and find his entry point that way."

Michael's entire mind lit up with objections. Although she couldn't hear them, she could feel him preparing to argue. "He'll feel you, he'll destroy your mind."

"He didn't feel it when I was in your head earlier." It bothered her to see the hint of anger before he hid it. She went on before she lost her nerve or they lost their interference. "Besides, I've done it before. He won't know I'm there until it's too late."

Michael's jaw dropped.

"By the side of the road, that night when I thought I saw someone with a flashlight." She watched as realization sunk in. "I don't know why, maybe it was because I wanted to see if I could do it for

Black, I don't know. But I did, and I was inside its head. I could see and hear. I know I can get what I need in there and send him back." Silently, she pleaded with him to help her, begged him not to see that she'd carried a piece of the demon with her since that night. Without him, she couldn't guarantee her body would be safe with her consciousness gone. Jumping into one person was one thing, a double jump combined with digging around inside a demon's head would take all of her concentration and she couldn't watch for an attack.

He tightened his lips and gave her the small nod that told her he was in.

With a sinking feeling, Becca pulled away from him and stood up straight. "Great. Now if you can get Black to make sure to keep me locked in with you, I'm going to try to take another hop out of my head and into him."

"Can you do that?" Anger was gone in favor of bald fear for her safety. "What will that leave behind?"

Faking a tight smile, she avoided his gaze. Staring at his furrowed brows was easier. "I can find my way back to you no matter where I am." She felt his eyes burning into her and feared that he was going to change his mind, until the band in his head clamped down and all but locked her in. The gasp that escaped her lips was as much from the mental squeeze she felt as the physical as his arm encircled her waist and he ran her up to the top of the seats.

Taking up position in front of where she sat, he raised his voice to be heard over the snarling din. "Ryan, Gabs, you got this? Things are going to get weird."

The answering crescendo of snaps and growls was enough. Michael settled his weight into the balls of his feet and waited. Becca could feel him holding onto her inside his mind as tight as she knew he wanted to bodily.

Splitting her mind three ways was new and she wasn't sure it would work, but Becca approached it much the same as when she needed to see out of her physical eyes even though she was in someone else's head. Following that tether back to her own head, she took a few seconds to firm herself up and remember who she was, what she was doing, and to feel for what she knew was the demon. Her concentration was complete. She didn't feel the sweat beading up on her lip or forehead, nor was she aware of the headache that blossomed from her muscle rigidity.

****

Michael milled closer to her, smelling the adrenaline rising inside her, escalating the strange scent in her blood, sensing her body's strain as it tested its limits. The demon caught it too and began to move, bringing the fighting wolves with him as he gained the first step.

The larger cinnamon wolf caught the change in direction and circled wide, throwing himself with jaws open at the demon's face. Luck or good timing, it didn't matter, granted him a mouthful of demon flesh. Sneezing at the release of sulfur when he pierced its flesh, he held on tight. Gabrielle's smaller body allowed her to run up the back of her larger shoulder mate and she landed on the far size, twisting in midair to manage a graceful landing behind the third row of seats. Lunging forward, she took a mouthful of belly and locked her teeth, shaking her head for maximum damage. The room filled with the smell of sulfur as the demon's "blood" was finally spilled.

Michael watched as the thing's body went still and its eyes hardened, turning its glare directly toward the defenseless woman seated behind him. At the same time, he felt her body fall forward into his legs as the last of her body control left her. Becca had jumped and he'd figured out the scent in her blood. For all new reasons he hoped she could locate its entry and they could shove it back in. The question was, would the demon take everything with it when it went? Even the piece it had left inside Becca?

Chapter 31

*The orange glow of fire all around her told Becca
she had been successful. The demon's mind was
filled with burning pyres and the smell of sulfur
combined with earth for an unusually tangy, acidic
flavor. The last time she'd been in his head, Becca
hadn't been sure of where she was and certainly
hadn't taken the time to dig around thoroughly. This
jump, however, was about exploration and she knew
her time was limited. As if to reinforce that
assumption, she felt a strong sideways push.
Dropping her weight into her hips, just like she was
dealing with a physical force, she settled herself to
push back. Her unwilling demon host growled in
protest, unable to dislodge her.*

*Pressing on, feeling the urge to move quickly, Becca
tuned into the tingling feeling she'd experienced
when walking on the ley lines. Closing her eyes in
her head, she let the lines tell her where they were.
There it was. The strongest vibration was to her
right. Twisting, she struck off that direction, feeling
it on some level when she moved beyond the theatre.
It was impossible to describe, but being inside the
demon's mind wasn't limiting like being in Michael
or even Ryan's. It was like it moved her to an
entirely different plane. Free to roam not just
remain where he was, she followed the vibration
past the shadow of first one building, then two. A
wide gap that could have been a street and then she*

*passed under another building. The vibration
continued to pull her, growing stronger as she
moved along.*

*She stopped when the vibration became so strong
she could feel it in her teeth. She let her head turn
slowly around, taking in all that surrounded her.
High rock walls rose all around her forming a solid
dome. Fires burned higher here. A circle of them
closed in and flared, blocking her view of anything
else. It didn't matter. Because at the center of the
burning circle was a wide, gaping hole. Blackness,
beyond which lay the scorching desert orange
moonscape that was this demon's home. She'd
found the doorway. Becca knew where to put the
demon back.*

*Backing up, she began to retrace her steps in order
to return to her mind and drag the demon if need be
back to its portal and shove it back in bodily. Only
when she turned around, she was no longer alone.
She ran into something very hard that had been
right behind her for who knew how long. Craning
her head back to see, Becca stopped breathing.*

*"Have you found something interesting?" The
demon grinned at her, orange fire matching those
surrounding them, flared behind black, pointed
teeth. "No, stay. I insist."*

Her scream froze in her throat as the fires flared again and blocked her off entirely.

***

Ryan picked himself up off the ground and shook his furry head. Gabrielle had to hit the brakes in the air to adjust and avoid landing on her face when the demon she'd been about to tackle disappeared. Michael froze, horrified, and turned to see the slouched form behind him remained unmoving.

Both still in their wolf forms and faced with definite nudity issues should they change back, Ryan and Gabrielle managed to communicate with a series of short barks and whines.

Michael felt his chest tighten. "She must've found the door and he figured it out." He turned back to Becca's motionless body, taking in the bluing lips and thin pulse. Her ties to her body were weakened by strain and distance; she couldn't have long. Ropes of fear wrapped themselves around his throat and middle, tightening as he grew more frantic.

A loud bark brought his head around and Michael snarled back. "I don't know what to do. If she left a trail I could smell her. How do I follow a trail I can't see or smell?" And then it came to him. She *had* left a trail. It was in his head. Everything he needed to find her was inside him.

The tingling she felt when she was near a ley line was stronger than what he felt, but, being a supernatural creature sensitive to otherworldly energies, he could sense them too. Plus, with her still held tight in his head, he could use her presence to boost his feel for the demon's energy. It was sketchy but he was going to try it.

"Ryan, Gabs, ready to do some hunting?"

Both whined eagerly, ready to chase the demon down and recover their compatriot.

Carefully, ignoring the grinding of broken bones in his ribcage, Michael scooped up Becca's near lifeless body and cradled her against his chest one handed. "Find us the path of least resistance."

Cinnamon and gold surged down the hallway, the door rattling on its hinges when first one, then the other hit it with their bodies to fling it open. Michael, unhindered by the insignificant weight of Becca's body, was right behind them. In the main theatre area Ryan and Gabrielle split. Ryan sniffed at the back door while Gabs scented along the corridor, pausing at the exit signs along the way. She yipped first, signaling the others to come. Nodding that he should go first, Michael shouldered past them and hit the door. It took two good shoves to open it and he stuck his head out.

He could see why no one was guarding the door. It opened onto a narrow alley barely wide enough to ride a bicycle. A half wall of cracked concrete rose opposite the door, snow and dormant trees making it feel even narrower. The only breaks in the foot-high snow between the building and the wall were the tracks of several small animals skirting the building and occasionally meandering into the open. No one came back here and, for most, the door would have been considered impassable.

They were out, now where did they go? Michael turned his focus inward, ignoring the tiny pellets of ice the gusting wind was blowing off the rooftop and onto his face and head. From within his mind, he felt a minor tug. Zeroing in on that pull, he turned right and headed down the narrow path. The wolves walked on either side of him, Ryan pushing ahead, Gabrielle lagging behind. When they reached the edge of the theatre, they flowed across the tiny chasm to the dry cleaner before they came to the street. A quick sideways glance and they darted across. Any attention being paid on this street was up at the theatre. It probably wouldn't matter if the wolves changed back and were naked at that point, no one would notice. And that was saying something.

A warm breath of air startled him as he reached the other side of the street. Feet stuttering, he came to a sudden halt; Gabrielle nearly crashing into his back. Only vaguely aware of the near run in or the irritated snapping of teeth precariously close to his ass, Michael glanced down. Color was returning to Becca's lips, her pulse had gained strength.

Ryan whined and Michael grinned. "We must be getting close." Gabrielle angled her neck around and gently poked Becca's leg. "Be ready," he cautioned them both. Two sets of canine eyes blinked and their shaggy heads bobbed understanding.

Becca continued to show signs of revival as they went, her pulse thrumming stronger until it virtually pounded in Michael's sensitive ears. The shudder that ran through her when they jogged past the backside of the bank, accompanied by the painful vibrations rattling through his bones, told Michael when they reached their destination. He stopped, as did the wolves. "We're here."

There was a back door to the bank, not that it was unlocked or unalarmed. However, those were both issues easily dealt with when one was a vampire. Laying Becca down to be guarded by the wolves, Michael walked around the front, asked for the bank manager, and immediately had a willing guide who not only opened the back for them and disabled the alarm, he opened the door to the basement. Once in the basement, they walked past the vault and came to a steel door in the floor. The manager unlocked it and stepped back, eyes not quite focusing. Michael led the way down a flight of rotting wooden steps that opened into a tunnel that branched into a series of tunnels below the building, not used since the days of Prohibition.

The dry tunnels led away from the bank and went next door, opening up to a large chamber that put them smack under the club where things had gone awry the night before. Michael followed the beacon that was the demon and the other half of Becca's mind down a side tunnel. A cluster of old wooden barrels, some intact, some broken from time or help from a thirsty traveler, sat forgotten in the far corner. Movement and flickering light on the far side sent all three into a crouch and Michael searched for a good place to hide Becca. Already one-handed, he couldn't hope to fight holding on to her. Their best bet was to stash her where she would be out of harm's way.

Fortune smiled and he saw a dusty pile of wood and an old threadbare blanket covering a heap of something not fifteen feet ahead of them. He could get there and have her safely tucked away before anyone saw him. Not allowing himself to think of the possibilities of failure or discovery, he lifted the blanket and laid her beneath it, making sure to rumple the pile and make it appear undisturbed when he was done.

Ryan and Gabrielle, growing impatient, moved on ahead and were following the signs of movement when Michael caught up to them. The chamber turned abruptly to the right and opened into a large cavernous room roughly the size of an elementary school's gym with jagged, pale limestone walls and the light of several fires illuminating the space in flickering orange light. The three exchanged a look. They'd found the opening. Now they just needed the demon.

Chapter 32

Becca cast a desperate look over her shoulder at the dark doorway to the world where the demon belonged and wondered how she would get him down there. Even if she were to fall through, she feared he wouldn't follow. Why would he? There was so much energy up here for him in this demon's playground he'd discovered. Manipulating people's feelings to extremes and then feeding off of them, even the windigo had fed him. Terror had filled each victim as they'd been torn apart and consumed before they died. The demon had only grown stronger with each battle Becca's unit had fought with it as well. After the theatre, it was impossibly strong. She couldn't think of how she would defeat it now that she was facing it alone. What had she been thinking? The demon was eyeing her hungrily, its orange sockets glowing bright with something akin to lust. Though not for physical desire, it wanted her psychically.

Taking a page from Michael's book, Becca shut herself down and locked her emotions away. Left staring vacantly at a spot just beyond the demon, she offered him nothing. If she couldn't figure out how to defeat him, at least she could stop feeding him. Time passed and her mind went blank.

"Becca?"

Her mind snapped back to reality. "Michael?" She turned to see him walking up behind her. "How did you find me?" She looked around, searching for the demon sure to be lurking close by. "Be careful, the demon's around here somewhere."

But Michael was unconcerned. Grinning broadly, he reached out and scooped her up in both arms, holding her close. "He's gone, the others are tracking him." He spoke softly in her hair. "I'm so glad you're safe."

Becca's arm tightened around her beloved's neck, ecstatic to be back with him and to be safe for the time being. "It was dumb of me to follow him." She laid her head on his chest, looking up. "I hadn't thought past catching up with him."

Michael was shaking his head, still grinning. "It doesn't matter. I'm just happy to have you back." Lowering his face, he captured her lips with his, his tongue massaging its way into her mouth.

Surprised at his carefree attitude, Becca pulled back and regarded him. "Not that I'm complaining, but shouldn't we be following Ryan and Gabrielle?"

Hand reaching around the back of her head, Michael brought her close again. "They've got it handled." His other hand slipped down her back and cupped her bottom, pulling her up against him to

feel just how excited he was to see her. Her eyes
and mouth popped open and Michael didn't let her
up for air again.

In moments, his expert use of his hands and mouth
had her mind miles from that tunnel and demon.
The only thoughts she had involved him and her,
and preferably nothing between them. If his body
was any indicator, he was thinking along the same
lines.

Breaking from her mouth, Michael's tongue flicked
over the sensitive skin of her neck and she felt it
warm under his touch. Moaning, she rubbed her
hips against his and slid her hands down his sides.
Lifting her up with both hands, he wrapped one arm
around her back, using the other to hint that she
should wrap her legs around his waist.

Reason itched at the corner of Becca's mind. Brain
clawing its way out of her pants, she opened her
eyes and gazed into his from inches away. "Wasn't
your arm hurt?"

Without answering, he pushed her face back to his
and bit her lip. Hard. When she tried to pull away
he grabbed a handful of her hair and held her tight.
Squealing, Becca frowned and pulled away, losing a
small chunk of hair in the process. She often
fantasized about making him lose control, falling to
the passions of his inner monster, but not like this.

This wasn't passion, this was cruelty. This wasn't her Michael. "Ow, Michael. You bit me."

"I'm a vampire," he growled, leaning in to lick her neck again. "We bite."

The heat of his tongue burned her skin and again she twitched away from him, only to have him clamp down, immovable arms preventing her from squirming. The scrape of teeth against her delicate skin registered just before she felt the pain as he sunk inch long fangs in to her neck. Mouth going wide, Becca felt her throat burning inside and out as she gasped and screamed; her blood ran down between her breasts.

****

Hesitant to leave Becca, helpless as she was, Michael lagged behind as the others led the way into the cavern. Her moan reached his ears and he stopped. It wasn't a pained sound. If he wasn't mistaken, it was one of pleasure. He was well familiar with it. Moving silently, he crept back to where he left her and crouched, being sure to tuck his wounded arm against his side. It would heal but not enough to be used tonight. Carefully, he lifted the edge of the worn blanket. She hadn't moved. Her body remained exactly as he left it. Satisfied, he lowered the edge of the blanket and stopped. Her hips shifted and her neck craned back. She looked like she was having an erotic dream. The corner of Michael's mouth twitched and he wished they weren't in the middle of something or he would happily wake her and help her to make her dream a reality. There wasn't time to get distracted. Michael let the blanket down. Right when he let go, she started to scream.

Whipping back the cover, he watched blood appear in twin spots on her neck. Two spots that weren't there before and were shaped in a very familiar pattern that beaded up and began to run down her chest, pooling in her shirt. Gravity would have dictated the blood run over her shoulder, not down. It trailed like she was standing. Brow wrinkling in thought, Michael watched her chest rise and fall. With each shallow breath, the strange smell rose up to his nostrils. Stronger now, he leaned down and sniffed at the punctures. Sulfur.

Leaping to his feet, he was through the mouth of the cavern before a human could have managed a sneeze. And that was where he froze, right between the wolves. Also stopped dead in their tracks. All three stood motionless, watching what couldn't be happening and not a one had any idea how to go about stopping it.

Michael's doppelganger was standing facing them, his arms pinning the ghostly image of a woman to his front, his head ducked so that his lower face was hidden by her shoulder, Michael's double was staring directly at them, daring them to come closer. Beyond him lay the black opening of what had to be the gate to the line he'd walked out of.

Ryan's huge furry head swung toward the real Michael, his green eyes clearly troubled. Gabrielle refused to take her eyes from the two intertwined bodies, her head hung low but focused. A bomb could have gone off and it was doubtful she would have twitched an ear. Her posturing was clear, she was waiting for any sort of gap between the bodies and she would attack. The green eyes asked Michael for guidance. More intelligent than a normal canine, the wolves were somewhat hampered in brain capacity while in their animal state. Hunting was where they excelled. Strategy was often left to the non-canine accompanying them.

Giving a small shake in the negative, Michael let him know he was equally directionless. This was beyond his ken and he found himself, for once, at a total loss. Fingers dipping into his pocket, he removed them just as quickly. What could Black tell him that he hadn't already? They had to get the demon through the doorway, and now they had the further complication of cutting Becca's psychic connection with him. He was fairly certain Black couldn't help him with the question of what to do when a demon was seducing one's woman while she was lodged firmly inside both their heads.

Seduction. It gave Michael an idea. Not one that made him feel happy and tingly, but one that might work if he could get through. Hoping she was still somewhat conscious, tethered to this reality, he retreated to the smaller antechamber and fell to his knees. Fingers delicately raised the cover he'd placed over her and threw it back.

"Becca," he whispered in her ear. It wouldn't help if the demon figured out what he was doing. "Becca, it's me."

Whimpering, her sandy brows were pinched together; clearly pleasure had turned to pain. Becca turned her face away from him so that he was looking directly at the dried blood along her hairline. "Please, no, Michael."

That she thought him the cause of her pain sent an icy blade tearing through his insides. Now wasn't the time to get caught up in personal drama, he reminded himself. If he let her be consumed, they had no foreseeable defense against this demon. Girding himself to face her torment, he tried again. "Becca," he continued to speak softly so as not to frighten her. "Becca, my love, I want you to dance with me."

Frowning already, she squinted. "You want me to what?"

A hint of a smile played at Michael's taut lips. That was his girl; she was still in there. "I promised, remember? I want you to dance with me." Keeping his gaze focused entirely on Becca's troubled face, Michael pictured the cavern and her positioning on the other side of the limestone wall.

The sound of a paw scuffing rock reached his ears and Michael glanced up to see that Ryan had backed up enough to check on what he was doing. By the puzzled look in his eyes, Michael imagined Becca was listening to his commands. Beckoning with a finger, he called the wolf to him and whispered in his large ear. A nod and Ryan trotted back to where he could keep an eye on the goings on in the cavern and the antechamber.

One eye on his scout, one on his unwitting accomplice, Michael grimaced when Ryan's head wagged back and forth. A scan of Becca's pinched features told him she was too frightened of him to function. Tentatively, he ran a finger down the side of her face and she flinched away from him. Knowing what her reaction would be and seeing it were two different things. Michael set about drawing her in. He had to be fast though, the blood trails continued and her flesh grew more pale by the minute. Thankfully the demon wasn't a real vampire or he would have drained her by now. Glowering at the thought, Michael kept himself from flying through the chamber and doing serious violence to the demon next door. This was what had to happen to get her back, all of her, or he would lose her for sure, he reminded himself and his vampire. The vampire was not happy but the thought of losing its mate was enough to keep it at bay for a little while.

"Do you remember the night we came home from hunting that rogue vampire in Albuquerque?"

The edges of her features relaxed. "Yes."

"Do you remember our first date?"

Her lips twitched and his did in reply. She remembered.

The mission had been short and sweet. The vampire was a bad one, a clear-cut case of termination. They were able to locate him quickly and return home. It was less than 24 hours. Unfortunately, they planned on going out before returning home but Black called, letting them know they were expected back right away. There was another mission waiting. They were going to Amsterdam after a vicious were with a taste for cross dressers from the red light district. Becca tried to hide her disappointment, but they had been together over a month without a proper date. She'd been looking forward to a night out together; no missions and no surveillance, maybe even some time on the dance floor.

After their back to back meetings in the war room downstairs at the estate, Michael had snuck off to the kitchen and threw together what he could manage, sending Ryan up to knock on Becca's door. By the time she made it onto the back yard, he'd arranged a small meal. Really it was pathetic by romantic standards, except he'd seen the way her eyes shone in the starlight. The moon was only a crescent, but by the light of the stars he'd seen how happy she'd been. Hands going to her mouth, she'd been genuinely and pleasantly shocked by his impromptu picnic.

A menu of crackers, three types of cheese and a few pieces of fruit had to do. Scrounging deep in the pantry had revealed a small handful of Andes mints and he'd tossed those on the tray as a sad answer to desert. A thick comforter served as their bed/table, making the baked ground a touch easier on them as they sat for hours and she ate the entire platter herself. The one upside was the bottle of wine he'd been able to scare up. It was a rare one and he'd paid Gabrielle handsomely for taking it. Still, the quality had earned the meager fare forgiveness and rounded out their romantic evening.

"I wish we could have gone dancing," Becca commented, her head in his lap while she stared at the hundreds of stars slowly spiraling above. "Not clubbing." She twisted to see his face. "Real dancing."

And Michael got up, dusted himself off and held out a hand. Becca laughed at first but he shook his outstretched limb at her, raising one eyebrow. She took it and, effortlessly, he helped her to her feet, wrapping an arm behind her back and pulling her close. No music save the night sounds of the desert and no lights but those nature lent them, the two had barely begun to move when the front doors creaked open and Ryan called, "Wheels up in fifteen."

He capitalized on the euphoric glow the memory created in her. "I want to dance with you for real." Both arms slipped under hers, the pain shooting through him bitten back and hidden by a skyward glance as he hauled her limp form up, tucking her against him. Dark eyes flicked up and caught green ones looking back. The wolf turned his head then came back, bobbing his snout confirming that Michael's approach had worked. Becca was indeed maneuvering the demon.

Now, more than ever, Michael gave Ryan his full attention. The big auburn head leaned right and Michael shifted her body in the same direction. The big wolfish head bobbed enthusiastically. It had worked; the ghostly version of Becca could be led with her physical form. Ryan tipped his nose up twice in rapid succession indicating they needed to go straight back. Uncertain how to make her do that, Michael whispered in her ear to go back, the footing was more even there and he didn't want her to turn an ankle. Apparently, Ryan heard him and the green eyes rolled before he turned back to the cavern. A muffled snort and Michael shot him a warning glare though inside he was elated. Ryan raised a paw telling him they had the demon lined up.

Good thing, Becca's exposed flesh on her chest and face had gone porcelain. Even the blue lines of her veins below the skin were visible. The blood trailing down her chest stained the light colored top a deep red and the spots where it was drying were turning brown. That all of her cuts' bleeding had slowed wasn't entirely a good thing. Michael could hear her heart and it was struggling. He knew that a taste of his blood could save her, but at what cost? On top of what she already had in her system, another infusion could prove enough to push her over the edge and into immortality or madness, possibly both. Anxious, he gave Ryan the signal that it was time.

"I'm so sorry Becca," he told her honestly, bracing himself for what he was about to do. "But I need you back right now."

"What?" was all she got out before the back of his hand snapped her mouth shut and her head lolled sideways. Already close, she lost consciousness completely and Michael caught the blur of cinnamon leaping from the room and into the cavern.

For several agonizing seconds, Michael waited. A quick series of yips, an enraged scream and then the air was sucked from the room. The fires that had flared and flickered in the cavern, lighting the antechamber in their dancing shadows, burned bright for one brief moment then went out, leaving them all in darkness.

His ears picked them up first, the sounds of their paws on the packed stone floor drawing near, then he saw them emerge from the shadows. Gabrielle was limping on her front paw but otherwise they were fine. Pausing, they waited for Michael to scoop Becca up and settle her against his chest. Her body was cold and her breathing shallow. If he could have anything at that moment, it would have been some sort of reassurance that he'd been able to return her to her body before they sent the demon tumbling back into the line where it belonged. Thankfully, demons can only cross when someone or something can be convinced to bring them over. Once the demon crossed the line again, it sealed itself. No doubt Becca would have been unable to assist in any sort of "witchy" capacity if additional help was needed.

Cold body pressed to his, which offered her no warmth, Michael carried her back up through the tunnels and into the bank. Once again, the manager was enlisted to let them out the back without the peep of a single alarm. After they were back in the alley, the wolves took to the woods and made their way back to the motel. No pockets or keys, they would wait nearby until Michael returned to let them in. He would face the police alone.

Years of experience told him to face the chief and detective head on. They didn't have a culprit to turn over but would guarantee that he wouldn't return. Briefly, Michael considered locating a petty criminal or homeless individual who wouldn't be missed to provide a body. No, he shook it off, although it would make things easier he couldn't do it. He would have to blame it on their shadowy partners and maybe a hint of black helicopters, and face the wrath of those less powerful.

So, beloved tucked safely in his arms, Michael stepped out of the theatre entrance where their standoff had begun less than two hours before and blinked in the midmorning winter's gloom.

Chapter 33

Becca woke to the sound of twin engines grinding away beneath her and the familiar scent of Michael filling her nose. For a few panicked heartbeats, she feared she was back in the demon's arms, him pretending to be Michael and failing miserably. With her head on straight she knew right away it was him because Michael's kisses might inflame her, but they were not in and of themselves warm. The demon's face was Michael's even if his temperature was not. Nor was his cruelty. The real Michael would never hurt her. That belief rang as true in her mind now as it did when she'd first seen him taking Black's beating for saving her life that first night. The way he'd looked at her, the reverence he held her in since, told her to trust her instincts. Michael was her ally, no matter what.

Opening her eyes, she stretched and stopped herself when the awkward adhesive square on her throat folded into her skin. Hand reaching up, she investigated. Remembering the rough details of what had transpired, she sighed. Another exchange with a demon and she'd come out victorious. How many more times could that happen? No human had any sort of long-running track record where demons were involved, did they?

The hand that squeezed hers brought her mind screeching back to the man seated in the cream-colored leather seat beside her. Peering up at his worried expression, Becca felt a twinge of sympathy. He must think she blamed him for what the demon had done. Only she didn't. As soon as it had been sent back into its line she felt her head come back. Both the part of her in the demon as well as the part in Michael had snapped back into her head simultaneously. Blinking, she leaned up against him only to jerk back upright. Hand going to her jaw, she rubbed at it delicately and looked askance at him. Had that part been real?

Michael's cool exterior warned her of danger. A quick glance around and she saw that Ryan was sitting up front with Gabrielle, their pilot. They were giving them space to talk. Nerves pinched at her stomach.

"Did you want to tell me what happened?" she asked evenly. There was no use beating around the bush. That never did anyone any good.

"We sent the demon back and it's possible we'll never be allowed in River Falls again." He forced a short laugh and Becca tried, wincing when the skin over her jaw tightened.

She caught the grinding of his teeth when she winced. "All of it."

If he were human, he would have sighed or at least taken a deep breath. Instead, he took in only enough to speak and stared past her, out her window at the blackness of the night sky. Night? "The demon had your mind and it was draining you. We were ready to throw it back into the ley line but we needed to get you out of it. You were out of it and we didn't have time to talk you back." He lifted his chin, refusing to look at her. "There was only one way I knew to shock you back fast enough. I hit you."

Becca sensed his shame; it was palpable. Fingers gently tracing what had to be a monster bruise forming on the side of her jaw already, she couldn't help but smile. That hurt and she winced, which made her smile again, and back to wincing.

When she glanced up, he was staring at her, a stupefied expression on his face. "Can I ask what you find funny about that?"

Stifling a giggle, she held a finger under her nose and sniffed. The giggles still wanted to come so it took a few more inhale/exhale cycles before she could trust herself. "How pissed was Salvo when you told him case solved but you don't get the perp?"

At that, Michael cracked a faint smile but it vanished just as quickly. "You aren't upset that I hurt you? A man hitting a woman…" he started, looking slightly sick.

Becca searched herself and found no sign of animosity toward her lover. "It's not like you poked me with sharp sticks for hours at a time." She bit her lip to keep from smiling at his expression at that one. "You did what you had to do to keep me from spending an eternity locked inside that thing's head while it slowly went mad." She laid a hand over his where their seat arms met. "A few bumps and bruises come with the territory. We aren't florists."

Leaning over, Michael kissed her lips gently and Becca oozed into it.

"You're an unusual woman, Rebecca Sauter." He grinned at her when he pulled away.

"I know. You're just lucky to know me," she shot back. Realizing she was oddly giddy, Becca had a sobering thought.

Sensing exactly where her thoughts went, Michael squeezed her hand. "I didn't give you any. You're lightheaded because of what the demon took. We considered stopping at the hospital and picking up human blood to do a normal transfusion but we thought it best to leave before too many unanswerable questions were asked."

By his level of discomfort, Becca could guess whose suggestion it had been that they get the hell out of town. The lack of blood explained her feelings of sluggish euphoria. It was an odd sort of high but one she was getting used to in her line of work. The fact that she was still bruised actually should have told her she hadn't had any of his blood. It would most likely be gone by tomorrow if his previous transfusion continued to linger. Not now, she told herself. She didn't need to revisit that worry tonight.

Nestling her head against his arm, Becca let out a big breath. "When are we due home?" she asked him quietly.

"Within the hour. The admiral's waiting," he told her gently.

Becca didn't need to ask what or why he would be waiting. More than just a debriefing, he would be looking for progress on her "homework." She wondered what he would think of the fact that not only had she figured out how to jump into a demon's head, but she could do two jumps at once.

Sighing deeply again, Becca felt her euphoria give way to exhaustion and she closed her eyes. Cool lips pressed against her temple and she smiled sleepily.

"We only have to answer the questions he thinks to ask," Michael reminded her. "There are some things even *he* wouldn't dream possible."

The End

About the Author

The Admiral's Elite is HK Savage's third series but not to be her last. Provided the ideas keep coming and her family doesn't revolt she intends to keep writing for as long as her fingers and computer hold out.
When she isn't writing HK practices martial arts, rides her horse or is out running her dogs. Family is important to her and HK is often found making time for the most special people in her life or asking forgiveness for staying up too late writing her next novel.

Check in at www.hksavage.com for the third installment of
The Admiral's Elite
Late Winter 2013

377